Praise for

'There are perhaps three or ... e
new books I seek out with a ... 1.
M. John Harrison is one ... e
power to leave the world about you unsteadied; glowing and
perforated in strange ways. He combines sharp clarity of vision
with deep compassion of heart; a merciful eagle. Once read,
these stories ghost you for days and weeks afterwards.'
– Robert Macfarlane, author of *Landmarks*

'M. John Harrison's slippery, subversive stories mix the eerie
and familiar into beguiling, alarming marvels. No one writes
quite like him; no one I can think of writes such flawless
sentences, or uses them to such disorientating effect.'
– Olivia Laing, author of *The Lonely City*

'These stories map a rediscovered fictional hinterland, one
tucked behind the glossier edifices of modernity and genre
with views down alleyways into pubs and flats where Patrick
Hamilton glares balefully at J. G. Ballard.'
– Will Eaves, author of *This is Paradise*

'M. John Harrison moves elegantly, passionately, from genre to
genre, his prose lucent and wise, his stories published as SF or
as fantasy, as horror or as mainstream fiction. In each playing
field, he wins awards, and makes it look so easy. His prose is
deceptively simple, each word considered and placed where it
can sink deepest and do the most damage.'
– Neil Gaiman, author of *American Gods*

'With an austere and deeply moving humanism, M. John
Harrison proves what only those crippled by respectability still
doubt – that science fiction can be literature, of the very
greatest kind.'
– China Miéville, author of *Perdido Street Station*

You Should Come With Me Now

Stories of Ghosts

M. JOHN HARRISON

First published in Great Britain in 2017 by Comma Press.
www.commapress.co.uk

'Entertaining Angels Unawares' was published in *Conjunctions 39*; 'Cicisbeo' in *Talk of the Town* (*Independent on Sunday*); 'Not All Men' in *Time Out* (as 'It Isn't Me'); 'In Autotelia' and 'Psychoarcheology' in *Arc*, the *New Scientist* magazine; 'Animals' in *Curious Tales*. Nicholas Royle published 'Getting Out of There' as a Night Jar chapbook. 'Babies from Sand' appeared in *An Unreliable Guide to London*, Influx Press. 'The Walls' and parts of 'Self-Storage' were performed by Barbara Campbell as part of her 1001 Nights Cast project (http://1001.net.au/). Paragraphs of 'Cave and Julia' featured in *Long Relay*, a collaborative project devised by Tim Etchells and Adrian Heathfield for the Serpentine Pavilion Gallery Summer Exhibition, 2007. 'Yummie' first appeared in *The Weight of Words*, edited by Dave McKean and William Schafer (PS Publishing, 2017). 'Imaginary Reviews', 'The Theory Cadre' and all the shorter pieces appeared on M. John Harrison's blog, which can be found at https://ambientehotel.wordpress.com/

A CIP catalogue record of this book is available from the British Library.

ISBN-13:   978 1910974346

Supported using public funding by
**ARTS COUNCIL
ENGLAND**

The publisher gratefully acknowledges assistance from Arts Council England.

To Sara Sarre

Contents

Lost & Found

Worn black and white linoleum floor tiles go back to a wooden counter. Furniture – mainly chromium diner stools – stacked in a corner. Some cabinets, you can't make out what's in those. Push your face up against the window on a dark night and a rain of silent objects drifts down slowly through this space like the index of some unreliable past: ashtrays of all types and sizes; geranium in a terracotta pot; thousands of 45rpm records; tens of thousands of abandoned paperbacks; stones off a beach; money and playing cards; the dustjackets of library novels 1956; black French knickers waist 24; cheap tickets all colours; suits, hats and shoes; bruised cricket ball, seams worn; a porcelain globe five inches diameter bearing a complex design of leaves and tendrils in delft blue; small chest of drawers, veneered; bicycle tire, gentleman's silver cigarette case, national insurance card: all gravityless and wreathed in Christmas lights like strands of weed underwater. One night you hear Frank Sinatra behind a door to another room. Go the next night: nothing. You turn up your collar in the rain. The card in the window says open but the door is always closed. Ask around, no one remembers seeing the owner. Open book, indelible pencil on a bit of string. 'Sign in here.'

In Autotelia

THE 10:30AM OUT-TRAIN from Waterloo lies abandoned by its passengers, who have, after half an hour's wait, decamped to Platform 9 and the 11am. I find myself sitting opposite a man in a dark pinstripe suit. Two women, who have lost their reservations because of the move from one train to the other, wander angrily up and down the carriage, followed by their defeated husbands. 'That's nice, innit? Chaos, innit?' they say to one another: 'There's no booked seats. It's disgraceful.' And so it is. Or at any rate tiresome. As the 11am finally pulls out, twelve minutes late, the pinstripe man and I exchange glances.

'It's getting worse,' he says.

For a moment I think he means more than just the railway service; but he's only being polite.

The train soon gets going and we are clattering through south London before swinging north and diving deep under the river. The trains are new but the lines are old, and seem to travel deliberately through the dilapidated back of everything. Rusty old metal bridges, trees invisible under Russian vine, short dense brambles on waste ground. I am just beginning to tell myself that despite all the changes everything is as useless as it ever was, only dirtier and more expensive, when the train emerges from London and the man sitting opposite me says suddenly:

'If they've got interim reports, it would be helpful to see those. It might save time if they faxed those direct to me.'

Then he closes his phone. He's a solicitor, as I half

suspected. He's travelling on business. He arranges some papers on the table, giving me a faint smile, and begins to use a yellow highlighter on them.

The train pushes its way through a shower of rain, then past a dilapidated farm, an abandoned house in a polluted fold of land. A woman standing alone in a channel of mud by a tiny two-arch bridge. 'Have a splendid weekend,' the solicitor says. 'My pleasure.' And then, looking at me affably and indicating the papers with their neat yellow lines, his phone, the laptop he opened as soon as he sat down: 'I hope this isn't a nuisance for you?' I ask him if he could perhaps not use the laptop. As he begins to reply we break out of the transition zone into the sunlight the other side.

'Good god,' he whispers, more to himself than me, staring out of the window: 'Look at that.'

I love the little steep crumbling valleys that run alongside the railway eastwards from where Norwich used to be, often bounded on one side by the line and on the other by a leafless but impenetrable thorn hedge or a wall of yellow local stone resonating with the early heat of the day. Thin terraces, irrigated by a stream or a well with its pony in harness. Dry willows. An abandoned car washed across from our side of things and already becoming part of the landscape.

Three hours later we are received in _____, by the regional president, a marching band, and an escort of police motorcycles as well. By the time we reach the main square, and see the vast buffet laid out on tables in a sort of outdoor auditorium, many of us are, if not exactly marching, then shambling in time to the music. It is all very stirring. I sit on a bench to take photographs. The solicitor has served himself a plate of food, mainly different types of sausage, on which he's concentrating with a kind of puzzled greed even as he looks for a place to sit. He's seen me and begun to smile and raise his free hand when a little local girl, perhaps three years old, grabs his sleeve and begins talking earnestly to him in her own language. She seems delighted by him, but puzzled that he can't answer. Eventually her mother succeeds in explaining that he's English. They whisper together for a moment; then the little girl turns back to him, holds out her hand and demands:

'Geev me five!'

She's full of life, she talks to everybody, all the way through the speech of the regional president.

I've spent so much time on trips like these.

I slip away to my hotel for a bath and an hour or two's sleep, then a drink at the Tristan & Isolde in Central Plaza. By then it's late afternoon. Until I order in English, Jack Daniels and a double espresso, I'm not so interesting to the young woman behind the bar: after that I can feel her approval. This, she believes, is how women can be; a role model brought to her from our side of things. My change comes in the local money, which I keep for my nieces and nephews. Espresso at the Tristan & Isolde always includes a small chocolate wafer wrapped in foil, the foil decorated with a picture of a gun and something which resembles a Tyrolean hat. I always take these home too. The children love the pictures, but are less keen on the chocolate itself.

After a while the solicitor arrives in the plaza and wanders about rather helplessly until he sees me. He's exchanged his suit for jeans. A proofed cotton jacket. Boat shoes and a pink shirt, the off-duty uniform of the West London professional. He's full of excitement. Down in the old town, on one of the recently-recobbled streets that runs towards the lake, he's discovered the shop everyone discovers on their first visit here, the one that sells the Stalin alarm clocks. The window is stuffed with them, enamelled or in brass or copper, in different sizes but all with quite large bells. He struggled with himself, then bought two, one of which he unwraps and places on the table between us. A quarter to three (not the real time): Stalin has an affable look as he stares out across the hands of the clock. He isn't looking at you, precisely. It's nothing you've done. He's looking at everyone. You aren't sure what he's thinking.

The solicitor doesn't seem to know whether to be amused or shocked. Perhaps he's both.

'Isn't it extraordinary?' he keeps saying.

'This is what they like most of ours.'

Two doors along the same street, he says, there's another shop, the window of which is empty but for a single oil painting of Adolf Hitler on a velvet-draped easel. 'They have all the bases covered, anyway.'

'It's not kitsch to them,' I tell him. 'It's a real sentiment.'

There is an uncomfortable silence, during which he rewraps his souvenir.

'Would you like another drink?'

'No,' I tell him, 'I don't think so. But do sit down. Please.'

A lake ferry must have arrived – people are pouring up the hill, some clearly tourists, some clearly locals, schoolchildren in woollen hats, teenagers dressed up as people who have an aching sense of how to dress as a teenager. An accordion has started up. A Volkswagon camper chugs its way across the square. The police keep their eye on all this. Regional police couture splits the difference between professional plumbing and special forces chic, a colour of blue you only ever see in cheap overalls and uniforms. Even their van looks as if they bought it from DynoRod. I smile at them.

'I'll buy supper later,' the solicitor offers eventually. 'Do you know of anything we could do until then?'

'I'm afraid not.'

After breakfast next morning I take a train to the New Ministries. I love the subway stations with their mosaic tiles and coloured plaster mouldings, their central girders marching off into the darkness in either direction. There seem to be far too many girders for any structural purpose and yet they have no decorative value. They are just heavily riveted I-beams, painted grey. The clean, brightly polished trains are the centrepiece here. They look nothing like the subway trains you see on our side of things. Interiors of brushed stainless steel, colourful, comfortable seats. Almost everything you expect – alcohol vomit, graffiti, burst styrofoam burger packages – is missing. They're cleaner than the trains in Stockholm, and they make the London Underground look like the on-the-cheap Inferno it is.

The 'municipal room' at the New Ministries. If you stood there with me this is what you would see: locals in an orderly line, not really a queue, facing expectantly into the room with their backs to the polished wood panelling. Facing them are looser groups of people clearly from our side of things, dressed with a certain formality though they're not sure how to behave in this situation. They seem uncomfortable, as if this is the first time they have been here, which, for most of them, it is. Hopefully it will be the last.

The room smells of cleaning materials and wax polish, as if it has to be cleaned thoroughly every early morning to remove the traces of the previous day's business. Names are called out. People step forward with hesitant smiles, papers are signed. To you this would seem like some ordinary, if rather old-fashioned bureaucratic activity. There is no true culture of information here, no digital culture. It's all still pen and ink. Maybe, you think, this is something to do with marriages, births or deaths, some kind of registration anyway; or maybe it isn't at all clear what's going on – just people from our side buying something, dealing in something. It's legal, though. It's intrinsically legal.

My part is to make the medical checks. They often aren't necessary, even so I'm required to make them. The same little adjoining room is put aside for the purpose every time, bare but very clean. Legal representation must be present, or no examination takes place; often, the representative is also the agent from our side. The women and children cover their embarrassment with smiles. The men, especially the older ones, do what's required with an appalled dignity, as if I am an outrage that could only happen to them during war or an epidemic, a breakdown of all values and infrastructures, something to be borne but never forgotten. They are so reluctant to loosen their wide, thick, hand-tooled leather belts – a poor-quality example of which can fetch two or three thousand euros in a London store – they tremble. To help, I sometimes joke:

'Where I come from, this is the cultural day of bad luck. Don't get married, or travel by boat! There, you can do yourself up again now.'

All morning, thunder rumbles across the capital from the range of limestone hills that gives the region its name. The air in the room stales and darkens with each peal, the low-wattage electric lights dim then brighten beneath their flat enamel shades. The door opens and closes an inch or two in counterpoint, admitting a draught from the corridor; the smell of floor polish intensifies. I see ten, I see twenty of them, mostly women and children. They have been advised to dress without underwear that morning, to save time. At mid-day the solicitor turns up, accompanying a tall woman who leads him into the room with such composure he might be the client; he is carrying her daughter in the crook of his arm. He looks tired already.

'She should carry her own daughter.'

'I'm sorry.'

I shrug. 'It's not a problem with me. But others.'

As soon as he puts her down, the toddler begins to scamper around the room. The woman chases her, then, to indicate harassment, fans her hand in front of her face and blows out through her lips. Like most of them she has ignored the leaflet and dressed the child in its best clothes, including pink knickers like a decorated cake. She has a sort of willing self-effacement, a giving up of herself to the child. 'I think of cutting down on the amount of food I give her,' she says to me. Then she laughs. 'I survived three of these but I am not sure I will survive this one.'

'Geev me five!' the little girl orders, flirting heavily over her mother's shoulder with the solicitor.

I push the forms across to him.

'Have you done this before?' I know he hasn't. 'You'll need to sign these. And witness here.'

'I know,' he says.

'You can use this pen.'

Thereafter the examination proceeds. I am careful with the little girl but she begins to scream and throw herself about as I feel under her skirt for signs of deformity, which can appear early. I ask the mother if she can calm her, please: 'A little thing but we must do it.'

'It's only that she doesn't understand,' the woman says gently.

Suddenly the child lies still and smiles up at the ceiling as if she has found a way to accept what is happening to her. After that, things go quickly, the mother turns away as she takes off her clothes, then forces herself to turn back. The solicitor watches all this, as he must: if the examination takes place behind any kind of curtain, it can't be said to have been witnessed As he leaves he looks to me like someone who is going to vomit.

That evening I visit the regional art gallery. 'If you look at too much art,' their national poet is supposed to have said, 'you will always leave your umbrella behind.' Perhaps it doesn't translate. Housed here are paintings from the last four hundred years, but the major collection is of Doula Kiminic, who went steadily mad as he painted the most recent wars and famines. Kiminic's rawness seems as deliberate as ever. It seems reductive, a deliberate sweeping out of other values. His world of endless injustice and pain seems as wilful a construct as LegoLand. Not so much *The Bombing*, which on our side of things long ago lost through repetition its effect as an image, as drawings like *Study in Composition VI*, in which the usual eviscerated horse competes for your attention with the usual howling woman and dead child.

I'm contemplating this little piece, which is perhaps twelve inches by twelve, pen and watercolour, mostly blacks and wispy greys, when I become aware of the solicitor, standing slightly behind me so he can look over my shoulder.

'What horror!'

'I don't doubt these things happened,' I say. 'That doesn't seem to be the point. The point seems to be that this culture expected them to happen. Its vision was already prepared.'

'This morning,' he says. 'At the Ministries —'

'You think I'm crass,' I tell him. 'You think I'm being unfair.'

'No,' he says. He thinks he's going to say more, but in the end he doesn't. He looks tired.

'Let's go to a bar,' I suggest. 'One of the bars in the square.'

Inside, the bar is full of laughter and shouting, smells of smoke and food. At one table, three women play cards; at another sit two much younger women in identical pink T-shirts. Outside, a dog sprawls among the empty tables, its body rocking with the evening heat. Someone has given it a hamburger which first it guards, then, eventually, eats. It's some kind of winter dog, a malamute perhaps, a dog of marvellous subtle greys and whites. Also of transparent intelligence, and less transparent motive. The beauty of an animal like this appears to fix it in our expectations. But while its beauty says one thing, its heart may say another.

I can't think of a way to put this for the solicitor, so I tell him, 'They are very popular over here, these winter dogs from our side. But they must feel the heat.'

Then I say:

'Back there, back in the gallery, what I meant was this: a culture to which the abuse of animals is so central should not use the pain of animals as a symbol for human pain. It's so inappropriate. You steal their lives and their dignity, then you steal their sign —'

'But,' he says. 'Don't you think —'

'— at which point, anyway, all it becomes is a secondary symbol of your talent for the abuse of human beings. What?'

'It doesn't matter.'

'You were going to say something more.'

'Really, it doesn't matter.'

On our way out, half an hour later, he scrambles past me to hold open the door.

'Can you do something for me?' I say.

'Of course.'

'Can you not do that? I find it so patronising.' After that we walk back to the hotel in silence and part in the lobby.

Next day, on the return journey, small fat Autotelian men in perfect Armani casual clothes go staggering down the aisle of the train with their arms outstretched, as if they have never had to walk in a moving train before. Perhaps they haven't. Perhaps it's the first time they have left their prosperous regional town. A woman further down the carriage sings a few notes of the same song again and again to her child. Her voice comes and goes like a subtext to the journey, monotonous and without meaning. She seems tired and sad, but the child laughs uproariously at everything. 'Geev me five!' it can be heard demanding.

The solicitor sits opposite me. Our reservations have brought us together again. He sets out his papers and marker pens. He opens his mobile phone.

'Aren't you in the pub yet?' he shouts into it, with every evidence of enjoyment. Then, after a pause, 'Well, let's see where we get to on Monday. Not at all. My pleasure. Have a splendid evening.'

He opens his laptop. Would I mind, he asks me, if he worked?

'It seems bizarre to me,' I answer, 'that you would want to use a journey for something other than itself.'

But really I'm too tired to argue this time. Looking out of the window, I feel as I always do, that I've lost an opportunity. I should be in some kind of contact with things. I can see dusty paths; a figure, perhaps a man, perhaps a woman, labouring up hill in shorts. There are trees and rocks, paths doubling along the sides of dry gullies. You could walk down there. It looks as if you could walk all day in the sunshine between the rocks and trees.

'Transition,' the guard tells us, 'will take place in half an hour.'

Up and down the carriage, people draw into themselves. Even the solicitor seems to notice something, though all he does is to look up from his work for a moment and smile. After all, it's only like going into a tunnel. The world will be more or less the same when you come out of the other end. You can, at least, expect something to be there. The last thing I see is a boy, standing in a glorious waste of flowers at the end of some gardens to wave at the train. This is such an old fashioned gesture I catch my breath. To wave at a train because it is a train is a vanished body language on our side of things, generous, unguarded, agonisingly naive. On our side, children don't wave at trains: they throw things. Their optimism has been replaced by something else.

'Transition —' the guard begins, but then interrupts himself.

The train slows to a walking pace. Different kinds of darkness flicker outside. There's some commotion further down the carriage, a woman shouting in the regional language, a child beginning to scream. My back is to all that; but the

12

solicitor, facing in the direction of travel, leans out into the aisle to stare.

'They've changed their minds,' he says. 'They don't want to go.'

'You were at the Ministries,' I say. 'It's all above-board. That's why the two of us were present.'

'Isn't there anything we can do for them?'

'Not now. It's all above-board.'

'I don't think you understand how awful this is for ordinary people.'

'I understand perfectly well.'

'No you don't. Not for ordinary people.'

We stare at each other for a moment, then, startled for the first time by the depth of our mutual dislike, away at the blackness out of the window. After a moment he clambers awkwardly to his feet and walks off down the carriage. Shortly after, there is a bump too loud for transition, an alarm goes off, the train shudders to a halt. Someone, the guard tells us, has jumped off. We are to remain in our seats. Three people have managed to get a door open, though this shouldn't be possible when the train is moving, and jump into the transition zone. No one knows what to do. No one knows what to do five minutes later, then ten.

When the solicitor fails to reappear, I turn his laptop towards me, expecting to see a report for his client, the broad outlines of his morning's work at the New Minstries. Instead I find this. It's a journal entry, perhaps.

'Outward journey. Sat opposite a woman in a reserved seat. Pale blue cardigan with gilt buttons. Cream shirt. Orange silk scarf worn over both, tied in front with a loose knot. (Hem slightly detached at one corner of the scarf.) Grey hair chopped off behind the ears, silver ear-rings in the shape of a four-petal flower. No one ever called her petal. 60 years old? Thin face, veins visible in cheeks. Lipstick. Copy of *The Guardian*. Copy of *The Private Patient,* by PD James.

Complained about my computer the moment I opened it.

'Added later: every movement on my part – getting out a book to read, or a notebook to work in – elicited a partly-audible sigh. Computer wasn't the problem, she simply felt that to reserve a seat was to reserve the whole table. Caught sight of her legs under the table, found myself looking away – like seeing her underwear. Skin of the ankles slack & wrinkled.'

I close the laptop. The guard is walking back along the carriage towards me. At least they've got the train moving again.

Cries

THEY START BETWEEN SIX and six thirty in the evening. They're usually distant. If they have a motive, it's internal and psychic: like the sounds of someone with a head wound, they are not rational except in relation to themselves. At times they seem to move closer, the way sounds do on a wind, especially in the night. For a moment, the listener is able to distinguish more than one voice, perhaps even differentiate male from female. There are qualities of both plaintiveness and aggression, but words are hard to make out. They reach a peak by ten in the evening. By midnight they have moved away for good, and the centre of the little town is dark and quiet.

The Walls

A MAN, LET'S CALL him D, is seen digging his way out through the wall of his cell.

To help in this project D has only the flimsiest and least reliable tools: two dessert spoons (one stainless steel, one EPNS); half of a pair of curved nail scissors; some domestic knives lacking handles; and so on. The cell wall, constructed from grey, squarish cinder blocks about a foot on a side, has been carelessly mortared and laid without much attention to detail. But this lack of artifice makes no difference; none of the knives is long enough to reach the last half inch of mortar at the back of each block, and the more D uses them the shorter they get. Each block must, eventually, be loosened and removed by hand, a task which can take several months, and which leaves him exhausted.

His hands become deformed and swollen. After a decade of digging, he breaks through, to find not the outside but a compartment about three feet in depth, full of dust, mouse-droppings and bundles of old newspapers tied with string. Collapsed against its outer wall he discovers the desiccated corpse of another man, surrounded by worn-down meat skewers, bent knife blades, and an artful device made by splitting and opening-out an old metal cup. This man is huddled up with his shoulder and one cheek against the wall as if in his last moments he was trying to push it over; or as if he had pressed his face up against it to try and look out through some tiny crack, the result of a lifetime's

17

effort. His skin, which has a patient look, is as yellowed as the newspapers.

Taking the corpse under the armpits, D drags it respectfully to one side, selects the best of the tools, and begins scraping where the dead man left off.

Years pass. He is generally full of energy; but, sometimes, when he wakes too tired or depressed to work, he'll spend half a day reading. In strong sunlight, newsprint can go yellow and brittle-looking in an hour, giving you the eerie feeling that the news is already old. The events recorded – some tennis matches, a bombing, a fake suicide – seem historical and quaint; the people oddly dressed, their figures of speech as hard to sympathise with as their values. After a few hours, D thinks, all newsprint and thus in a sense all news, looks the same. It looks like the paper with which someone lined a drawer thirty years ago. By the same token, the news of previous generations, the kind of news he is now forced to read, looks about six hours old.

A decade of intense effort and focus enables D to break through the second wall. Disappointed to discover another musty compartment, another corpse with a puzzled expression and a selection of home-made tools, he sets about the third wall – only to reveal a third compartment; then, after a further decade, another, and another: until he has made his way through six walls, past the six dead men who can be said, in some way, to have preceded him. Like D, all these men wear the grey civilian cotton jacket in which they were arrested, over combat trousers with a beautiful if rather faded dazzle pattern of blues and browns. Their hands are as bruised and dirty, their nails as broken, as D's. Their hair and clothes are equally impregnated with dust. But he is glad to see that each one has made some individual addition to the basic toolset – a cut-down trowel from the prison garden, a snapped hacksaw blade, a short length of soft thick metal which he suspects began life as a fire-iron in the prison governor's quarters – and though they are dead, some of them have quite satisfied expressions.

They died, he thinks, doing what they wanted to do.

Before he breaks through the seventh wall, D decides to see how his escape is progressing, so he makes his way back, through compartment after compartment, to the cell from which he started. Accustomed to living in the spaces between the walls, he has forgotten how relatively large and comfortable it was, with its white paint, metal bed, keyhole toilet and barred window (through which he can hear, still rumbling on, the tail end of the afternoon storm). There's even a small shelf of books!

D stops to touch the spine of Dino Buzzati's masterpiece *The Tartar Steppe*. He takes it down and riffles the pages, looking for the marked lines he knows by heart. Then he opens the cell door and steps out into the dazzling light and humid atmosphere of the prison compound. The rain has already evaporated from the bare, reddish earth. High above, a brahminy kite patrols the air, all its attention focussed on something D can't see.

It takes only a moment to walk round the cell block to the place where he expects to break through. Though he taps the wall here and there, and bends down once to touch the mortar, he finds no sign of his own efforts; yet he still feels optimistic. Before he goes back in, he looks over at the wall of the compound itself. It's six or seven metres high, and featureless but for some black stains. Once he's got out of the cell block, he thinks, he will have to start on that. It will be a new challenge. D's quite excited about the prospect, so he goes back inside and starts digging again with renewed enthusiasm.

Rockets of the
Western Suburbs

LISTEN, AND IT'S STEADY straight-down rain. No wind. A car halts at the corner, pulls away in acknowledgement of its own muffled existence. Tyre noise louder than engine noise. Against this, the tendency of things to be. The rims and ribs of terracotta pots hard and slick with light. Roofs like mirrors. The bricks suck up water. Everything supported by the perfect angle of a drainpipe. This afternoon Barnes is quiet. This afternoon every garden plant is one uncanny green or another. The visitors ring the bell, wait in the doorway, too polite to come in immediately but chatter a lot when they do. They are nice. Their children always have some new practical thing, less a toy than the beginnings of a fruitful lifetime interest. Without warning (an act in itself 100% pure communication) the camera cuts away from this: very fast, upwards, turning in a series of vertical 180 degree snap rolls, so that first you see the world kaleidoscoping rapidly from a thousand feet up, then from low orbit. By the time everything's returned to the right scale again, the rain has stopped and the sun is coming out.

Cicisbeo

SUMMER WAS HALF OVER before it had even begun. With a sense that my life was in the same state, I phoned Lizzie Shaw. She hadn't changed.

They lived in East Dulwich now, she told me, her and Tim, in a little house 'practically given' them by a friend. She had worked for a while as a buyer for John Lewis. 'You'd have been proud of me,' she said. 'I was properly industrious.' She had bought a Mercedes. Enjoyed the money. Missed her kids. 'I wasn't getting home 'til eight. I had a seventeen year old Polish girl looking after my family, I mean can you believe it?' Jobs pall, she said, as soon as you start thinking like that. She said she couldn't wait to see me. 'People count more as you get older.' She was thirty seven now. Then she said: 'I'm pregnant again,' and burst into tears.

That house was always full of sex.

'You will come and see us?' Lizzie said.

'I'm not sure,' I said. 'Would that be a good idea?'

'Please,' she said.

I thought about it. I drove across London, intending to go there, but lost motivation somehow and fetched up in Brixton or Blackheath instead. Lizzie kept phoning. Would I go and see them again, or not?

'Why don't we meet where we used to?' I suggested. 'Just the two of us?'

'It can't be like that again,' she warned me.

23

'I know,' I said.

I wanted to put the phone down and not speak to her for another three years.

'All right then,' she said. 'When?'

We had lunch at Angels & Gypsies on Camberwell Church Street. She was late, a little nervous. 'I can't get over you,' I said. The pregnancy threw her off-balance a little, but it suited her. 'You look so well.'

We talked about her boys for a bit. She had got them into a good school. They were so grown up, she said. So emotionally intelligent. 'I don't know what I'd do without them, especially Ben.' Of the buyer's job she would only say: 'I felt it was right at the time. But now I feel it's right to be pregnant again.'

'And how is Tim?'

'Just the same,' she said 'You know Tim.'

I smiled. 'I do,' I said.

'He's converting the loft.'

'Is he now?' I said.

'It's such a little house,' she said off-handedly. 'He thought it would be a good idea. He thought it could be a studio.' She ate some olives and then some bread. She sat back. 'This is nice,' she said vaguely. 'I always loved this place.'

I knew that tone of voice.

'What's the matter?' I said.

'Oh, you know.' She looked away suddenly. 'It's all he ever does now, really. The loft.'

I reached across the table and tried to take her hand.

'No,' she said, 'I don't want that.'

She told me about Tim. Something happened to him, she said, the day he was forty. He went up into the loft. He liked it there, the very first time he stuck his head and shoulders up through the trapdoor. He called down from the top of the ladder, something like, 'Hey!' or, 'Wow!' and that was it. Something clicked for him. Soon he was up there every available day, working, but not at his job. He had started out to

24

store things up there. Then he was going to convert it. Then he was moving himself into it, bit by bit. He even had his own TV up there.

'He was forty,' she said. Looking back, you could see that's when it began. 'His life was so good,' she said. 'But something went wrong with his view of it.'

After a pause she said, 'He misses you.'

I couldn't take that seriously.

'I bet he does,' I said.

'We both miss you.'

'I've missed *you*,' I said.

'I know. I know,' she said. 'So you will come over? To supper?'

I began to say, 'I'm not sure that's such a good idea,' but she was already adding:

'Perhaps you can even talk some sense into him.'

'I'm not the best person to do that.'

'At least come to supper,' she said. She put her hand over mine. 'It's so good to see you again,' she said.

I shouldn't have gone, but in the end I couldn't see any reason not to. I was bored. I thought she might light my life up again.

Their street was like all the others packed between the railway and the hospital. Tubs of geraniums outside narrow-fronted terraces. Roadsters parked two wheels up on the pavement. The house was nice but far too small for them. By the time you had a family you were supposed to have moved down the road to the Village, or out of London altogether. East Dulwich – or Dull Eastwich, as Tim called it – was for younger people. They would have done better, he said, in Herne Hill: but you didn't get the resale value.

He hadn't changed much since I last saw him. You found people like Tim all over London. They had rowed a little at school. At the weekend they wore chinos and a good quality sailing fleece. Boat shoes with no socks. They all had the same

tall, polite good looks. They never seemed to age: instead, their
self-deprecation matured into puzzlement. They began to look
tired. Tim liked to cook. He had his treasured cast iron
saucepans from the 80s, his five-hob Lacanche range. I watched
him, and drank a beer, and asked him how things were.

'Oh, you know,' he said vaguely. 'Could you pass me that?
No, the little one.'

Once we sat down to eat it became harder to sustain a
conversation. 'I wish I'd learned to cook,' I said, as if I'd lived
the kind of life which makes a thing like that impossible. He
didn't know what to say to that. Who would? This left things
to Lizzie, who grew impatient. 'It's a chicken,' she explained to
me. 'A child could cook it.' He was quick to agree. 'You could
soon learn, you could soon learn.' He slotted the plates into the
dishwasher while she banged pudding down on the table.

'Well that was good,' I said when we'd eaten it.

'I'm glad,' Lizzie said. 'The kitchen cost him twenty
thousand pounds.' When he only smiled at this, she added: 'No
one puts a twenty thousand pound kitchen in a house in East
Dulwich. In the Village, yes. In East Dulwich, no.' Tim
shrugged a little. He looked away. Twenty thousand pounds
was an exaggeration, the shrug said. It said that if you were
going to cook you should have the right things.

While Lizzie made coffee in the kitchen, he gave me the
tour. 'We'd gone as far as we could without opening the loft,'
he said. You could see they had. 'It was a bit of a push to find
somewhere for the boys.' Tim, you sensed, had turned his
talents as easily to family life as to sport: but now he wasn't
quite sure how he came to have a family in the first place. I
poked my head into the little room he used as a study.

'No computer?' I said.

He'd moved it up there already, he said. There had never
been enough room down here. 'Lizzie told me you were up to
your neck in it,' I said. The study was a mess. He laughed and
looked rather tiredly at the heaps of stuff. 'Eventually all this

will go up there.' I asked him if I could see the loft. 'It's a bit dusty at the moment,' he said. 'Probably better to wait.' I didn't press him, even though I knew Lizzie would have wanted me to; and I left not long later. Tim had his problems, I had mine. One of mine was that I didn't really care one way or another about him. It's hard to hide that. He knew it as well as I did, and she was the only one pretending not to know. I kept in touch. I went over there once or twice, for a meal, then let it lapse again. I was working anyway.

Three months later the phone rang.

I answered it. I said, 'Hello?'

'Hi. It's Lizzie.'

I caught my breath.

'Hi,' I said, 'I —'

'There's someone on the other line, hang on,' she said. Then, 'Hi. How are you, I'm sorry about that.'

'No, it's OK.'

After a pause she said: 'It's a girl.'

'I can't believe it,' I said.

'I know,' she said. 'A girl!'

I sent flowers. I sent a card. I telephoned my friends as if I was the father. In two days Lizzie was on the phone again.

'The baby's home,' she said, 'but he won't see it.'

'That's ridiculous.'

'We're both back from the hospital, but he won't see either of us.'

'He won't see his own baby?'

He wouldn't see his own baby. He sent notes down from the loft.

'I don't know where to turn,' Lizzie said.

'Come on,' I tried to encourage her, 'he was a bit like this with the boys.'

'Well now he's got a girl and he won't come down out of the loft to even look at her. What am I going to do?'

So I found myself in East Dulwich again, hoping to get a word alone with her. The house was full of wellwishers. Her women friends had long backs and sexy voices. The men were packed with the aimless brutal confidence of people barely thirty years old earning large sums of money at banking. Even their children were successful at something. I felt old and immature at the same time. Tim was nowhere to be seen, but no one mentioned that. He was in the loft of course, but no one mentioned that either. They had called the baby Emma. I held her while Lizzie had a proper drink. I couldn't believe her fingernails.

'Look,' I told anyone who would listen, 'they come with a manicure!'

The boys stared at me as if I was simple, and Emma started crying. I took her outside. I brought her back in. It was no good. She looked up at me angrily and flexed her spine. Her face went bright red.

'Give her to me,' said Lizzie. 'She wants something you haven't got.'

This drew laughs all round.

I was there a lot the first few weeks. I helped with this and that. I learned to change a nappy. Lizzie sat up in bed, looking exhausted but pleased. 'They've taken it well,' she said of the boys. She was proud of them. After a few days, though, they grew thoughtful, painted their faces, spent money on slime. They ran in and out of the small garden whooping and shouting: but magical thinking would not save them. Change was inevitable. The tribe was doomed.

Tim watched it all from a distance. His idea, you could see, was to ride it out. Six months after his daughter arrived, the loft was his home. He cooked up there, he slept up there. 'He's living on baked beans,' Lizzie said. She looked down at the baby. 'Essentially,' she said in a tragic voice, 'he's left us.' No one had any idea what he was doing. He hauled stuff up in a plastic dustbin. Whatever it was began coming down again within a few hours. There was a lot of bumping and banging which sometimes went on all night. She asked me, 'What's he doing up there, with all those power tools?'

I said it could be anything.

'Is this something that happens to men?' she said viciously, as if I was doing it too. Shortly afterwards he installed a good-quality pull-down ladder, but he rarely used it himself and the boys were forbidden to go near it. He was a man living away from his family.

'He might as well have gone to Blackpool,' Lizzie said. 'You've got to talk to him.'

I tried. If nothing else, I thought, it would give me a glimpse of the loft. I went up the ladder. I stuck my head through the trap door. I got a confused idea of a much smaller space than I had expected, most of it curtained off by heavy tarpaulins which sagged from the roofbeams. He had put a floor in. Piles of eurothane insulation lay about under an unshaded low-wattage bulb, everything thick with damp-looking dust. It all seemed thoroughly miserable. Tim sat at an old school desk, his legs sticking out awkwardly at the sides, writing something on a sheet of ruled A4. The computer components stacked on the floor beside him were still done up in bubble-wrap. He hadn't even bothered to unpack them.

'Hi Tim,' I said. 'When do you think you might be finished?'

He got up quickly.

'Probably better if we talk downstairs,' he said.

He looked embarrassed. You don't want your wife's best friend to see you living in your attic. You don't want him to think about what that means. I'd hoped I might shock him into talking about things. But in the end we just stood there awkwardly on the landing looking past one another, and all he would say was:

'You have to get away somehow. You have to get away from it all.'

'I don't think Lizzie sees it that way,' I said. 'You know?' This sounded futile, even to me.

After a moment I added: 'I think she'd like to see more of you. The kids would too.'

He studied the floor and shook his head.

But Lizzie did want to see more of him. She wanted to see more of someone, anyway. She called me.

'Come and meet me for a drink,' she said. 'I'm in need of, oh, something.' She laughed. 'I don't know what I'm in need of.' She left a pause and then said: 'We could meet somewhere in town.' I didn't ask who would look after the baby.

All afternoon she seemed nervous. She kept taking her phone out of her bag, studying it with a faintly irritable expression, then putting it back again. She swirled her drink around her glass. She looked up at me once or twice, began to say something, decided not to. She was wearing skinny, low-cut velvet jeans. When she saw me looking at them she said, 'Do you think they're too young for me?' They were a champagne colour, and they fastened at the back with a lace, like a shoe. She touched my arm.

'It's odd, isn't it,' she said, 'how things happen? I always loved this suit of yours. Your only suit.'

She said, 'I've never seen your house, have I?'

She drove us over to Walthamstow in the Mercedes. They always called it that, her and Tim: the Mercedes. As if they had other cars, two or three of them. When I showed her into the house she said, 'It's bigger than I thought it would be.' She stared into the kitchen for a moment, then out into the garden. We went upstairs. She looked at the bicycle in the bedroom and said, 'It's so like you, all this. Really it is.' She got her phone out again. She put it next to her ear and shook it. When nothing happened her expression hardened. Then she laughed. 'It's just what I expected, all of it.'

I don't know what I expected. I'd been waiting for her for three years; longer. After about ten minutes I said, 'I love your neck. The nape of it, here.' Then I said: 'I can't believe this is happening.' She twisted away immediately and we lay like that for a minute or two, awkward and embarrassed. My hand was still on her hip.

'This is stupid,' she said.

'Why?'

'Because it just isn't grown up.'

I got off the bed angrily. When I looked back she had covered herself up with the sheet.

'What *do* you want then?' I said.

She shivered.

'Can't you get it any warmer in here?'

'No.'

'I just want him the way he was. I'll have to leave him, if not. I don't even know what's going on in my own loft,' she told me, with a false laugh. 'Can't you at least try and find that out from him?'

I shrugged. 'Why should I do that?'

'Don't sulk,' she warned.

The second time I went up into the loft, I heard a regular metallic scraping noise, more distant than you'd expect in a space that size. The light was off and something was happening behind the tarpaulins. 'Tim?' I said. But I said it cautiously, to myself, as if I didn't want him to hear. I was curious. As much as anything else, I wanted to poke around. The tarpaulins were new, but they looked old. They sagged under their own weight, stiff to the touch, with fixed folds as if the dust had already worked its way into them. Perhaps it had. Around their edges I glimpsed the eerie white flicker of a butane lamp, or perhaps one of those portable fluorescent tubes.

I examined the desk, the abandoned computer, the piles of other stuff. Why would you keep a garden spade in a loft?

'Tim?'

This time the noises stopped immediately. For a moment we were silent, each listening for the other. Then a draught seemed to go through the loft, along with a smell which reminded me of old-fashioned house gas. I saw the tarpaulins billow, hang, resettle; and he called from just behind them, 'Hang on. I'll be with you in a second.' I backed away until I bumped into the desk, then descended the ladder. He followed me down and stood there rubbing his hands on an old towel as if he didn't know what to do next. He was covered in white dust. His hands were scraped and banged, the knuckles enlarged as if he'd been doing manual work, outside work. His fingernails were broken.

'I wasn't expecting you,' he said. 'Lizzie shouldn't really have encouraged you to come up.'

I couldn't let him get away with that.

'Tim,' I said, 'for God's sake. What are you doing?'

'I'm converting the loft,' he explained patiently. 'I'm converting the loft to give us more room.' He didn't want to be understood. He was exhausted, and that made me feel exhausted too. In the end I said:

'You hire people to do the work. You don't do that yourself.'

He shook his head.

'It's my loft,' he said, with a certainty I admired.

While we were talking Lizzie came up the stairs carrying the baby. 'Do either of you want coffee?' she asked. Then she said to Tim: 'I heard all that. What rubbish you talk.' She began to cry. 'You know it's rubbish.' Tim pulled himself to his feet and looked as if he might try to comfort her. She backed away. 'No,' she said. 'It's just an excuse. It's just another excuse.'

'Lizzie's frantic, Tim,' I told him. 'You've hardly said hello to your own daughter.'

'Don't talk about me as if I'm not here!' she said. She stood in front of me and wouldn't let me turn away. 'Can you see me?' she demanded.

'Lizzie –'

'Well I'm real,' she said. 'You always pretend I'm not.' Her voice went from contempt to puzzlement. 'You're as bad as he is.' The baby wailed and waved its arms. 'Now look what you've done, both of you.'

'You asked me to come here,' I reminded her.

I left them to it and went downstairs.

'That's right,' she called after me. 'Walk away. Walk away from everything, like you always do.'

After I left, I drove about in the dark, through Balham and Brixton, jumping traffic lights to the accompaniment of a Sonny Rollins CD. By the time I got home it was three o'clock in the morning, and she had left messages with my answering service. They were a mixed bunch. One said: 'I'm sorry. I'm really sorry.' Another said: 'Is it any wonder no one will have you? It's just so easy for you to leave people behind, isn't it? Just so *fucking* easy.' A third said, 'Please don't do this. Please answer, oh please, please.' I could hear the baby crying in the background. 'Please answer.' But I didn't; and I didn't hear from her again for two or three months.

June.

The evening air was hammered like gold on to the rubbish in my front garden. I had been thinking about her all day.

Early summer had always been a dangerous time for us. Tim would be at work, we would go to the park. I would put my arm round her while we sat on a bench and watched the boys running about in the distance and she told me, at length but without ever saying it outright or irreversibly, why nothing could happen between us. 'I'm making such a fool of myself!' she would decide at last; then appeal, 'But you do see some of what I mean, don't you?'

'Lizzie, I haven't got the slightest idea what you're talking about.'

I knew she would call, because in early summer, desperate with the smell of her, I had always been ready to give her the reassurance she needed.

'Hello?' I said.

'Hi,' she said. 'It's me.'

'Hang on,' I said. 'There's someone on the other line.'

'Don't do this,' she begged.

'Can I ring you back?'

She said: 'You've got to come. It's Tim.'

There was a confused scraping noise as if she had dropped the phone, and then all I could hear was her breathing, and a shout in the distance which might have been one of the boys.

'Something awful's happening,' she said. 'In the loft.'

She dropped the phone again.

By the time I got to Dulwich it was dark. The front door of their house was open on the empty street. Lizzie stood in the hall at the bottom of the stairs with the baby held along the crook of one arm. She was wearing a white bathrobe and she had her phone up to her ear. The hall seemed too hot, even for a night like that. It seemed packed with heat. Why would they have the heating on in June?

'He's up there now,' she said.

I wondered if I should take the baby off her.

'Lizzie? What's wrong? What's the matter?'

'I thought I could get him to answer his phone. Get him to answer his bloody fucking phone for once,' she said.

'I'll fetch him down.'

She stared at me. 'That's not it,' she said.

'I'll just go up.'

There was fine white dust all over the stairs. I could hear the boys in their room, quarrelling over the PlayStation. The house seemed to get hotter from floor to floor, a dry heat which caught at your throat. 'Tim?' I called. Then louder: 'Tim!' No answer. I had caught Lizzie's mood. I felt nervous, jumpy, angry with both of them. Why did I always have to be involved? Why couldn't they put on their futile theatre without me? 'Tim?' Dust had silted down all over the upper landing. I stood at the foot of the pull-down ladder and listened. I went up far enough to poke my head into the loft. The air was full of a grey light which, dim and distributed at the same time, seemed to come from everywhere at once. I could hear a distant, measured chunking noise. It sounded like someone using an old-fashioned pickaxe to break concrete.

'Tim!' I called.

Almost immediately there was a loud crash. The house lurched, a powerful draught parted the tarpaulins. That was enough for me. As I went down the ladder I heard him tottering about up there, coughing in the dust. He seemed to be trying to drag some item of equipment across the floor. 'Tim! For God's sake!' I called up from the landing. His face appeared briefly, framed by the trap.

'The whole lot's coming down,' he said. 'Tell her to get the kids out. See if you can persuade her to care about someone else for once.'

Lizzie, halfway up the stairs, heard this.

'You sod,' she said. 'I'd do anything for those children.'

Everything seemed to lurch again. I got her by the arm and pulled her down the stairs and into the street. The boys, sensing the future like dogs before an earthquake, had already saved themselves. They couldn't believe their luck. Their house was falling down. The hall was full of plaster. Cracks had opened up in the exterior walls. From above came the shrieking sounds of joists giving way under huge loads. It was *so cool*. They stood in the quiet street in the hot night air, staring up at the line of the roof where it had sagged into the void of the loft. Their father came running out, then stopped and turned as if he had forgotten something.

His house was done for. Window frames popped. The facade deformed and began to slip. Just before the roof fell in and it became obvious that the whole thing would come down on us if we didn't move, I saw the tunnel he had been digging out of the loft. It hung in the air, transparent but luminous, perhaps three feet in diameter. Travelling north towards the river, it rose steeply until, at perhaps a thousand feet, it linked up with a complex of similar tunnels all across London. Hundreds of them, thousands, more than you could ever count, they rose up from the houses. A 787 Dreamliner was making its way down between them towards Heathrow, engines grinding, landing lights ablaze. When it had gone, the tunnels hung there for a moment like a great shining computer-generated diagram in the night sky, then began to fade.

'See?' Tim said. 'What would you have done?'

'We'll come back,' I promised him. 'We'll come back and find another way in –'

Lizzie didn't seem to hear this. 'Twenty thousand pounds on a kitchen,' she said. She laughed.

Later, she sat on the kerb a little way down the street, with the boys on either side of her and the baby in her lap, thoughtfully watching the fire engines and drinking tea. Someone had given her a man's woollen shirt to wear, wrapped a foil blanket loosely round her shoulders. The street was full of hoses and cables, generators, powerful lights. Firemen were picking over the rubble, and a television crew had arrived.

Imaginary Reviews

(1) THE HERO'S ANXIETY

IN THIS CURIOUSLY INVOLUTED thriller of the near future, the father is not dead but absent, if only temporarily. The son must act for him, whether he wishes to or not. They exist in the most ideal loop of anxiety, the father a ghost in the son's brain, the son a sub-routine of the father's competence. They are a single entity, the hero only completed by his father's wealth and prior achievement; the father present in the world only through his son's ability to act in it. Whose anxiety is the greatest? It is hardly possible to venture a guess. They describe between them not so much a main character as a desirable state, a circle whose perfection is forbidden to the son, no longer obtainable by the father.

(2) INERTIA, ANIMALISM & PARANOIA

The humanity of the world is maintained only through constant effort. If you learn to grow flowers as a child – if you understand how quickly they die without water – you become a better adult. People think of love as a given. Love is made. Maybe it does come out of nowhere but it can't support itself here, and it would soon go back there if we let it. To occur at all, festivals, celebrations, civilizations must be constructed; sustained by contribution. The nightmare of this novel is that among its characters nothing is being constructed. The only alternative to inertia, animalism and paranoia is magical thinking. Nothing practical is being done. The curve of humanity bottoms out.

From here the only way is up. Where its author sites herself in relation to this understanding is uncertain.

(3) 1973

1973: The whole of a small desert town is inhabited by aliens who have taken on human form. They escaped the disaster that wiped out their planet, but denial and post traumatic stress have erased this from their memories. The TV series, based quite closely on the original film, constructs itself as a phased revelation of their state. Imperfect recollections of life and death on the alien world are seen to be symptoms of what look like new psychological disorders. Dr Bax Fermor, drawn to the desert by convoluted Lacanian flexures in his own personality, understands their situation by an intuitive leap, and becomes town psychiatrist. He must spend the rest of his life taking care of them – some he helps to remember, others he gently encourages to forget.

(4) RIPPED, CUT & LOADED

The contemporary investigator is loaded. He drives a Porsche and wears Versace overcoats. He is as big as he is charming, as cultured as he's ripped and cut. He got his self-defense training from an ex-KGB agent. He has a connection to the CIA; or to a mysterious agency which has only twelve clients worldwide, and which can get him information about anything or anyone, any time he needs it. His family runs every part of the infrastructure of this major American city. The contemporary investigator is PC, and even when he isn't, even when he falls from grace a little the way every man can, well, his girlfriend is rich too, and equally well-connected, and she won't take any nonsense from him. His assistant's a Goth, tattoos all over. She won't have truck with that male manipulative charm either. Even when he's arrested in what he calls 'Buttfuck, Iowa', the contemporary investigator's connections are there for him. Despite that, he can get in trouble! Just in case that happens, he carries with him 'four inches of money' (ten thousand dollars) along with unimpeachable false identities for himself and his assistant. Because even when the he's not in charge, the contemporary investigator is in control. Even when contingency rages, it isn't entirely contingent, not for him.

(5) BUTTERFLY

This novelist's characters are like himself. They speak in clever and rounded sentences. They have caught life in a linguistic net, and found some odd fish there, and now they are going to tell you about it: not really at length, but in the end at more length than you suspected in the beginning. The impression of wisdom radiates from the feeblest of their jokes. You look covertly at your watch even as you think, 'How delightful!' It isn't possible at this distance – the distance between writer and reader – to tell how much of the novel is 'autobiographical'. If some of it is, there's nothing we can do about it; if none of it is, well that's a joke some decades old by now, and perhaps a little less joyful than it seemed in 1980. What is possible to say is that the acknowledgements page, written in the same tone as the book itself, is a very self-indulgent piece of work. A butterfly landed on page 52 while I was reading it in my garden. From that single event I learned nothing about the book, or reading, or writing, or anything at all.

(6) SCIENCE & THE ARTS

A clear and useful bridge between science and the public is constructed by this empathic literary novel of a boy and how he comes to terms with his world. Explanations of everything from black holes to epigenesis demonstrate the author's engagement with the scientific worldview, acting as the pivots of metaphors for a full range of human emotions and concerns. The total effect is one of numbing boredom and of a mind which has carefully removed everything of excitement from its encounters with physics, cosmology and molecular biology. A Hay Festival version of the *Popular Mechanics*-style science fiction of the 1920s, this novel has a similar mission to educate its demographic – primarily 40/50-year-old reading-group members with humanities degrees. As a result, the very last thing its author has managed is to be, as his dustjacket claims, 'boldly imaginative'. The most interesting thing about the book is its title, the literary referentiality and linguistic quirkiness of which promise more than they can ever deliver.

(7) READER, I WROTE HER

'What's your book about, Carlos?'

'It's about the romance & holiness & mystery & paradoxical matter-of-factness of all books. & it's about my struggles with this book, my book, the one you hold in your hand. & it's about women, the romance & holiness & mystery & paradoxical matter-of-factness of women, & about my struggle with this woman, the woman you –'

'Next.'

(8) AN UNIMPRESSIVE WAR

The interception of incoming rockets – silvery elliptical explosions seen through the clouds – reminds the viewer, at best, of the closing sequences of *This Island Earth*: special effects put together long ago by a team not of the first rank. Missiles that get through make a hole no bigger than a V-weapon made in the East End of London in WW2; far fewer of them have fallen. Meanwhile the corporate-class civilians video themselves in state of the art gas masks in their sealed sub-basement, footage they will later edit and label: 'How we spent the war. The little boy was so frightened.' Of what? The awful events they had explained to him? Their panic at the things that might almost be happening? He could have had very little direct evidence. It's all a bit histrionic, a bit unstoic, after such an inaccurate bombardment, so few deaths. On the other side, meanwhile, we see the civilians walking about almost cockily while the smart weapons, each one guided by a small part of the cloned neural tissue of a pigeon, moan and fizz down the line of the main street above them, en route to their very exact targets.

(9) DINNER IN THE BROWNOUT

In this novel of alternate history, Thatcherism inadvertently drove the Left into the tertiary education system, where it became a permanent nuisance. In a world separated only by the thickness of a cigarette paper from our own, the ruling Right Wing coalition's economic measures are aimed at driving it out again, a program which will fail to the precise extent that it succeeds: indeed at the outset of the novel, the Left, outraged, disoriented and under pressure, is already regaining its lost enthusiasm for actual Leftism; while the associated mayhem is as good as a rebrand. Even as student action weakens the walls of the ideological kettle from one side (reminding the Left that it *can* still act despite long term bans on unregistered strikes and street demonstrations), the collapse of the aspirational model for the majority of the population erodes it from the other. The middle aged (portrayed with amusing accuracy as the 35 to 50 year old default constituency of the UK Centre – established yet for psychological reasons still insecure, embittered in a curiously comfortable way by the life-defeats they're required to call 'realism') begin to lose control of the people who most frighten and enrage them: the young who will replace them and the old who know more than they do. A purge of the universities, one of the central characters remarks at a candle-lit dinner in the brownout, is one of the first and most satisfying revenges the business-culture imagines for itself; but when you succumb to that temptation, you deal yourself a whole new hand of nightmares.

(9) SCIENCE FICTION

In *American Ruminant*, self-replicating machines arrive from the stars. Implacability is their signature characteristic. Their mission: to cannibalise our planet for parts! Life as we know it – the life of well-fed science wonks and policy advisors and their resilient, generally likeable, dependent families – seems doomed. But though the planet dies, home and hearth live on. The author recommends a spirited response to life but demonstrates only repression, invokes the concept of total loss but in the end preserves everything. You could slice big pieces off the ideological carcass of *American Ruminant* and, like a fortyish academic from a prairie state, it would still walk around, feeding, digesting and congratulating itself on its own gravitas and of the worth of the herbivore life in general. It might stumble occasionally or feel tired; but it would have an explanation for that.

(10) DISSIPATIVE SYSTEMS

In this novel of worldbuilding, future psychoanalyst Diana Sontag-Cohn recklessly intertwines her own imagination with that of an unnamed patient known only by the letter X. X has failed to construct himself and invites the psychiatrist to extend her own self-constructive efforts on his behalf. The two of them are immediately looped into the construction of a third thing – their relationship – then a fourth and fifth – each one's perception of this relationship under the shifting terms of the old pre-analysis selves – and so on. Out of the patient's perception of emptiness and the psychiatrist's gesture of filling, they build not one but several 'worlds'. In the end, has the psychiatrist helped X to identify, find, or make himself? No: but between them they have made an incalculable number of new psychological spaces, their exploration of which has made an incalculable number more. This labyrinthine dissipative system fails both of them and everything they have consigned to it re-emerges sooner or later in acts of insane violence.

When I received this book from the *Times Literary Supplement* for review, it was under such heavy embargo that minor reviewers like myself weren't even allowed to know who had written it. The name of the author would be backfilled into our copy on delivery. I would be required to show evidence that I had destroyed my Advance Reading Copy by an accepted secure method. At first I thought I must be reading a lost Richard Powers, written in the mid–80s and for some reason remaining unpublished. But at 120 pages the volume seemed too slim; and the text didn't, in the end, seem recursive enough. Then I began to count the author's many uses of the acronym DSC, the initials of worldbuilding psychiatrist Diana Sontag-Cohn, whose name comprises the first three words of the novel. With the exception of X, all the central characters share these initials; and in one entire – thankfully short – chapter, every character's name is made from an anagram of Sontag-Cohn's. This led to the inevitable recognition that I was holding in my hands an early product of the legendary Dynamical Systems Collective – perhaps their first and only foray into the literary arts! You can imagine my excitement. A tragedy that, in the end, it was withdrawn a week before publication – although the occasional ARC, untitled, unattributed and unread, can still be found in the Oxfams of Clapham, Highgate and Cambridge.

(11) KICKASS CULTURAL PROPERTIES

The behaviouristic universe, controlled from outside the text. The meaningless anxiety generated by a plot trope carefully isolated from any actual plot. The meaningless preparation for action. The preparation for meaningless action. The Proppian magic object, its discovery being the next item on a to-do list checked from outside the text. The freedom motif and its meaninglessly glib reversal. All of it makes a Skinner box look like *To the Lighthouse*. The actant has nice muscles but you feel only compassion. Not because she's haggard from the effort of keeping in shape; not because she's trapped in a scenario one millimetre deep; not because she's encumbered by those risible poses of faux-aggression and off-the-shelf feistiness; not because her humanity has been reduced to an algorithm, a schematic whose tragedy is to make Lara Croft seem complex: but because she exists only as cultural property at the beck and call of the rights holder & the male player. She can escape the prison but not the game.

(12) LIQUID ARRANGEMENTS

In this novel without urgency, there's a carrot but no stick. Chapter by chapter, a Team of Friends, driven by what they'll gain when they solve a problem rather than by what they'll lose if they don't, solve problems. Once a problem is solved, the next problem is presented and the drive to solve it lies simply in the fact that no solution has yet been found. At the same time this isn't a puzzle novel. Neither does it seem to be an attempt to write an exciting story without resort to violence, sensationalism, othering, etc. Once all the problems have been solved the novel ends. The same applies to each scene, each sub-plot, each arc of character-relation among the Team of Friends: the momentary problem and its solution drive development at every level. People live alone, but come together easily in cafeterias, offices and public spaces. Their arrangements are liquid. Spirits are usually high, but even where there is physical danger – or loss or heartbreak, or at least the possibility of those things – work on the current problem places it somehow at one or two removes: so that while the Team of Friends may be threatened, threat converts fluidly into an issue of morale which in itself slides away in the corner of the reader's eye as a new problem captures the attention. Violence is deferred or confronted by proxy. In moments of great doubt there is always an authority to be applied to. It's a structure which appears to be written out of – and directed back into – a culture or subculture in which, although society is often depicted as collapsing, work and its aspirations remain the only conceivable drives. Whatever its motive or audience, this assumption about the world comes over as a soapiness in the feel of the narration, as if no one is really there and nothing is really being told.

(13) THE LAST FISH

This short novel's central character stares out over a deserted coastal town, entangling himself with mysterious couples, psychiatrists and airmen as the world around him falls slowly but irrevocably into a beach-fatigued 50s science fiction version of itself. 'Every so often, as he waited for nightfall – signalled by the long repetitive sweep of the old Ferrari's headlights against the greenish afterglow above the esplanade – Carson would force himself up and down Hermione Miro's small swimming pool at a slow crawl, these few enervated daily laps a way of convincing himself that he still existed.' We read this as a metaphor: but in Carson's world, as in ours, everyone without sufficient ego is vanishing. As the novel progresses, we see that Carson is vanishing too.

Entertaining Angels
Unawares

I GOT TWO OR three weeks' work with a firm that specialised in high and difficult access jobs in and around Halifax. They needed a labourer, someone to fetch and carry, clean the site up behind them. The job was on the tower of a church about thirty miles northeast of the town. I wasn't sure what I thought about that. I wondered what I'd say to the vicar if he ever appeared, but he never did.

Generally it was a quiet job. I was there on my own with the supervisor, a man called Ed Brinklow.

Brinklow picked me up every morning in the firm's van. He drove the van as if he expected it to be a motorcycle, changing lanes at high speed among slow traffic, overtaking on the inside. He made the engine rev and snap so that other motorists stared suddenly over their shoulders. Until I was used to this I didn't have much to say, but we got on well enough, and after a day or two he began to tell me about a recurring dream he had. In it he found himself chasing people through a city.

I asked him what sort of city. Larger than Sheffield, he said, but not as large as London. It was old. 'Not right old – not ages and ages ago – but not right modern, either.' It was a Victorian city, blackened with soft coal smoke, rotten with industry. In the dream Brinklow went up and down the stairwells of factories and tenements, sometimes at a run,

47

sometimes a floaty dreamlike walk, broken glass and iron pipework all around him. 'It were the usual thing wi' dreams – corners turn into dead ends just as you get there, even though you've seen people go round them. Anyway, there I were, going along, and I had this absolutely *mega* sword.'

I stared at him.

'A sword,' I said.

'Biggest fucker you've seen,' he said. 'Biggest fucker you've ever seen.'

His memories of this sword were vivid and exact. It wasn't new. It had been resharpened many times. He could tell from irregularities in the chamfer of the blade. Its hilt – which he called 'the handle' – was built up out of gold rings; and it came in its own long leather scabbard – which he called 'the holster' – fastened with a press stud for quick access. 'I can just imagine it now in front of me. I feel as I've got one of these somewhere. Anyway, this dream basically consisted of walking around, then going on to tube trains and stuff, and –'

He stared at me, unsure how to proceed.

'– and, well, just basically hacking people's heads off.'

'Fucking hell,' I said. 'Steady away.'

'Weird, eh? Isn't that fucking weird?'

I had to say it was. 'Do you have it a lot,' I said, 'This dream?'

He thought.

'Often enough,' he admitted.

To get to the job you had to drive through wooded hills on steep, narrow roads. It was beautiful country, even the way Brinklow drove. What the fuck, I thought, I might as well sit back and enjoy the ride. The trees were green and lush, oaks and birches. It was rainforest Britain in the second year of Century 21. Then you turned a corner suddenly and the church was in front of you, a blackened square edifice flanked on one side by a farmyard full of wrecked machinery, and on the other by a neat garden in which tame rabbits lolloped stupidly around all morning. Its blue and gold clock had stopped at half past five. They had strung the site sign across the tower near the top:

GEX ACCESS.

No one, Brinklow admitted, was sure what GEX stood for. But the story on the church was this: when it was built in 1830, the buttresses were an afterthought. They had no real engineering function. Instead of supporting the building they were just leaning against it. By 1900 they were beginning to sag and banana away. A hundred years later, eight inch gaps had opened up, and the church had been condemned unless it could be fixed. That job was finished now. The GEX team had gone in and driven thirty six ten-foot, 12 tpi, stainless steel bolts through the buttresses into the fabric of the tower itself, cementing them in with aerospace resins. You had to hide that, of course, so afterwards the restorers came along with something called 'gobbo', a kind of grout made from mud and goat-hair, and sealed it all up. There were a lot of jokes about gobbo. Not counting assessment and planning it had taken less than a fortnight. All that remained was a bit of repointing. Brinklow had also promised he would take the rotten stone louvres out of the belltower.

'They're all laminated,' he told me.

'You mean they're fucked,' I said.

'That too.'

We decided to do the louvres first. We spent three or four mornings dropping them eighty feet to the floor where they went off like bombs. It was tiring work getting them out of their slots. We would chuck a few of them down then go up to the top of the tower and have a drink of tea. From up there you could see that the church stood at a confluence of valleys, streams and lanes. You would never have understood that from the ground, Brinklow said, because of all the hills and ridges.

It would have been impossible to unravel by eye. I drank my tea and said:

'That dream of yours. The one with the sword. I mean, what's the point? What's the story on that?'

He shrugged. 'I don't know. There's no story. It's more like a video game. Hacking people's heads off, that's the point. And it's not just the odd person. It's doing a lot. That's the tick: getting loads of people all at once. Five or six people are stood round you, and you just sort of start *spinning round* with this thing – *footoof!* – and getting all their heads off.' While he was talking two houseflies landed on the parapet and began to copulate on the warm stone. The sun glittered off them blue and green, and off the mica crystals in the stone around them.

'Hey, look at these fuckers,' I said. 'They're at it.'

'Leave them alone,' Brinklow said. 'You wouldn't want people watching you.'

I watched the flies a minute more. I could see they were unaware of me, unaware of anything. Every so often they buzzed groggily and lurched into a new position. 'I hate flies,' I said. 'I hate the dirt of them.' I crushed them with my thumb, then I wiped my thumb along the parapet to clean it.

'Jesus,' Brinklow said. 'They were only fucking.'

'Are you yourself?' I said.

'What?'

'In this dream, are you yourself?'

'I suppose I am,' he said. 'I never thought about it.' Then he said: 'I'm taller.'

We never ate lunch at the top of the tower. It was too hot by then. We could have gone to the local pub, but Brinklow wasn't much of a drinker. Anyway, as he said, at lunchtime it was always full of locals playing Fistful of Money. If they weren't doing that they were selling one another shotgun cartridges. So most of the time we took sandwiches down into the back of the church, whatever that's called, which had been converted into a miniature parish hall. It stayed cool there all day. They had a kitchen where we could make tea. There were chairs and tables, and a piano. It was all separated from the rest of the church by a long glass screen. Pictures and bits of writing by Sunday school kids were displayed on red felt pinboards. Every morning we found a fresh display of leaflets on one of the tables. Someone had arranged them carefully in a fan.

'"Keep Yourself Pure"!' Brinklow quoted. He laughed. 'What's the difference between perverse and perverted?'

'I don't know.'

'You're perverse if you tickle your arse with a feather. If you're perverted you use the whole chicken.'

'How do you feel,' I said, 'in this dream you're having?'

'Weird,' he said. 'I feel weird.' He drank some of his tea. 'I'm myself, but I don't feel as if I'm inside myself.'

'You're watching yourself,' I suggested.

'I suppose I am.'

'That's what you're doing.'

He was watching himself stalk this gloomy industrial city, getting their heads off. One night adults, the next night children. One moment he was in a huge park with silent blackened monuments, the next following a woman and child along a disused gantry. Suddenly he found himself, hours later, in a tube tunnel. 'All these kids came on to the tube-station platform —' Or was it a platform? At its shadowy edges it seemed to him to blend into a kind of courtyard, with a ramp for wheelchairs. 'It felt like you were on a platform. But at the same time you could feel you were somewhere else — in this courtyard.' Anyway, he was with two lads off the hi tech team, Steve and Paul. He told them to lie down quietly on the ramp out of harm's way. 'Then all these kids came running round the corner — you know, eight, nine year old kids, and suddenly it went really dark, and I just remember squatting down to get the right height and —'

'*Footoof!*' I said.

'– all their heads off, five or six heads at one go.'

I went and looked at the noticeboards where the Sunday school kids had pinned their work up. A recent drawing exercise for the boys had been 'My route to church'. They had made light work of it, drawing themselves in red Ferraris and adding commentary: 'My house.' 'Whooosh!' 'Hinchcliffe Arms.' 'Screeech!' 'Church Bank Lane.' 'Bang!' The energy of these journeys undercut the cheap parsonical metaphor they were based on. The girls had done paper samplers which read JESUS IS LORD OF LIFE.

Brinklow came and looked over my shoulder. 'See that?' he said. 'One of them's written BORD OF LIFE. Little tinker.' He studied his watch. 'Hey, time to drop a few more bombs,' he said.

'I'm having a piss first.'

'You can do that if you want,' Ed Brinklow said. I went into the lavatory. 'Remember though,' he called after me: 'More than two shakes is a wank.'

The graveyard was famous for something, but Brinklow couldn't remember what. I ought to go and have a look at it anyway, he told me. It was worth seeing: there were graves out there the size of supertankers. I went round one lunchtime. He was right. The graveyard was also full of fantastic stone obelisks and gesticulating angels. Insects whizzed through the air between them. Brambles, thistles and fern had sprung up in one corner. Elsewhere it was the kind of grass you only ever see in cemeteries.

There were more children out there than I expected. They buried them close to the church. The ones that died before 1900 were miniature adults full of some earnest future. They got proper graves, serious graves. Today's kids slipped their moorings in childish boats piled with toys. If the older graves were like supertankers, these new ones went bobbing along in the church wake like condom packets behind a ferry.

I had a look down at them. LOVE NEVER DIES. But we all know it does. Clarence and Katherine lose John, their beloved son. Not much later, Clarence loses Katherine. Two years after that the world loses Clarence, and that's that until GEX arrive. Thrash metal blares from their radio. They hang a yellow plastic bucket out of the belfry. They bolt everything back together with fucking great bolts. Thinking about this, I went back into the church where Brinklow was finishing his tea.

'What do you reckon then?' he said.

'It's disgusting. People are expected to leave monuments to their tragedies, even though that makes them harder to forget.'

He stared at me uncertainly.

'Here's that goat's hair you wanted to see,' he said.

He threw it on to the table, where it settled next to my cup, a dark brown swatch flecked with grey. It was full of goat dandruff, the biggest dandruff you've ever seen.

'Thanks a lot Ed.'

'You said you were interested,' he said. 'That's what they bound the gobbo with. Don't ask me how successful it was. In the end they just poured a couple of buckets of it down between the tower and the buttresses. Lo-tech fuckers. Sand and cement, bound up with that stuff. They just call it gobbo to distinguish it from structural concrete.' He said: 'We could make some up if you like. I mean, if you're that bothered. Apparently the hair needs to be fresh.'

I was fascinated by the whole idea.

'So do they have to keep a goat?' I said. 'The restorers?'

'Feel it,' he said. 'It's just like women's hair.'

'Fucking hell. What sort of women do you go out with?'

He was right though. With your eyes closed it felt exactly like human hair.

'We had a chemistry teacher at school called Gobbo,' I said. 'But that was because he spat a lot when he talked. Really thick spit.' We were thirteen, we loved that. We also loved the rubber tubes that fed the Bunsen burners; after six months or so, I told Brinklow, we stopped laughing at Gobbo's spit problem and concentrated on setting them on fire instead. 'Do they still have Bunsen burners?' I said, but he didn't know what I was talking about. 'It was a fair old time ago,' I had to admit.

Another thing that struck me about the graveyard was this: some of the headstones had undergone such mechanical erosion you couldn't read what they said. Despite that the words on them seemed to remain beneath the surface, as if now was just water running over them. 'In memory'; 'also of three infants'; 'a glorious eternity'. With the right focus, you thought, you might be able to bring them back. But in the end no meaning swam up into view.

Brinklow had done every kind of difficult access engineering, from avalanche-netting in Gibraltar to cleaning windows in the City of London; but his fame came from stabilising the chalk cutting at the entrance to one of the big rail stations on the south coast. The problem was, in that environment explosives couldn't be used to remove the unstable stuff: so he drilled rows of holes one metre apart which he then pumped full of a fast-expanding chemical grout. 'Levered it off nicely. Not a bad solution.' He'd been on the tower blocks too, everyone in that trade has. He wouldn't go back to it. Gangs of kids wreck your work behind you. The adults steal your equipment: they aren't much more than kids themselves, and they couldn't give a toss about where or how they live.

He'd spent years on that. Even so he was quite a lot younger than me. He had a wife and two kids in Rotherham. He didn't get on with her any more, but he saw the kids every weekend. He showed me a photograph of the whole family on some flat northern beach. The tide was out as far as you could see. The wife was nice, a looker in an ordinary kind of way. One glance at her face and you could understand why they were separated. She didn't trust him, she didn't trust the job with all its risks and its foreign travel opportunities; she didn't trust the tattoos up his arm. Who would? Still, the kids were beautiful – two boys, five and seven, in their England football shirts – and he clearly loved them. In the end that's why I couldn't understand the dream he was having.

'So how do you do with it?' I asked him. 'I mean, having these kids of your own? You must feel pretty shit about killing children in a dream.'

He thought for a moment.

'I felt like an animal,' he said, 'the first time I had it.'

It always ended the same way, he said, that dream. *Footoof!* – off came the heads of all these kids. One little lad lost only the top of his head, 'the top bit like the scalp. I have to give it three or four goes, so it comes off in slices –'

'Christ, Ed!'

'– and eventually I get it. Oh, it doesn't look like you're cutting somebody's head,' he said. 'It looks more like a cabbage or summat.' He paused to consider this. 'Coming off in slabs.'

After that he always ran for it, in a convulsion of fear and glee – 'I can really feel me heart pounding, every step' – and then the dream seemed to jump very quickly and he was out of the city altogether, with a job selling agricultural machinery in some great prairie farming waste, somewhere where the dust boiled off the landscape all summer. 'There I am, talking about experimental tractors to some old bloke in a farmhouse but thinking all the time:

'I'm going to get caught. I'm going to get caught.'

He wanted to get caught.

'They're never my kiddies,' he said. 'But I feel like an animal every time I have that dream, and I want to get caught.'

The job went well. We pried the rest of the louvres out and replaced them with brand new stone a rosy colour so faint it was almost white. The church people weren't up for sandblasting the rest of the building to match, so we started in on the pointing. Good weather was a requirement for that, and we got it. At the same time we needed shade and cool air. Nine in the morning, we'd already been working three hours. We hung off the abseil ropes, pointing as fast as we could, trying to get a section done before the grout dried up in the bucket. We were working in shorts, drinking four or five litres of water a day, gasping like animals. From up on the tower, the surrounding hills resounded with light. By noon it was so baked and airless the only place you could bear was the inside of the church. About four days of this and the job was finished.

'We'll clear the site tomorrow,' Brinklow said. 'It'll be a late start. I've to go to the dentist in the morning.'

'Ouch.'

'I don't mind it, me,' he said.

He had an interesting relationship with his dentist, who had once dared him to have a filling without anaesthetic. 'It won't take a minute,' he promised, staring steadily at Brinklow. The challenge was obvious. Brinklow looked steadily back at him for fifteen seconds and bought it.

'Did it hurt?' I asked.

He shrugged. 'It were bearable. But I love those fucking dental drills! Watercooled, five hundred thousand rpm. Shit hot. You can see this fucking *aerosol* of stuff flying out of your mouth when they're working. Tooth debris, water droplets, saliva, blood, bacteria. The fucking works.' Seeing my expression, he laughed. 'Anyway we're done here. We'll have a nice short day tomorrow.'

He got out his cellphone. 'I'll just make arrangements for someone to collect that laminated stone.'

He drove me back to Halifax in his usual way, overtaking people on blind bends as if the van was some Kawasaki he'd once owned. I got him to drop me in the centre of town, so I could go round Sainsburys and buy a few things; then I walked home with the stuff in two plastic bags.

It was nine o' clock by then, a Tuesday night in high summer. Something was different about the air: it was filling with humidity. I could see clouds up over the moor outside the town. I cooked. I watched a TV programme about a footballer accepting a challenge to be an interior decorator. After that the news came on, the usual stuff, children without anything to eat enlisted as soldiers in some fucking African war; kids at home suffering all kinds of abuse. It was dark by then. Outside it had just begun to rain, big slow drops then smaller and faster. I fell asleep in front of the TV and woke up at two o' clock in the morning to find it still on. I went over to satellite to get the adult channels, but after five minutes I couldn't be bothered. I couldn't imagine having sex any more. The water was more interesting, sluicing down the windows, rushing down the gutters in front. I got up and switched the light on. The house had been a rental when I bought it, a one-up one-down furnished in the 70s with fitted carpets in swirling patterns of purple and green. The bathroom suite and kitchen cupboards were purple too. Nothing got done because I couldn't get the energy up after work. There was grease and dust on top of the cupboards that had been there twenty years.

Looking round, I wished I'd done more. Then I thought if I just went to bed maybe I'd go to sleep again. But I lay awake listening to the rain and thinking about the sword in Ed Brinklow's dream. I thought about Brinklow himself, and the sense of him I had as feral, full of caution and daring as he went about getting their heads off. I thought about him taking the dentist's bet, bracing himself against the vibration in his jaw, trying to bring on anaesthesia by staring up and away from the dentist's blank intent face into the spray flying up like fireworks through the tight beam of the overhead lamp.

Why did I like his smile so much? He didn't smile often but when he did it was hard not to respond. All I could think was that it reminded me of my father's smile. It had the same quality of being too young for his age.

'I'm too old for mine,' I thought.

I was awake most of the night.

It was still wet the next day, Wednesday, which made it hard to wake up. The light was poor. The air had that grey liquid look it gets in West Yorkshire, where the chemists are still filling prescriptions for seasonal affective disorder in July. Brinklow arrived ten minutes late. I was already outside the house waiting for him.

'You're keen,' he said.

'Good time at the dentist's?'

That got a grin off him.

'Not bad,' he said. 'But I had a right epic wi' the van this morning. Smoke coming from under the dash, all sorts. I can see something sparking back there but I just can't get at it with my fingers.'

By the time we got to the job the sun had come out a bit. A light breeze was helping to dry things out, moving the leaves of the birch and oak above Church Bank Lane. Church Brook, swollen by the night's run-off, rushed along in its narrow defile. The porous old gritstone they'd built the church from had sucked up the rain; it looked blackened and fucked, like a ruin in the valley. Brinklow wouldn't have the radio on, he didn't feel like it. That made us slow. We had trouble getting the GEX ACCESS sign down. CPTs and other tools, locked into the vestry at night, had to be checked into their plastic bins and stacked in the back of the van. Brinklow did this on his own, then wandered about the site looking for things he thought he might have missed. He seemed sad the job was finished. 'People should look after places like this,' he said. If he had his way, he'd always do this kind of work, restoration work. Looking out at the graveyard I wasn't so sure. Eventually we were finished.

'How's that dream of yours?' I said.

'Eh? Oh, that.' He rubbed the back of his neck. 'Like

clockwork these days,' he said. 'Night after night, getting their heads off.'

'I want to be in it,' I said.

He grinned.

'What?' he said.

'I'm serious,' I said. 'I want to be in the dream. I want to share it.'

'Come on Mike,' he said. 'What's the joke?'

'I mean it, Ed.'

He began to look embarrassed.

I said: 'There's no joke here.'

He laughed.

'Come on Mike,' he repeated. 'It's a dream.'

I kept looking into his eyes, but he shook his head and walked off. 'You're fucking mad,' he said.

Two hours later I watched him go round the graveyard. I was on the tower by then, hidden down behind the parapet. Brinklow was calling, 'Mike? Mike?' The humidity in the air made his voice sound unpredictable, close by one minute, far away the next. 'This is fucking stupid,' he said. He looked at his watch. 'I'm giving you another five minutes, then I'm going.' He waited slightly less than that. 'Fuck off then, you stupid fucker,' he shouted. I watched him drive the van away, then I went back down into the church. I pulled one of the Sunday school drawings off the pinboard and wrote on the back of it:

'Places like this reek of death.'

I signed that as if it was the visitor's book and put it on one of the tables next to the careful fan of leaflets. As an afterthought I added, 'Anyone can see that.' Then I went out between the graves with the bucket of gobbo I'd mixed that morning and started smearing it over them at random with a pointing trowel.

Elf Land: The Lost Palaces

ELDRANOL THE ELF LORD is wheeled to bed every night on a reinforced composite and titanium gurney. Two or three attendants lift the thick laps of flesh and lovingly clean out the sores down in the creamy, lardy folds where his genitals still nestle. He has lost some of his right foot to diabetes. The Queen left him a hundred years ago, with her dwarf, for the North. But none of this will ever spoil his dream of finishing an ultra-marathon. At night in a secondary world of his secondary world the Elf Lord runs, barefoot and effortless, across the Great Erg Desert (see map), wearing only the traditional leather kirtle, while his favorite daughter keeps watch over his sleeping body with its faint, calming smells of ketones and antifungal cream. She's a feisty urban vampire princess but her heart is so in the right place. She can't help but wonder how things will go with them when the Horde arrives at the Gate next Wednesday. Tomorrow, in a final attempt to reach out to his people, the Elf Lord will feature kingdomwide in the Don't Do This To Yourself segment of *Supersize vs Superskinny*; while for the Princess it's a Kickass Battle Looks last chance on QVC.

Psychoarcheology

I KEEP GETTING FLASHBACKS to provincial streets. You're driving. We're touring the big civil engineering projects, looking for dead Royals. We found a minor Plantagenet earlier today, crouched in bad cement beneath a Midlands motorway pier for all the world as if he'd been garotted on the lavatory. Yesterday it was a previously unknown illegitimate Stuart, two meters under the floor of an HS2 station with her two children, some scraps of religious writing and an older man (he's related, maybe a brother or cousin, molecular biology will sort it out). She's no longer the fairest of them all.

Now that science tells us they're a good place to look, we're finding kings and queens under every parking structure in the UK, just lining up to present their DNA for inspection. They choked on items of food, bled out on a moor during some predictable turf war, suffered a beheading they might have avoided if they'd learned how to work a room and not piss off the archbishop. There's no more sense to the way we find them than in a feature length re-run of *Waking the Dead* or *Silent Witness*: their circumstances seem no less incoherent, post-historical; their post-death narratives no less fatuous. Their hands are clenched and presented in the boxer position, as if to hang on to the good things they grabbed in life.

'We're coming up on the airport now,' you say. 'The data indicates Hapsburgs. Lots of them.'

I say: 'I think we should get takeaway first.'

DNA, the last word in personal identification. Along with

every one of these corpses there's a buried irony. It's to do with privilege transmitted in the blood. DNA, after all, was the reason for their hugger-mugger in the first place – the plot in the provinces, the rat in the arras, the neck bent before the axe, the smothering of little princes, the slaughter of serfs in an open field somewhere near Bosworth, the unrelenting sexual intercourse – the dogged monotony of the Royal way of life. Now here they are, their hack-marks intact, identified – betrayed, some might say – by the very chemistry that drove them through their crap lives. DNA is the meat of it.

So we eat in the car on the South Perimeter Road, staring through the chain link fence, and you say:

'What will the heritage industry do when it runs out of kings?'

The airport is like a vast construction site. In one corner, heavy duty ground-penetrating radar is still grinding to and fro; if there's a pea left under this mattress, the radar will find it. Elsewhere the field-walking and heritage solutions teams have been and gone; trench trials are over; 'strip, map and record' is under way. Ranks of powerful backhoes, on standby for a month, manouevre in and out of the shadows. The Dreamliners are mothballed, the runways are up. The overburden is off. They're ripping down to the first archeological horizon. The schedule's tight: time is money in more ways than one. Generator exhaust drifts through the cones of light from a thousand portable halide lamps, under which celebrity academics gang-bang the 'past' in front of the cameras in hi-viz wear and sterile paper suits. There's a palpable sense of excitement. Can they hear us, the queens and kings, through the impacted earth? Do they know we're on our way down?

For them the truth will soon be out. They come to light pre-butchered, grinning shyly, stripped to the bones and teeth for on-site strontium isotope analysis. There's no option but honesty for them in this respect; after the imbroglio of history, chemistry must seem simple, even refreshing. But things are more complex for us, especially when we work for the Heritage Police. There's always a rights issue. Where does the latest Tudor belong? Does he belong where he was found? Or whence he came? Who gets the brown sign? One wrong decision and York won't talk to Leicester, the knives are out again after hundreds of years of peace. Contracts torn up, the industry at war with itself, we all know where that can lead: diminished footfall in the visitor centres. No one wants to see that. In the end, of course, presentation is nine tenths of the law: dig for the evidence, develop the interactive exhibit, crowdsource the story the public wants to hear.

'It's the contemporary equivalent of the religious relics industry,' you say, winding down the window and chucking the remains of your burger into the shadows of the layby, 'only this time the relics are real.'

'Very postmodern,' I say.

It's as if our obsession with dead Royals has in itself made them available in such numbers. Why have we suddenly started digging them up like this? Out of nervousness? Out of the need for a psychic anchor? Out of economic desperation, so that, having run out of each other's washing to take in, we now take in one another's ancestors? Why not let them lie? It's certainly not possible to learn from them. All they mean to us is what we want them to mean. To claim we can learn from them because they had, at base, the same emotions as us, the same satisfactions, the same fears, the same 'needs', is in itself a projection. They aren't the past in any material sense: brought to light, they're what they are now, not what they were then. At best they're a geological resource, not perhaps as valuable as coal, but more easily available and each containing enough energy to power a couple of careers, a biography, an MA course, a BBC4 series.

'All this is so hackneyed and played out.'

I've heard you say as much before, so I shrug and start the engine. 'Let's get this over with,' I say.

It can't be long before the DNA of Richard III's horse is detected in processed food in the Republic of Ireland. That'll open up new fields of research.

Royal Estate

THE PALACE TURNED OUT to be a stuffy, disappointing warren that just *reeked* of dogs. The Queen showed us around lots of small low-ceilinged rooms with fitted carpets, not what we were looking for at all. No real Elfland values or internal architecture left, except for that rather gorgeous river-frontage. She kept saying that she and her husband had been going to make this or that improvement, but everything was interrupted when, 'They came back'. At one point she said, 'We were going to sell up, go to the Deep West, but they came back. They came back, you see, and what can you do?' She never said who or what they were. There was an old labrador sleeping outside the back door. They also had a really quite smelly chihuaha, always gazing up at you, and when you petted it, 'Oh she'll go to anyone, that one. When you're shopping she'll go straight in your bag.' Meanwhile, honestly, Eldranol just vegetated there in the front room, watching cable TV on satellite and in the end we decided no matter how close it was to the Evening Harbours it just wasn't for us.

Yummie

IN HIS LATE FIFTIES Short experienced some kind of cardiac problem, a brief but painful event which landed him in an Accident and Emergency unit in East London. From A&E he was processed to Acute Assessment, where they took his blood pressure at two-hourly intervals but otherwise didn't seem to know what to do with him. Everyone was very kind.

His second night on the ward, he stood in the corridor where it was cooler and looked out over a strip of grass. An iron staircase was off to one side. He could see bollards; what he imagined was a car park; behind that a few trees quite dense and dark against the sky. He rested his forehead against the cold glass of the fire door. Propane tanks, portabuilding offices, everything lighted grey and blue. He had a short clear glimpse of himself opening the door and walking out. It wouldn't have required a decision; to some degree, in fact, he felt it had already happened. That glimpse had lobed itself off immediately, becoming its own world. He could see himself moving away between the trees, tentatively at first but with increasing confidence.

Late the next evening, a bed came free in Coronary Care, a wheelchair ride away across the architectural and procedural grain of the hospital, from clean and new to grimy and old, past stacks of mysterious materials, parks of apparently abandoned medical electronics and radiology machines, and into a narrow slot deep in the original building. 3am, he found himself awake again. Someone further along the slot was

69

moaning. Someone else had a cough, long and retching, full of sad self-disgust.

'Make no mistake about this,' the consultant advised him next morning: 'You've had a heart attack.'

Short, who had never believed anything else, waited to hear more; but that seemed to be it. The procedure he now underwent was an experience very much like an amusement ride. He was placed carefully on a narrow table. The nurse gave him an injection of diazepam she described as 'the equivalent of three good gin-and-tonics', while someone else demonstrated the bank of cameras that would image his heart. The table stretched away in front of him, elongated, bluish. The cameras then groaned and slid about, pressing down into his space. Soon, off to one side, someone was putting in a lot of effort to push something like an old-fashioned drain-rod up the femoral artery and deep into his body. It was a struggle. He had the distant sense of being smashed and pummelled about. He couldn't feel anything, but sometimes their voices made him nervous. 'He'll have a bit of a bruise,' someone warned; someone else said they would put some pressure on that. Every so often they asked him if he felt ok. 'I don't know what I feel,' Short answered. In fact he felt violated but excited. He felt as if he was whizzing along some blue-lit track, he could come off the rails at any time but thanks to the diazepam he wouldn't mind.

'I'm quite enjoying it,' he said.

They laughed at that, but when he heard himself say he thought there might be a sensation in his heart – not a pain precisely, but some sort of feeling he couldn't quite describe – there was a silence then the thud of some more powerful drug hitting his system like a car running over a cattle grid.

Back on the ward, he felt embarrassingly optimistic, though a list of possible changes to his life (scribbled under the heading 'Opportunities' in the blank space next to the Guardian crossword puzzle) proved vague; turning out when he consulted it later to be couched in the self-improvement languages of the 1980s. How, for instance, could Short be 'kinder' to himself? What might that actually mean? Deep in the night, Coronary Care became a site of hallucination, like the woods in a fairytale: he was woken by a child's cough, sometimes seeming to issue from a ward directly beneath this one, sometimes from the wall of monitors and tubes behind his bed. It was a careful, precise little sound, urgent yet determined to attract no attention. Towards dawn a tall languid-looking man of his father's generation stood in the corridor by the fire door, calling, 'Yummie? Yummie?' in tones pitched between puzzlement and command. His head was almost entirely round, his expression in some way surprised. He looked Short up and down, made eye contact and said, 'Let's not be mistaken! You will have a hell of a bruise!'

An empty trolley clattered past unseen behind them.

'Are you even here,' Short whispered. 'Because Yummie is not a name.'

'Those chickens,' the man said, 'waiting outside for you now? They are your chickens. You deny them, but I see they follow you with great persistence.'

Though no chickens were visible, he was right: if Acute Assessment had been like the lobby of a cheap but comfortable hotel – air too hot, coffee bearable, quiet conversations at reception – Coronary Care was where events played out the way Short had been taught to fear. It wasn't the bottom of things by any means, but it was the beginning of the bottom of things. Those chickens, having come home to roost, would eye him now and until the end, heads on one side, mad little combs flopping.

The next day, he was discharged.

'Isn't it a bit soon?' he asked the rehab nurse.

'You'll be fine,' she said.

She said people often felt a little anxious. But it really was a safe, easy, walk in, walk out procedure, and he could plan for a good outcome. She asked him if she could take him through some leaflets. 'For instance,' she pointed out, lowering her voice, 'as soon as you can manage two flights of stairs you can have sexual activity.' There was also a list of foods he should avoid. Short had a look at it. Before the attack, his diet had been sourced almost wholly from the red end of the scale. He wondered what he would eat.

'I don't drink much alcohol anyway,' he said.

She gave him a number to call if he needed any further advice. 'If you're worried about anything at all,' she said, 'just ring.'

He wrote 'sexual activity' in his notebook.

'That seems fine,' he said.

Soon afterwards he found himself wearing his own clothes, carrying a two-day-old copy of the Guardian and some hospital toothpaste in a plastic bag, waiting for a cab to come down through the traffic and turn on to the hospital apron. When he got home he was exhausted just from leaning forward and telling the cabby how to get where they were going. He lay down on the sofa and pulled a blanket up over him and went to sleep. When he woke up it was on the edge of being dark. The street outside was quiet. The light in Short's room had a kind of sixty-year-old smokiness, as if he was looking at things through nicotine-stained glass. The door of the room was open, and the man he had met in the hospital corridor now stood at the window, holding the net curtain back with one long hand so he could stare down into the street. He was whispering, 'Yummie? Yummie?' to himself.

I'm moving forward into something here, Short thought: but I don't know what it is. He fell asleep again. The next day he rang the number the rehab nurse had given him and told her: 'I don't think I'm half as well as I feel.'

'People often report a sense of vulnerability,' the nurse explained. 'It's nothing to be ashamed of.'

'Do they report a man with a round head?' Short said.

'Let's get you to come in and have your blood pressure taken.'

In an attempt to normalise himself, Short walked around his neighbourhood, not far at first, twenty minutes here, twenty minutes there. He knew it well, but there are always a few little corners of a neighbourhood you don't know. You always meant to explore them: today, perhaps, you do. Or in the end you glance into that short curving street – with its blackened gap halfway along where a woodyard used to be, or the Memorial Hall with the three tall cemented-up windows and stopped clock – and decide again that it only connects to some other street and then another after that. All the pubs down there, you suspect, have yellowed, patchy ceilings and a feeling of grease under the fingertips wherever you touch.

At home he slept a lot, dreaming repeatedly of his angioplasty – the bunker-like underground theatre, the table too narrow to rest on comfortably, the banks of cameras, the lively technicians and nurses in their colourful thyroid protectors, the air dark but also displaying a slight bluish-grey fluorescence in the corners as if it had absorbed the radioactive dyes from Short's bloodstream. 'How are you getting on,' someone would ask, 'in your ongoing struggle with the world of appearances?' Short's responses became increasingly facetious. He was embarrassed for himself. He woke sweating, his pulse a hundred and fifty beats a minute, experiencing such premonitions of disaster that he had to get up and move around the room. In these moments of unconscious hindsight, the essentially violent nature of the procedure – the feeling of racing feet-first forward on rails under a weird light while your heart is reamed, plumbed, measured to its full physical depth and found wanting – was only heightened. By day he thought he felt a little better. His blood pressure remained too high.

'Whatever you say,' Short told the man in his room, 'Yummie isn't a name.'

'Who are you to tell me that?' the man said. 'It was your mother's name, and her mother's before her. It was your sister's name.'

Short was becoming embittered with the whole thing.

'I never had a sister,' he said. 'How did you get in here?'

'I'm always here. I was here before they christened your father, and before they christened your mother, and before they buried the poor unstained sister you say you never had.' His eyes were as round as his head, entirely without expression and yet somehow both confiding and expectant, as if he knew Short would soon admit to something. 'The poor sister,' he repeated, with a sentimental emphasis. When Short failed to answer – because this was not a past he could recognise, let alone own or identify with in any degree – he waved one hand dismissively and seemed to fade a little. 'How are you getting on with those chickens?' he said. 'Yummie.'

Short made another appointment at Rehab and told them, 'I think my medication might need adjusting.'

'How do you think of me?' the heart nurse said.

'I think of you as the heart nurse,' Short said.

'Well, I am a nurse,' she said. 'But my name's Linda.'

'Then I'll think of you as Sister Linda.'

They laughed and Short left with his new leaflets. A minute or two later he went back down the corridor to her office and stood in the doorway and said: 'I'm supposed to talk when I'm walking?'

'We recommend that,' she said. 'We need you to exercise, but we need you just to make sure your breathing stays inside the range: if you can walk and talk, you're inside the range, you know your heart is fine.'

'I can't think of anything to say.'

She stared at him. 'Well, for instance, you can just have a nice conversation with the other person.'

'The other person,' Short said: 'OK.'

He wrote 'other person' in his notebook.

'I'm usually on my own,' he said. In fact, he was hearing voices in his room at night. One voice would say, 'You're accepting more, aren't you?' and after a pause another would answer, 'Oh yes, yes, I'm accepting more. Definitely. I'm able to accept much more now.' They sounded like an old couple, talking in the tea room at a garden centre. Short couldn't quite locate them, or tell if they were male or female. They seemed to originate quite high up, in a region of discoloured wallpaper, then, in the weeks that followed, still invisible, lower themselves down until they were able to occupy the room proper, pulling themselves about quietly but jerkily between the larger items of furniture, murmuring, 'Two funerals and now another house move. No wonder I can't take anything in,' or, 'Look at this one, dear. He's young enough.'

Once he had noticed them, he noticed others. Sometimes he woke in the night and it was quite a hubbub in there. They were everywhere. They were looking for the toilet. They had opinions about Catholicism and walking. Short had the feeling that they gathered round him while he slept, looking down at him considerately and with concern. Perhaps they even discussed him, and these fits and starts of language were the only way they could express what they knew. As their conversation decayed further, into a mumbled repetition he could hear only as 'Yummie, yummie, yummie,' he would see the tall, calm, round-headed figure waiting by the window, pulling back the curtain to look out, smiling a little. One night it whispered: 'Research shows how rats dream repeatedly of the maze they have not yet solved.' Short woke up with a sharp pain on the left side of his chest and called an ambulance.

'The paramedics said I was fine,' he told Sister Linda at his next appointment. 'They said it wasn't the right kind of pain. They were very kind.'

'I should hope they were,' she said.

'It was just a moment of panic,' Short admitted. He tried to think of a way to qualify that, but could only add: 'My parents were the same.'

'You're due for the three-month echocardiogram anyway.'

On his way to Sonography, Short became lost in the hospital basement; then the technicians didn't want to admit he was in the cubicle with them, but carried on checking their equipment as if they were waiting for some more significant version of him to arrive. After a brief glimpse of what looked like a translucent marine animal pulsing and clutching inside his chest, Short kept his gaze directed away from the monitors. He couldn't so easily ignore the swashy emphysemic whisper produced by this monster, surfacing in his life as if from the depths of a Hollywood ocean. He went back upstairs to Rehab and asked the nurse, 'Have you heard that noise? It's like a 1950s Hotpoint washing machine. Do you remember those?'

She stared at him, then down at the echocardiogram result.

'This is all good,' she said. 'You can take it from me. You can look for a very positive outcome with results like this.'

'So, a heart sounds like obsolete white goods.'

'Really, no one's surprised if you have some anxiety.'

That night he dreamed that a great hoard of household rubbish – broken beds, cheap soiled mattresses, used unpaired shoes stuffed into plastic shopping bags – covered the floor of his room. It smelled of urine. It smelled like a slot deep in the old hospital building. The ceiling was off, and the ceiling of the room above that, and the one above that too: all the way to the roof, which was also off. The room was open to the night sky. In some way, Short's original procedure was still going on. The cameras whirred and shook above him. The walls, bluish with radioactive dyes and ruined by moonlight, were crawling with slow old people pulling themselves head-down towards the floor. 'Where's the toilet here?' they whispered. 'I think it's over that way, dear.' The tweed jackets of the men, the old fashioned wool skirts of the women, fell around their heads, muffling their dull talk; while by the window, Yummie the watchman kept his eye on the street below.

'Why are you doing this?' Short said.

'You think you are alive. Have a closer look. These people were victims of that thought too. People come home from a visit and discover they've never left. Or they have a wall knocked down in their attic and find this behind it. Do you see?'

'I don't see, no.'

'People imagine there will be no upshot from this, no discovery, that it will be the end of the story. Or so they hope.'

'Another thing,' Short said: 'I don't want you here.'

'Good luck with that.'

That was a low point, Short was forced to admit; but afterwards his life seemed to improve. He found another room, not far from the hospital. He went to the gym every two or three days. From being a zone of anxiety, the weekly act of transferring his medication from its calendar-packaging into the dispenser became a comforting regime. Bisoprolol, losartan potassium, atorvastatin, lansoprazole like a cheap holiday destination in the Canary Islands: their side effects were legion, though in three months Short had suffered only a sudden but unimpressive swelling of the inner lip. He bought himself a blood pressure monitor. The clutch of its cuff was like a reassuring hand on his upper arm, although inevitably it reminded him of things he didn't want to remember. Once a major organ has failed you – or you have failed it – your relations with the world become more tentative, more grateful and fragile. He had never liked to feel the beat of his heart. Other emotional reactions he experienced: a kind of protective reluctance; easily-triggered startle reflex; fear that every internal sensation might be the symptom of another event.

'But there's something else too,' he told Sister Linda. He experienced it as 'a kind of lifting up away from life and towards it at the same time. You can't avoid it any more, so all you're left with is to engage it.'

'I'm not sure I follow you,' she said.

'The other thing is I'm determined to be kinder to myself.'

By day he walked the streets – chatting out loud to no one, maintaining a brisk pace but always checking that his heart rate remained safely within the range – or toured the supermarket aisles foraging for products at the green end of the scale. At night he watched on-demand television; worked on the Guardian crossword puzzle he had begun in hospital. He had to admit now that he had enjoyed his stay there, the warmth at night, the regular coming and going of the staff by day. He had felt safe for the first time in his life. He went through his belongings until he found the toothpaste and toothbrush he had brought back with him from Coronary Care, laying them out on top of his chest of drawers where he could see them, along with a pair of red non-slip ward socks still in their packaging. While he was doing that, Yummie climbed slowly down the wall behind him and said:

'You needn't think collecting a lot of old rubbish will help. They all thought that.'

'Those chickens you used to mention,' Short said: 'I never saw them. How are they now? I often think of you on the street, waiting outside the hospices and care homes in all weathers. I worry on your behalf.'

'Worry about yourself,' said Yummie, 'not me. That's my advice.'

Places you Didn't Think to Look for Yourself

IN THE LIGHT FALLING horizontally along grey lapboards. In very fast light, as on any seafront. In the idea of coughing up your large organs due to drink even though you don't drink very much. In a related feebleness of your own actions which is not physical. In a tendency to hate being followed, especially in October. In the sense of things adding up or ticking away or both. In such a perfect empathy with other people it enables you to do what they want before they know what it is. In Rotherham. In any real sense of looking at yourself from outside. In the softness of your decisions. In a tendency to copy down signage. In failures not your own which, when you read about them, make you feel uncomfortable for two days or give you the feeling you are living out the ending of a Robert Stone novel. In any town in the US. In any town in which people's lives are directly determined by local economics. In decaying trajectories. In Portsmouth. In real dejection, not just the kind we have now. In the sense that you have reduced your options according to an inner program you don't understand but which is obvious to anyone who has known you longer than a year. In the failure to be shameless. In a concrete pipe, or on a large ship. In a Turkish film.

Not All Men

When you email me and say you've seen me on the train again, I don't know how to answer you. Those people you see aren't me.

I thought you weren't going to send me any more video? I thought we agreed that? This stuff is just so dark and blurry it could be anybody. It doesn't even look like the inside of a train, which is what you say in your mail, 'I took this on the Central Line in the rush hour yesterday morning.' No you didn't, Julie, because you're always at work before the rush hour starts. Anyway it just doesn't look like a train. The seats are wrong.

I don't care that you've started following people again. You'll get in trouble for it the way you did before. Don't blame me. I could feel sympathy for you the first time because you were hurt. Anyone can be hurt, and we often do unpredictable things because of it. But you weren't that hurt, and in the end just nobody believed what you said you saw.

Another thing, I never travel on the Central Line now anyway.

The sound file that came along with the video is wrong too. Tube trains don't sound like that. It sounds like somebody making a noise into a pipe. Some child. I don't think it's clever, you making a noise into a pipe like that to imitate the noise of a train when it doesn't sound anything like it.

I don't think we can ever get back with one another again, no. For one thing I'm with someone else now. I've been completely honest about that from the start, whatever you say. Not all men are liars. Another thing, we just didn't work out. It's no good you saying we wanted different things out of life. Wanting different things out of life is being incompatible. That's what being incompatible is.

And why send me all this stuff again?

I remember perfectly well what you claim happened. I didn't believe it then, I don't believe it now. I'm not stupid. I understand what you're saying. What I can't understand is why you think I'd believe it. You went out in the morning two weeks after we broke up. You got your train, the same train you always get from Shepherd's Bush, that's fine, I'm sure you did, because you were always completely anal about that. But then you say you saw me in a carriage on the Central Line, and you said hello and I just flat-out ignored you like that, even when you got right up close to me and tried to make me speak.

Well, it wasn't me, Julie.

You know why? Two things. Firstly from your own description. In your latest mail you say, 'It was you, but with different clothes and a different haircut.' For God's sake, Julie, how could it be me if I was different? Also you say, 'There was something different about your face.' If I had a different face, and different clothes, and a different haircut, how could I be me?

The second thing is this: I don't remember that, Julie. Don't you think I'd remember that if it happened?

One thing about our relationship and how it ended. I never once told you to leave. It was you who said you wanted space, whatever that means. I was the one willing to work things out, right up until you threw the scissors. Now you tell people I dumped you for Fareda. Well, that's really hurtful, you know. Because I didn't meet her until two months after you left. It wasn't me who threw things and walked out. I would never treat anyone like that. Just because it didn't work out between us, why would I ignore you in public? I know you were hurt. I always tried to make it as easy for you as possible. People owe each other that. By the way, it wouldn't hurt you to call her by her name.

Could you explain one thing in your mail?

It's where you say, 'You had a shoulderbag with something in it, something with an odd shape.' *Well the person you claim is me in the video isn't carrying anything.* He's a man in what looks like a corduroy suit, reading *The Guardian*. And anyway, can you tell me when I ever owned a shoulderbag? Can you tell me that? I hate men who carry shoulderbags. You know I do. That's just another reason it couldn't have been me. 'A shoulderbag from some shop in Camden,' you say, 'a bit knocked about and dirty, with something in it.' I can't think of anything that sounds less like me. I wouldn't be seen dead in a corduroy suit for that matter either. You must know that.

If you were going to palm this off on me, you might have made a video that matched the description in your mail.

'Something in it,' you say, 'a shoulderbag with something in it.' What do you mean by that? And what music was I listening to? Was it John Coltrane or Sonny Rollins? Because if I wasn't, I don't think it was me, do you? I mean, with what you and everyone else in the world knows about me?

You say that after I wouldn't say hello, I got off the train at King's Cross. That's another mistake, because why would I get off there? I never worked there. It's just such a big hole in your story. I can't think of any reason to get off the tube at Kings Cross at ten o'clock in the morning when I work in NoHo. You say I got off the train and you followed me out of the station and down to the canal. I went to the Regents Canal at eleven o'clock in the morning? I don't think so. I think *Get.This.com* would have something to say about that, don't you? If I hadn't turned up for work by eleven o'clock in the morning?

Then there's all this stuff about the empty building. That's sick, Fareda says, and I can understand why. She says I should get an injunction.

If you want to know how I met Fareda, I put an ad in *Time Out*.

'Man 35 seeks interesting woman 25-40. Must have broad but individual taste in books, music, films and be able to tolerate a high degree of individuality in other people's taste. Must like men but not football. Nobody who thinks of the South Bank, the Arts Council or the ICA as repositories of culture. Nobody who thinks a good haircut is important. Nobody trying to make a career in TV, journalism, or TV journalism. Nobody who wants it all. Nobody trying to fit a man into the vestigial and precisely-shaped space left by a tightly woven support structure of family, friends and work.'

Recognise anyone in that paragraph, Julie? Well it's you.

That's how hurt I felt. You say Fareda broke us up. You say I was fucking her. Well, that would have been something. I wasn't fucking anyone, Julie, not even you, because you were always too bloody busy. How do you think I felt about that? How good did that make me feel? Now you say that I won't speak to you on the tube. Well maybe if I saw you I wouldn't. What's sauce for the goose is sauce for the gander. *But I never see you on the tube!*

You know, sometimes I just play the files you send and I laugh. These people are not only not me, they're all different. You've followed a lot of different people to this building with the broken windows you claim is by the canal in King's Cross. You've taken some blurry DV stuff of them standing there looking at the walls and corners. It's filthy in there. Dirty people, looking up at the walls like that without moving. I don't know how you got that, but it isn't very nice, and I don't want you to send any more of it. None of them look like me. They're older, they're younger, some of them are obviously women. You should get help if this is what you're going to spend your time doing. I mean, are you paying them to stand there like that? Or what?

It isn't any good, all this. I'm with Fareda now and we're happy. I wish I could have been happy with you but I wasn't. You weren't happy either, you said as much. You should stop this and give yourself a new start, you owe yourself that. You owe it to me, too. It would be easy for you to meet someone, easier than it was for me. Another thing you say is that you regret what happened between us. You say, 'Every night I wish things could be the way they were.' You say you cry every night. But you never cried then, and now it's too late.

I left you, Julie. I changed offices and I never use the Central Line for work any more. I don't know how you found that awful building. You should get some help, because these people you see aren't me.

Dog People

I MET MYRA AT the Arts Club. It was lunchtime on the sort of summer day which makes you want to eat outside, off a table with a luminous white cloth. The girls touch the statue of Aphrodite for luck, imagining her to have blonde hair and bare arms like their own. They look down admiringly at the healthy balding suntanned heads of the men who have signed them in. My own date had failed to appear.

The Arts Club isn't a good place to be blown off in, especially at lunchtime. People who have also been blown off, or are about to be blown off, or are about to admit to being blown off, eye you with hatred as you walk past. They want no reminders. Among them that day was the ugliest woman I had ever seen. Her head had the qualities of an ethnic bronze, massive and massively-proportioned, all the features of which overstate some powerful but recently obsolete cultural dictum. She swung it slowly left and right. She stared at her watch, ordered a glass of house red.

'I'm waiting,' I heard her tell the barman, 'for this wretched person I wouldn't even recognise.'

I asked him if I could have a club sandwich. Recently he had stopped cautioning me, 'And you are a member, aren't you sir?' every time I ordered a drink. I told him I would have the sandwich outside. 'The table nearest Cupid,' I said. Cupid, a rational little deity, perches out there in the Arts Club garden, on a mossy clam shell between two terracotta urns, shooting his arrow of water into the air above a black pond decorated with green weed. He presides over affairs, one night stands, change. He serves the club members with the endless debacles they mistake for an emotional life. I was ignoring him when the woman with the massive head came and stood by my table.

'You don't mind,' she told me, 'if I sit here.'

In a way she was right.

'These bloody people who say they'll meet you,' she complained. She pulled my *Telegraph* apart and began to read the food page. 'I can't stand octopus,' she said, as if she had caught me eating one. Then: 'You don't say much, do you?'

'I'm sorry?'

'I can't stand fish of any kind. I suppose you're doing something this evening?'

We went to my flat. 'Flat' is perhaps the wrong word. I was renting a room from some friends of mine who lived in a maisonette on a council estate in Bow. The estate was constructed like an open box, so that it captured every passing sound. Even the silence was full of ghost aircraft descending far away, a shim or resonance of cries and traffic. At night you could hear young Asian men having their heads kicked in outside Mile End tube station by cheerful BNP members over from Leytonstone for the dog fights. I was as far east as the Arts Club is west, but I could come and go as I liked, and I was never uncomfortable there until Myra said:

'They're very tidy, aren't they? Your friends?'

Then she said:

'My god, is this actually a futon?'

She was wearing a white linen suit, the skirt of which she soon pulled up round her waist to show me the sandy coloured fur between her thighs.

'What do you think of that, then?' she said.

As soon as I got close enough to have an opinion, she turned away from me and lifted her great haunches in the air, laughing.

'Come on.'

'Can't we talk first?' I said.

When we had finished – or rather, when Myra had come, with a sudden series of barks and groans, shaking her head from side to side and looking back at me over her shoulder – she seemed to expect something else. There wasn't anything else I could think of. That was the first and last time Myra ever came to Bow. If I suggested it thereafter she made excuses, and we always went to Chiswick, where she owned a garden flat thirty seconds away from the Thames. There she had, as she put it, La Trompette for evenings, Richmond for Sundays, and the kind of neighbours who can easily afford an Audi cabriolet. In Chiswick, sex was noisier. I wondered what people made of us. 'So long as you can avoid Hammersmith,' Myra said, 'Chiswick is heaven.' To her, Hammersmith was less a place than a condition.

She was already anxious when we were apart.

Is 'anxious' the right word? It was an anxiety which revealed itself, like most of Myra's emotions, as irritation. Where it proceded from, I don't know. 'You'll go to seed in that place,' she would warn me, if I spent a day working at home. 'I'm your last chance at a normal life.'

Eventually I gave in. After Myra's remarks, Bow had lost its gloss anyway, though I still quite liked the strange shop signs along Roman Road – Spoilt Bitch, Blisters, Shuz-A-Go-Go. (For a while there had been a lingerie shop called Bare Essensuals. It didn't prosper, and though the sign remained the shop began to sell mirrors instead, as if its owner had decided to cook the impurities out of the narcissistic act and leave only the really good stuff.) Myra hardly seemed to notice when I moved in with her, except to warn me, 'Don't get in my way in the mornings.' The only other thing she said was, 'Don't offer to do my washing and I won't offer to do yours.' She could see I had been tempted by that. The bedroom smelled of overused bath towels, Myra and Nonoxynol-9. On the bed, the sheets were always pulled about untidily into heaps. Perhaps that was because we were always having sex there.

Myra hated it if we didn't have sex, or if I seemed to lose interest in her for a moment. I could see there might be problems with that. Around then my mother, who was seventy three and lived with mixed success in the Midlands, had a small stroke. Unlike Myra's, my mother's anxieties had always revealed themselves as anxiety: when she saw the ambulancemen in her front room, she fought. Just as she feared, worse was to come. Her struggles brought on a further stroke, and a coma, and then, for a month or two, Bramley Ward in the local hospital, which she shared with a transient population of equally unconscious but always slightly younger women.

Most of that time, my sister watched over her. My sister, like many relatives of stroke victims, had convinced herself my mother was still somehow there. The nursing staff explained to her that passing expressions don't signify awareness, but she couldn't accept it. My mother wasn't helping with this. She was smiling as happily as a girl. Some of those smiles were surprising to me, they were surprisingly sexy. It was as if she wanted to share something with us. Sometimes she wanted to share it so much that she was practically winking at us. I didn't want to know what it was. These were the opposite of a baby's practice smiles, they were what you got when there was nothing left to practise for. But my sister kept saying, 'We can't give up, we mustn't give up.'

I didn't know what to feel about it. I had my own difficulties, sitting by the bed on a plastic chair for an hour in Bramley Ward trying not to interpret that smile, so all I felt was my sister's need. It pressed me into the walls. She had me cornered there twice a week in the hospital smell and the light of an internal window with a kiddie's picture taped to it, entitled, probably, 'My Gran doesn't say anything any more.' There were other issues. I had been looking for a better family than ours, my sister said, since I was thirteen.

'Something's the matter with you,' she said.

There was some justice in that: as soon as she spoke, the world had tilted to one side and started to rotate slowly.

'Look,' I said, 'she's not going to wake up.'

The vertigo wore off in the cab on the way to the railway station, but though I felt fine by the time I got back to London, I'm not sure I was ever fine again.

The hospital gave fruit and flower names to all its wards. Bramley Ward. Daffodil Ward. Cherry Ward. Wards were grouped into wings which had the names of famous local people. Despite that, it had no integrity, it wasn't even itself, and was run as a satellite from some other hospital in the nearest big city. My sister explained to me they were always threatening to close it down; it was probably another thing we shouldn't give up on.

So that was the way things worked out. I went up and down to the Midlands, sometimes by car, more often by rail. Each visit, I tried to avoid my sister and catch the early train back to London. At night I lay in the dark imitating my mother's depthless, lively, transient expressions, thinking we were more alike than I preferred: both of us were afraid of death. As a result my dreams were full of the surprised humiliation I used to feel as an adolescent when forced to see things from someone else's point of view. I would wake up to find the room rolling slowly to the left and Myra staring intently down at me as if she knew something I was keeping from myself. Whatever it was, it still didn't enable her to understand me.

'Can we not fuck?' I would hear myself beg.

It was another climate-change summer. The light, like seaside light, seemed to make the streets wider and more spacious. Even London streets had a promise about them in that light. They became esplanades luring me upriver towards Richmond, or, less advisedly, north through Turnham Green until I lost myself in the tissue of residential streets

91

which had worked its way into the fabric of Acton then died; a place neither clean nor dirty, new nor old, inhabited by mid-day joggers and almost defunct pigeons, organisms like me. One afternoon I got back early and sat out under the cherry tree in Myra's garden. Chiswick Eyot smelled of exposed mud. A dog barked, an engine fired two streets away. A man was saying 'Yes,' and 'Hm,' into a cellphone, his voice close and slightly hollow, as if he were talking from an empty bath. It was another afternoon of hyperaesthesia. A breeze started up and though the sun was still beating down, the rustling cherry leaves made it sound like rain. Lulled by this, I fell asleep.

When I woke up ten minutes later, a rhythmic sound was coming from the garden next door. It had a shuffling, plodding quality, like the sound of someone exercising on a treadmill. The rhythm of it was metronomic. Then a voice said: 'Venice is nothing but souvenir shops. You wonder how they make any money, with such a high ratio of shop to customer?'

It was Myra.

Instead of calling over the hedge, I went upstairs to look out of the bedroom window. Two people were down there, but I couldn't get enough of an angle between the hedge and the wall to see what they were doing. 'Mind you,' Myra said, 'I did hear of a *blind man* who, whenever he was abroad, went into souvenir shops to touch the goods. He would run his fingers over a Tower Bridge or an Eiffel Tower, whatever, to get some idea of the shapes of the city he was in.' There was a pause. 'On the other hand,' she said, 'I don't suppose there are enough blind people to keep Venice above water.'

Later, when I asked her, 'How was work today?' she answered, 'Oh, the usual bloody grind.' Then she added, in a voice not quite like her own, because sympathy was a difficult thing for Myra, a response drawn forth only with the aid of deep resources of patience and stamina:

'And how do you feel?'

I wasn't sure. In one way at least, I said, I actually felt relieved. Once my mother had suffered this disaster I could embrace it as a possible fate of my own. In a sense I could even look forward to it, because prior to that I had only my father's death as a template. For years I'd expected to die suddenly and be removed without warning from other people's lives, the way he had been when I was thirteen. 'I'm not sure you'll understand this,' I told Myra, 'but now I can imagine something different for myself.' I had something new to look forward to.

'Jesus,' she said. She said that if I needed to see someone, she could get me a recommendation. She said, 'Look, do you want the rest of that?'

We were at Le Vacherin in Acton Green. It was late. Our waitress had an inturned look. Outside, Acton Green Common lay in a moonlike trance all the way to the tube line. Apart from ours only a single table remained occupied, by a young couple who had brought their very small, quiet baby with them. It didn't look more than a day or two old, and they were obviously delighted by it. Every ten minutes they lifted it out of its carrycot as if they had just been given it, passed it to and fro across the table, then settled it back again. Myra had lost patience with this pantomime early on, but seemed undecided how to respond. Now she put down her spoon in the remains of my prune and Armagnac tart and said in a loud voice:

'Did they order that? Only I can't find it on the menu.'

They stared at us in surprise. Didn't we like their baby? No one disliked their baby.

Myra shivered.

'They hate me,' she said. 'I'll see a cat when we leave here. There'll be a cat out there now.'

Myra hated cats. She claimed they were sly and untrustworthy; their love was cupboard love and without looking hard you could find something flat in their eyes. A dog's eyes, on the other hand, had depth. A black cat crossing their path, some people think, brings luck. Myra wouldn't walk down a street if any kind of cat had crossed it that morning. She said they smelled.

'I don't know how you can bear the touch of them,' she said with a shudder.

At a loss, I could only tell her the following story –

'Things were chaotic and miserable during Adam and Eve's retreat from Paradise. The children squalled endlessly. There hadn't been time to pack. Adam, who regretted the whole episode, blamed Eve; Eve realised for the first time that Adam was a wimp. Jacob, the third son, was particularly upset. With the whole tribe cowed and disoriented, less by God than the weather outside, only the family cat Mau had the presence of mind to memorise the route. A few years later, driven by her love for Jacob, who had allergies and never came to terms with the world, the cat led him back. Impressed by the boy's obsessiveness, the angel on the gate that day offered Jacob a piece of the maternal fruit. But as a reward for Mau's loyalty, he franked the route permanently into the blank back pages of her DNA. From that time on, there has always been a cat who remembers the way back to the Garden of Eden.'

'I heard it was their dog,' Myra said.

Talk to someone in a coma and you are talking to yourself. When it's your mother there are further complications. What do you say to her? I really liked your meringues? That time when I was eleven and threw up on the tea table from eating Heinz spaghetti on toast – Do you remember? – sorry about that! The things you expect to say, you don't. The things you want to say don't seem quite right. Eventually I began to talk about myself. I gave her progress reports dating back as much as twenty years, from the parts of my life she had missed. I listed my divorces. 'It took a long time to learn to like myself,' I concluded, 'but I'm doing quite well now. I don't think I'm as angry as I was, not as angry or as scared.' It brought her up to date and it was therapeutic for us both. I used all my charm on her, son to mother, and she used all hers on me, mother to son, staring coyly up at the ceiling of Bramley Ward, bursting with the secret no one wants to hear.

My sister left a message for me with the nursing staff.

'She does seem rather anxious to get in touch with you,' they said, handing over the damp, heavily folded piece of coloured paper on which was written, 'You'll have to talk to me in the end.'

I stared at these words, then out of the window of the 1.50pm to Euston. Now, I don't know. Or do I? What I would say now is that until the thing with Myra happened I didn't feel enough terror. I would say that like everyone else I ate too much; looked forward too often to the evening bottle of Chilean red. That's what I would say now. But that afternoon all I could do was smooth out the paper until you could barely tell it had been folded, and leave it behind me on the table when the train got in.

Back in Chiswick, someone was in Myra's house. The truth of this visited me not experientially — as a smell or faint sound, a sense of occupation, of usedness, in the air — but as a kind of prior knowledge validated by my sister's note, the moment I opened the door. I stood just inside the hall, the way we all have done at one time or another, and called:

'Hello? Myra?'

They were in the bedroom. She was on her hands and knees and he had got up on her from behind in the gloom. They were panting harshly, and their faces had a stunned look as if something was happening they didn't understand. He had a thick ginger beard. She seemed to have one, too, but I suppose that must have been an effect of the shadows in the room, the few thin slats of river light angling in through the blind. As I watched, he began to turn round so that he faced in the opposite direction to her. It was a slow, awkard procedure if he was to keep his cock inside her. But he did it eventually, and they remained like that, motionless and uncomfortable-looking, until I closed the door on them. They hadn't seemed to notice me.

That had to be the end of it.

'I hate dogs,' was my parting shot to Myra. 'I hate their shit. The smell of it makes you heave.'

When I'm in Chelsea I still look for her, listen for her voice, watch for the swing of the head slowed by its counterweight of vanished meanings. I see her there sometimes with other men. They're over-attentive, but then this is the Arts Club. Myra's sitting at the same table she sat at with me, staring at the Cupid fountain. 'You've got to understand,' she's telling someone, 'that other people are as confused as you. Just not so self-involved.'

My mother clung on for a while then died. The funeral went well, in that none of the relatives fought; although one or two refused to attend. Perhaps to help make up the numbers, my sister brought her dog, an English bull terrier with a big white blind-looking face. Two months later she was telephoning me every other day to ask for money; once a week she would write a letter summing up the injustices done to her by the remains of the family.

She lived with the dog, on one of those estates financed by the optimism of the late 1940s, a hundred and ten company houses in light-coloured brick set down around bleak flat squares and triangles of grass. She made some sort of life for herself there. Eventually I drove up to visit her, and we leafed through the family albums. There was my father, Guy Fawkes night 1968, thirty three years old but laughing as fatuously as a boy, in a boy's red-and-white football scarf, with the bonfire lighting up one lens of his spectacles. I never liked him. He died not long after the photo was taken, and that only made things worse. It reduced the chances of settling anything between us.

After his death my mother couldn't stand mess. She decorated often, bought new furniture and carpets; cleaned and cleaned. I can't stand mess, she would tell us, meaning, I can't stand the mess you've made of my life. I don't think there was any doubt she loved him, and adored him, and depended on him. She grew roses in the garden he had measured out so exactly with pegs and twine. She grew them in the way he would have approved, pruned to stumps in severely rectangular beds, surrounded by grey, cloddy, heavily weeded earth. Even at that age I could feel her looking around in a numb way and wondering how she would make sense of it all, which I don't think she ever did. It all fell apart when he went. Things were too much for her. That was the feeling I had from my mother around then, that her hold on things was marginal, that we were a difficulty hard to contend with: things were difficult enough without the demands we might make.

'Our mother always preferred you,' my sister said. 'We need to talk that out. We need to talk about it.'

I asked if I could go to the toilet.

She looked puzzled. 'Of course you can,' she said. 'Of course you can go to the toilet.'

It was another greenhouse Sunday, high humidity and temperatures in the 30s. Every so often she coaxed the bull terrier on to the steps outside the kitchen door and poured a two-litre bottle of Evian water over its head. For the next few minutes it sat in an evaporating puddle with its tongue lolling out of the side of its mouth and an expression of bliss on its face, while its pinkish eyes remained as hard as marbles. The back yard was full of dogshit, and stacked up on the hard earth was all my mother's furniture – two double mattresses, a thirty-year-old Creda gas cooker, armchairs and sofas the vinyl of which had already faded and split in the sun and rain. My sister was in dispute with the council over this. She was in dispute with her neighbours over it. 'But be honest with me,' she said, 'where else could I put it all? I ask them that and they can't answer.' She was in dispute with almost everyone about almost everything, and in addition genuinely disabled by asthma. The house smelled of the dog, which rarely took its eyes off me.

Driving back down the M1 an hour or two later, I spotted a couple and a child in a splash of sunlight, waiting by their car for the breakdown service. The woman and her little boy smiled at every passing vehicle; the man only seemed embarrassed. You often see families like this, poised on the hard shoulder of the motorway where woods and wildflowers spill down a shallow bank to the edge of the tarmac. Their afternoon is already ruined. The AA has been called, the outing postponed. It's a cracked radiator, it's electrical, it's something none of us, any more, can fix. There's nothing left to do but wait. At first they stand awkwardly in their careful high street clothes, unable to find a body language for the situation. Then, after five minutes, something happens. They move away from the vehicle, shade their eyes, peer at one another or back at the motorway, torsos moving one way, legs another, in the long grass. From the nearby woods a bird sings, there is a flicker of movement. The child tilts its head alertly to listen; the parents look at the child. Suddenly they hang between choices, up to their calves in moon daisies and cornflowers, surrounded by a froth of elder blossom and pink dog roses. Possibilities stretch away in the form of field and hedge. Scents, sounds. For a moment it's likely they will abandon the car and disappear, having mistaken this strip of woods between the motorway and the low-lying pasture for something they can run off into for good.

Jackdaw Bingo

ALIENS ARRIVE ON EARTH after a long journey, only to find that humanity has died out. The aliens have never used writing or paper, so they don't understand books; they've never stored data digitally, so they don't understand computers. They recycle the books for fuel and the internet servers for chemicals. But their own typical data storage system looks and acts very much like a jackdaw, so they value the jackdaws and put them in beautiful jackdaw-friendly environments and spend the next five hundred years reverently trying to decode the messages of hope they're sure humanity left encoded in jackdaw behaviour. Jackdaws can't believe their luck.

Earth Advengers

As SOON AS WE get the alien starship I will be known as Ms Jet, or Lady Jet. You will be Lemmy. Other members of the crew will be Spike, Smork, Cookie & The Crow. & we will have jokes, for instance in any bad situations – like we are running out of ammunition & surrounded by enemies – I will always say, 'Cookie, this is the worst porridge you ever cooked up!' & we will all have a favourite weapon. Spike's favourite weapon will be his rusty Earth .40 snub. & I will say, 'Seriously Spike you expect to hit anything with that, anyone is always better with the four inch barrel & the adjustable backsight.' & Spike will always say, 'Captain Jet, a four inch barrel is for vermin control.' & I will say, 'That's what we do here in space, Spike.' Then I will give him a significant look & add: 'We control vermin.' & everyone will laugh and Spike will admit ruefully, 'Guess you got me there, Ms Lady!' Spike makes his own bullets & has Outworld hair. Cookie is always 'Fat Cookie'. My special weapon will be a fifteen petawatt proton gun which only I can lift, aimed telepathically through advanced radio telescopes distributed in the Cat's Eye Nebula & accurate to less than one Planck length. Our main enemies will be: Bizarro Nazis & The Junk. Our signature will be: Earth Advengers!

Keep Smiling
(with Great Minutes)

VOLSIE CAME OUT OF me in a room at the Les Halles Citadines, from somewhere near the top of my left leg. It was hot and soft, a lot of discrete masses like grapes, or the inflationary universes of the new cosmology. I got hold of it in my hands and struggled with it and pushed most of it back in. I had just that moment arrived – it was my first time in Paris – so I let the rest sink into the carpet and went straight out. I didn't think much of it. That was my mistake.

Pere Lachaise cemetery, the Metro gate: a lunatic, bearded and dreadlocked, spun round and round at the top of the steps, raising his arms to bless us as we entered, while he recited an endless list of the fallen.

'All those who failed to find the ashes of Max Ernst,' I heard him say, 'in the columbarium in the year 2006. All those who failed to kiss the tomb of Oscar Wilde. All those who wandered about looking for Colette but found only Jim Morrison. All those who went to the wrong place.' It was hardcore rant, rich with the sheer physical sweat of a world being held together for the benefit of the tourists, with their unknowing souls and dormant sense of the relations between the spiritual and the spatial. 'All those,' he concluded, as if only now testing the pivot of his argument, 'who *gave up*, but later found a monument to the death commando at Buna Monowitz work camp, and couldn't for once think of anything cheap to say (being instead silent).

'This song,' he told me, 'is respectfully dedicated to all those who refused to sign the truce because it was written in the wrong colour ink.'

Too late I understood that he was Volsie too, and so we wandered together in and out of the little unkempt tollbooths and wrought iron urinals of the many dead, up and down between the cobbled levels, dirt paths and exposed tree roots in the sunshine.

'What are you on?' I said.

'You'll find out,' Volsie said. 'See that man there?'

I said I saw him.

'Stepped on a grave this morning. Dead within the year.'

He looked ordinary enough to me. He looked like an American.

'Which grave was it?' I said. 'Out of interest.'

'Someone called Darjou, 1757 to 1843. But see the expression on his face? Dead before August.'

I was puzzled by that: by what it meant for me. I went back to my Citadines apartment with its chic, nervous little kitchen and the special bed from under which a second bed slides suddenly and bangs your ankle. I listened all evening to the quiet yelps of laughter from down in the central courtyard.

You ask how it is that Volsie manifests as an episode of psychic piles one moment, a madman in a famous cemetery the next. You ask what its voice sounds like. Volsie will come out of you soon. It might be in the form of the oyster, it might be in the form of the pearl; it might come out of your mouth in the form of the Teratoma of Entitlement, a ball of dry Victorian-looking gristle, horsehair and compacted papier-mâché complete with a single eye from a species on the extinction list. You won't ask questions after that. Answers will be the last thing you want. If you didn't have bad teeth before, you will now. That cough of yours will soon appear to be the worst thing that ever happened to you; the glaze of the eye – the passive eye of a dead seal, the button eye from a French teddy bear bought years ago by some old friend of the family – will encode all the information you need.

Next morning proceeded with fine rain. Paris rain, not enough to stop anyone going out but enough to soak them piss wet through in half an hour. I walked around. I began by crossing the river a few times, going the same way each time, over by the Pont des Arts and back across the Ile de la Cite, looking down at the tents of the homeless pitched along the bank. I took to the Seine on a sightseeing boat and watched the rain run down the curved viewing glass. I saw Concorde Square, I saw the Alexander III bridge, 'the most luxurious bridge in Paris'; I saw the Eiffel Tower lurch abruptly out of its own fog. Arches of blue and yellow plastic flowers ran the whole length of the boat inside; also lines of fake lamp posts with dim lights behind bright orange glass. Right down the middle of the boat. What do you say about something like that? I didn't get it. I debarked cold, and had to have a calvados in a café near the Musee D'Orsay.

Volsie came out of me while I was there.

This time it came out from a bit higher, somewhere around the upper bowel, and slithered into my lap.

'I know how you feel,' it said. 'You feel like an outsider, as if you ought to be living in a tent near the Pont-neuf.' I felt soaked. I felt odd to be sitting with all those purple grapelike universes inflated over my thighs as warm as a pet dog. 'Not one of your contemporary lifestyle-choice outsiders either,' Volsie said. 'Just some old bloke who can't fit in. Maybe you're allergic to the pace of the modern world. I know I am.' There are those who believe Volsie is synonymous with death. Others associate him with any journey by train. He was with me in Paris and he was with me on the return journey, where he gurned up and down the aisles of the Eurostar in the guise of a food steward.

'All those,' he said, 'who ate Ghent ham and Westland salad, all those who ate 'macaroon au chocolat noir.' You never look me in the eye, but I piss in your mouth while you sleep and you taste it when you wake. Oh, don't thank me, it's what I do.' He pushed his face into the face of the woman sitting next to me across the aisle. She was reading the *Sunday Times*. 'Watch this,' he said to me over his shoulder, before slipping his face right through the paper and into hers: 'They fall asleep like children, clutching their smartphones.' The *Sunday Times*, he said, was a red-top for people who thought they were special. He said, as if it was connected, 'All that counts is the individual moment of suffering.' He said that everything else was ideology, hypocrisy, lies, claim and counter-claim, bullying and self-serving and pretending to be the victim: everything else was the financial news. 'The only time people are human any more,' he said, 'is in the moment of having their humanity taken away from them by other human beings. Being killed revalues your life, it's a way of choosing dignity. Another thing,' he said, 'I never saw a nuclear explosion I didn't enjoy. You think that's all over? Think again.'

He showed me his own phone, black, rubber-coated, the size of a fox. By then we were in Waterloo.

'This is my stop,' I said.

Volsie walked me as far as the Dali statue. Then he got smaller and smaller across the polished concourse floor and went spinning into the crowd – like a dropped coin of small denomination no one bothers to pick up any more – towards the Embankment. He was going to the Tate Modern. After that he was off to Clapham to undermine a reading group. I thought I'd got rid of him but I hadn't. The next time I saw him it was three weeks later, in the Pret A Manger on Cranbourne Street W1. He was a thin man about sixty years old with cheeks hollowed by a fanaticism like the desert wind etc., etc., and he was eating the All Day Breakfast with Free Range Mayo. He watched the women going to and fro along the pavement outside, up and down the kerbs, waiting at the junctions. It was Thursday lunchtime. After a while he put the

All Day Breakfast down with an impatient sigh.

'You think you see the real world,' he said to me.

'Pardon?'

'You heard. You think you see the real world. But you don't.'

I had a bite of my sandwich. He watched me with satisfaction, as if he was eating it himself. 'Good,' he said. 'Good!'

'There's a world, then?' I said. 'Somewhere round here?'

'A world, but not the real one. The real one would –' he shrugged. 'I don't say what the real one would do to you,' he concluded.

'How could I see the real one?'

He shrugged. 'It's easier than you'd think,' he said. His watery blue eyes measured me. 'In your case,' he said, 'I wouldn't recommend it.'

'Thanks,' I said.

'Some are strong enough. Some aren't.'

'I'm going to get a pecan slice,' I said.

'Get me one, too,' Volsie said.

When I came back with the pecan slices he was looking out of the window again. I didn't want to disturb him so I drank my mocha and unwrapped my pecan slice, which I ate in silence. After a while, he smiled to himself.

'Ask me another question,' he said, still looking out of the window.

I woke up this morning from the same old dream.

New Year's Eve, I'm at someone's house. It's in the Shires. Snow falls on and off all evening. Every so often someone opens the curtains and reports, 'It's wet. It won't settle.' Then at half past twelve, adults and children alike, everyone puts on their coat and boots and they run out into the village street. One three year old, rather bemused, wears her little Boden parka over her pyjamas. In the orange lamplight every snowflake rushes down to meet its own shadow. The sky shakes with fireworks from some other party, red, greeny-silver and a strange heavy blue, a blue too dark to be seen yet visible anyway just for this one night. Two inches of snow are on the ground. The parents can't believe it; the children easily can. Christmas at last! They dance in the hallowed empty street. They throw snow at one another. I watch from the window with a woman I have just been introduced to, like me she's down from London to see friends. We kneel on the leather sofa with our champagne glasses, looking out, saying things like, 'This is amazing!' and, 'Isn't this amazing?' We don't know each other. We don't even like each other much. But we can't stop smiling and saying, 'This never happens!' and, 'I mean you couldn't wish for more.'

You can't wish for more than snow falling after midnight in the lamplight at the start of a new year, to structure the children's expectations, remain as a memory, magic their lives forever.

After that everyone goes safely home wrapped up in a suit of initials, SUV, BMW.

At the end of any dream Volsie comes out of you whether you welcome it or not. It flops down your leg or swells up under your arm. You find yourself at the foot of the stairs still half asleep. Volsie is half outside you, you are still all the way inside it. It is a condition. It is a space or state. You don't have any further queries when you understand that. What a sight you've become. You look even worse without clothes than with them, some old desert man or woman with long hair and half focussed eyes, emaciated or running to fat, with spectacles or without, still reeling about under the impact of having once been born. It's never any less than that. Some of us are just shocked and appalled to find ourselves alive. It keeps echoing on. For me that's the meaning of it, anyway; for you, perhaps, it'll be something else. There are those who equate Volsie with the conceptual motor of the heart, those who know him as lovely food and drink. They are not right but they are not wrong either.

Every time I travel into central London by tube, Volsie comes out and looks at the debt-servicing ads. He looks at the ad which tells you everything is possible. He looks at the ad that reassures you: *Fly Business and be as cosseted, as protected, as the handsome, lone, powerful-looking wild animals in a conservation park.* 'The strangest thing,' he says in a kind of gentle wonder, 'is to live in a time like this, both bland and rotten.'

He says, 'Keep smiling with great minutes.'

The Crisis

YOU SIT OVER A one-bar electric fire in a rented room. As soon as you feel recovered from the commute you'll boil some potatoes on the gas ring, then, three minutes before they're done, drop an egg into the same water. You can hear the family downstairs laughing at something, some dressed-up cats or something, on the internet. After people have cooked, they can often get use out of their gadgets – join a world-building game, preorder the gadget they want next – although the load soon precipitates a brownout. During the day you work in a fourteenth floor office in the stub of the Shard. Publicity for a fuel corporate. It's nice. All very heads-down but worth it to have the security. A few years ago you got involved with an East Midlands junkie who claimed to have a telepathic link to another world and to be able to control a 3D printer with his mind alone.

This was how he told it: he came down from the North and to begin with lived on the street. He was young for his age. He started at Euston where the train emptied him out, then moved into a doorway near a bus stop. It was all right for a while. Then he met a boy called Alan and they went up to the centre together. Alan wasn't that much older than Balker. They were about the same height, but Alan knew more. He was a London boy, he had always lived there. He had bright red hair, an alcohol tan and a personalised way of walking. He could get a laugh out of anything. For a while Balker and Alan did well out of the Central London tourists. But Alan's lifestyle-choices moved him along quickly and he started to limp up and down Oxford Street at lunchtime saying, 'I'm in bits, me!' and showing people the big krokodil sore on his neck.

'Hey, look mate, I'm in bits!'

After Alan died, Balker stayed away from the other street people. They had a language all their own he never learned to speak, but he knew the same thing was happening to them as to him. He knew about the crisis, and the iGhetti. He knew the same thing was happening to everyone. There were new needs, there were new rules in. New rules had come in, and everyone in London was in the same position: if you couldn't look after yourself there was a new way to pay.

Sleeping on the street is hard. All the reasons for this are obvious. It's never quiet. The police move you about, the social services and NGOs won't leave you alone: everyone thinks the boroughs belong to them. You're hungry, you've got a cough, there's other stuff, it's an endless list. No one sleeps well in a doorway. You get fragments of sleep, you get the little enticing flakes of it that fall off the big warm central mass. Wake up, and everything seems to have fallen sideways. You guess it's four in the morning in November, somewhere along Bloomsbury Street; but you could be wrong. Are you awake? Are you asleep? Rain swirls in the doorway. You've got a bit of fever and you can't quite remember who you are. It's your own fault of course. You wake up and he's there in front of you, with his nice overcoat, or sometimes a nice leather jacket, to protect him from the weather. You never really hear his name, though he tells you more than once. He seems to know yours from the beginning. 'Your health's going,' he says. 'You want to start now, before it goes too far.'

So he leaned into Balker's doorway – maybe it was the night, maybe it wasn't – and took Balker's chin in his hand. He turned Balker's face one way then the other. He was gentle, he even looked a bit puzzled, as if he was wondering why anyone would choose to live that way, what bad choices they must have made to find themselves sleeping in a doorway behind the British Museum.

'You want to start now,' he repeated.

Later, when Balker told you all this, you weren't sure you believed any of it. It was difficult to believe anything then. The most difficult thing to believe was the crisis itself. No one was certain whether the arrival of the iGhetti was an invasion or a natural catastrophe.

They resembled stalks of fleshy, weak rhubarb, which appeared and evolved very quickly from nothing, like the tentacles which seem to bulge out of nowhere when you burn a piece of mercuric sulphocyanate. You would see them for a fraction of a second just at the city skyline behind the buildings, just under the cloudbase, evolving very fast like stopframe film of something organic growing, then running out of energy, then growing again. They seemed like neither a thing nor a picture of a thing: they seemed to be extruded from a space that wasn't quite in the world. The sirens would go off, all across the city from Borough to Camden. The artillery would fire and recoil, fire and recoil. The iGhetti would pulse and grow against the lighted clouds. Then they were gone again for another day.

Various simple beliefs surrounded the invasion. Some people associated the iGhetti with Dark Matter; some with the banking crisis of the late Noughties. Others believed that they 'came out of the internet'. (Indeed, this was the favoured theory of the internet itself: the medium still firmly − if a little desperately − casting itself as the message.) While none of these theories could be described as true, they did, perhaps, mirror the type and scale of the anxieties that led the iGhetti to us.

The truth was simpler. Originally they had leaked into our world from the astral plane. Most of them were found dead. At first they could manifest only as a kind of transparent jelly. This was spread on grass and the trunks of trees. In this form, for hundreds of years, they were known as 'astromyxin' or 'astral jelly'. Then, quite suddenly, at the turn of the 1980s, their efforts became both more determined and more successful. The new form appeared only in West London and only near water. Lakes and reservoirs were their preferred location, but they were also found on the banks of streams, and on one occasion at the edge of the carp pool in the Temperate House at Kew Gardens. Soon they had rolled down the River from Chiswick to Chelsea, and thence to the Square Mile, although no one could say by what means, or what that meant.

Balker started, anyway. For the preliminary tests they took him to a place in Aldgate. It was full of hospital beds. You'd get a meal afterwards, they said. They warned him that you could expect your head to swim a bit, but come on: somebody in Balker's condition was going to notice that? In the end it was easy and it was a bit of money in your hand. It was a way of being responsible for yourself. Balker passed well, they said. He showed real ability. That could be a beginning, they told him; or he could just leave it at that. But what Balker liked most was the clean bed, the warmth and the calm. It was worth it just to lie down and not think about what to do next. He looked around and fell asleep. When he woke up again, he said he wanted to go on with it.

'You want to go all the way?' they asked him.

'Yes,' Balker said. 'I want to go all the way.'

That was where it started for him, really. Aldgate, on the edge of the Square Mile, was where his whole life started, and where it finished, too, although he lived on afterwards.

All those streets – residential now, along with everything around Liverpool Street station – were in perfect condition despite the constant bombardment of the City from positions in Camden, Peckham and Borough Market. Restaurants remained open and ready to serve, in a wide arc from the

Duck & Waffle round to St John. It was as if nothing had changed, as if the City fringe, like West London, still believed itself to be intact, functioning, the heart of what we used to call, before money lost its confidence, an 'economy'. Brokers were commuting into Liverpool Street every morning, where, puzzled by the disorder, they attempted to do handshake business with one another in the cafés and bars. Others, unable to place themselves, feeling that the Square Mile was still in front of them yet somehow no longer visible – like some location beyond the reach of SatNav – had chosen to become lodgers in the fringe, renting the Barbican one-bedroom of some old friend from St Paul's and on Friday evenings making the short but by now increasingly confusing train journey back to Sussex. They wouldn't give up the working week.

After he passed the preliminaries, Balker was placed with a family – Jack and Jane, erstwhile investment bankers who, though they now ran a business organising outdoor activity challenges for young adults, still hoped to return one day to the abandoned financial settlements between the river and the London Wall. Jack collected first editions of children's books from the 1950s. Jane did triathalon. Their Georgian terrace had a garden, Fired Earth on the walls, the remains of quite a nice old staircase. They thought a lot of Balker.

During the day he took the more advanced tests. The point of these wasn't clear, but they fell into two types.

The first type was held, like the preliminaries, in a dormitory furnished with hospital beds. It was a big room, Balker said: in the late afternoons, when the majority of the tests took place, the rows of beds would seem to stretch away forever into the shadows. They were firm, cool, always freshly made and clean. Balker was given pills to take, then connected up to a drip. The big idea, he told you later, was that the chemicals sent you somewhere: in reality or only in your head, he didn't know. The medium was viscous and dark. Sometimes he seemed to be in the past. Sometimes he seemed to be thrown forward into futures even more confused than the present. They called it travel. The same word could be used, by extension, as a noun for the breadth or quality of the experience. Sometimes he heard a calm, insistent voice repeating, 'Are you getting good travel?' If he agreed that he was, it told him to stay calm and look for astral jelly, or any other sign of the iGhetti; if he said no, they increased the dose. What he brought back from the journey, Balker had no idea. They debriefed him while he was still off his face and thinking was difficult. Meanwhile the chemicals made him increasingly ill. In the end the only images he remembered were meaningless in the context: a half-timbered village, thatched roofs, long rosy winter dawns and sunsets. Gorse, mud, sheep. 'It was the olden times,' he told you later, trying to describe this Victorian idyll.

★

Adolescence. West London. You always believed a hidden war was being fought, a war nobody would ever admit to. You lay awake at night, listening to bursts of corporate fireworks that seemed too aggressive to be anything other than a small arms exchange; while by day, ground-attack helicopters clattered suddenly and purposively along the curve of the Thames towards Heathrow. You held your breath in moments of prolonged suspense, imagining the smoke trails of rockets launched from the bed of a builder's pickup in Richmond or Kingston. These fantasy-engagements, asymmetric and furtive, a kind of secret, personalised Middle East, left you as exhausted as masturbation. There was something narcissistic about them. A decade later, everyone was able to feel a similar confused excitement. With the coming of the iGhetti, everyone had a story to tell but no one could be sure what it was. Information was so hard to come by. Between anecdotal evidence and the spectacular misdirections of the news cycle lay gulfs of supposition, fear, and denial. People didn't know how to act. One minute they heard the guns, the next they were assured that nothing was happening. One day they were panicking and leaving the city in numbers, the next they were returning but rumour had convinced them to throw their tablet computers in the river. The thing they feared most was contagion. They locked their doors. They severed their broadband connections and tanked their cellars. They avoided a growing list of foods. They clustered round a smartphone every summer evening after dark, eavesdropping on the comings and goings of the local militias as they scoured the railway banks and canalsides for telltale astral jelly. Were the iGhetti here or not? It was a difficult time for everyone.

When he wasn't taking the tests Balker hung around in the coffee shops and cafés and, at night, ate with the family at a table in the garden. Jane and Jack talked about the art events they'd seen in galleries in Paris and Tokyo, while Balker entertained them by catching moths unharmed from around the table lights. They taught him to play chess. 'Now he can beat us easily,' Jane often said with a laugh, 'he wants to play all the time!' On Saturdays he learned to make breakfast for everyone, poached egg on rye with salmon, roast pepper and faux hollandaise. He loved that. It was the secure point of his week. He'd never known anything like it, just calm and middle class comfort, life lived simply for being life. That was where the two of you met, at a dinner party of Jane and Jack's. He was standing in the garden with everyone else, staring out towards the shadowy zone beyond the Minories where something could be seen moving above the roofline and between the taller buildings. They had cornered one of the larger ones somewhere in the warren around Threadneedle Street and were pounding it with 155mm smart artillery. Airbursts lit it up in syncopated, carefully-judged sequences, but you couldn't tell any more than usual what it was. You watched Balker, and you could feel Jane watching you.

'Don't you ever wonder what's in there?' she said, and you said you didn't. You shivered. You didn't want to know, you said.

The pull of the Square Mile was still strong for people like Jane and Jack. Everyone knew someone who, unable to bear it any longer, had found their way in, to re-emerge weeks or even months later after wandering puzzledly about the empty towers, lost souls eyeing other lost souls in the deserted corridors and partner washrooms. With a good pair of binoculars you could see them, staring out of the Lloyds lifts – which still travelled in their stately way up and down the outside of the structure – in despair. In a way, the Lloyds building, designed to question the relationship between the inside and the outside, remained the great metaphor of the disaster. It was the centre of the zone in that sense, even though geographically it lay towards the western edge.

'And this is only the beginning,' Jack said. 'They've been here less than a decade.' He stared at the towers for a moment longer, then added, 'If "here" means anything at all.'

'*I* wonder,' Balker said, emphasising the pronoun to get Jane's attention. '*I* want to know.'

His voice already seemed rueful.

Eventually, when he became too ill to continue with the first type of test, they moved him on to the second, which took place under different protocols. The test-site itself could only be reached by use of a modified GABAA agonist, a fungal preparation rubbed into the skin between the shoulder blades. It smelt, he said, a bit like Germolene.

After a few hallucinations of flying you arrived in what looked like the boxroom of a provincial house at night. Out of the window you could see the slope of a hill. Fireworks flickered intermittently across the darkness. The walls of the room were papered, in a faded primordial pattern of cabbage roses. Above the tiled fireplace a brown print of 'The Light of the World'; on the mantelpiece a tin alarm clock, the nauseous, literalistic tick of which seemed to control rather than register the passing of time. There was always a thick warm smell of talcum powder as if some old aunt had just crossed the landing from the bathroom looking for a towel. Obsolete CRT monitors were set up on every flat surface, ten or twelve of them linked through a rat's nest of cable. Everything was thick with dust.

When you arrived, Balker said, and sat in front of the keyboard, you could bet that four of the screens would be full of interference. Three would be blank. Until you looked at them closely, the rest seemed to be showing a blurry grayscale image of the room itself, from the point of view of a cheap webcam mounted high up in one corner. But things weren't entirely right with the wallpaper; and the person sitting there wasn't you. After a moment or two, someone else seemed to come into the room. Then everything vanished and those screens showed interference too. For a moment the air smelt only of dust recirculated by the system's cooling fans, as if the drive towers had briefly cooked. In all the time he spent there, Balker found only one interesting item. This was a loose-leaf journal in a black leather cover – squared paper, handwritten in coloured inks, each entry carefully timed and dated – which always lay open in a different position in the dust and tangled wires between the monitors. He would leaf through it while he waited for the drug to wear off and snap his connection to that world.

'The future doesn't make sense,' it began. 'I know that because I've seen it. In some way, to some extent, I've seen the things that happen. They make no sense.' Then, a few evenings later: 'The original figure always turns its head slowly and begins to stand up, perhaps in some kind of clumsy welcoming gesture.' Among these observations, queerly personal statements were interspersed. 'I moved back into this house twenty years ago. By then both my parents were dead.' And: 'When the work isn't going well, sleep becomes tiring and I dream I am dead.' Balker could make nothing of this. When he reported it no one seemed interested. It was the screens that interested them, they said: he should concentrate on the screens.

He often thought of adding something to the journal himself, to see what would happen; but though he found fresh entries whenever he went there, he never found a pen.

In the end, it didn't work out for him. He didn't have quite the talent they were looking for. Sometimes, as the high came groaning and roaring along his upper spine and into the amygdala, he looked along the darkening rows of beds and counted fifty or a hundred people dreaming at the top of their game in the motionless gloom. They were arriving at the house, flowing through it like a gusty breath, a flock of bats: they were making sense of the things they saw, taking notes on what they found. Balker didn't have that kind of travel. He knew he wasn't up with the best. He suspected his friend Alan would have done better. By then he had understood that the test-destinations weren't the issue anyway. All those travellers were being prepared to enter the Square Mile – not physically, but on the astral plane, the way the iGhetti themselves occupied it.

As far as you and Balker were concerned, that didn't last either. You made a stab at it, moved into a flat in Shepherds Bush together, but he turned out to be seventeen not twenty seven as he said, and after his staffie/mastiff cross, which he was looking after for a friend, bit two fingers off your ex's left hand when he came back from an oil-exploration contract in one of the 'stans – you forget which one – he fitted all the lights in the house with blue bulbs while you were out then tried to commit suicide in your bath in an excess of adolescent self-disgust. It was a cry for help. That had to be the end of that. Balker went back to the street. Jane and Jack searched for him for a month or two, Jane especially has been cold towards you since. Later you heard he was with a grindcore musician in Peckham. You were glad, although you missed his smell, which was instantly exciting; and his dysfunctionality, which you remembered as 'character'. And the sex was tremendous, if a little full on and tiring.

That was it for perhaps two years, perhaps three. Although their influence spread from primary nodes in New York, Dubai and especially the great Chinese banking cities, in London the iGhetti seemed content to be contained by the Square Mile. You had the sense they were focussed on other projects. New buildings began to appear, for instance — vast, not entirely stable parodies of Noughties vanity architecture which lasted a week or a month before toppling slowly away into a kind of dark blue air. For Londoners, things went downhill during that time. It was a different world. Life was patchy. Whether people could rescue anything from their individual circumstances depended very much on how determined they could be. It was a different kind of existence. You welcomed the challenge; it was the arrival, finally, of your teenage fantasy. Then one day you took two steps into a house by the river in Barnes, and there was a face, white, with skin like a layer of enamel paint, thrust in close to yours. It was breaking up with some emotion you didn't recognise. A voice was saying, with a kind of meaningless urgency:

'It's me! It's me!'

He was shaking, whoever he was. You couldn't process it: you had come expecting a party. You were thinking, 'I must have had a stroke on the way here and not noticed, and this is what the world's going to be like for me now.' Then the face was just a boy you once knew, wearing a cheap Paul Smith summer suit looted from some outlet in Twickenham.

'Jesus, Balker,' you said, shoving him away.

You didn't want to be important to him any more. You didn't want him in this part of your life. You wanted him tidily in the part labelled 'the past', where he had never had much time to be a player anyway. He bumped into a wall and slid down it slowly. No one was eating much, that summer. They all had estuary fever, but Balker felt like a bag of sticks. His condition was further along than yours, and that should have been a warning in itself. You pushed him out of the hallway and watched him stumble off along the street.

Music came from somewhere at the back of the house, dance hits from the mid 90s. It seemed distant, then someone opened a door on to the terrace. A hot evening, a wedding party. The river stank. Bright flashes in the sky, heavy, muted thuds off in the north around Camden Town. You leaned on the balustrade and stared down into into the space between the house and the river, a dark strip of trampled turf – littered with discarded paper plates, beer cans and discarded condoms – where the bride, oblivious to everything but her own happiness, was dancing alone, skipping and spinning, dipping and bending, trailing her arms. It was, depending where you stood, a simple expression of joy or a complex expression of nostalgia for a time when all such moments were fuelled by money, aspiration, and a true, fully functional narcissism, a performative sense of self only hinted-at by the Twentieth Century – days when it was still possible to see yourself as a great silent beautiful blossom opening up to the economic light.

An hour after you sat down, Balker came in again, wiping his mouth as if he'd only recently thrown up. By then the party had retreated indoors, folded itself into the warm reek of beer and smoke. Shadows, beats, weird coloured light. Everyone's hyperactive kids like a billowing curtain around the dance floor. You could see what was going to happen. You made sure the two of you stayed at tables on opposite sides of the room. You kept the dancers between you. You made sure you were always talking to someone. But finally he came over anyway and tried to speak.

'For fuck's sake not here,' you said. 'On the terrace.'

'I only came to talk –' he said.

'Talk? Jesus, Balker. You should have stayed where you were.' You meant, 'in the past.' You meant, 'forgotten'. You didn't really mean anything else, but there was always more to Balker than that.

You took him by the elbow and half-led, half-pulled him out there. 'Before you know it,' people used to say, 'the worst has already happened.' We think of extreme events as abrupt in that way, but they're always the result of more than one border being crossed. An action that feels instant and seamlessly impulsive is actually very graded. By the time you got Balker out on to the terrace you knew you were going to hurt him. In the end you didn't need to square it with yourself: you were pushing him about, whispering, 'For God's sake, what do you think you're doing here?' or something like that, when his coat fell open and you saw what had happened to him.

'What's this?' you said. 'What's this?' You were frightened, but not, it turned out, for yourself.

'I don't know,' he said. 'I'm not in any pain.'

'There's something coming out of your chest.'

He looked hard away from himself. The tendons in his neck stood out. He moaned. 'Don't tell me any more. I'm not in any pain.'

'It's like a cauliflower, but bigger.'

He made pushing motions with his hands. 'Please don't tell me any more,' he said.

'I'm just trying to tell you how it looks. It's like a wart.'

Whatever it was, it was grey and pink colours, very muted and toned. 'A wart,' you said. 'Or broccoli. Like pink brocolli.' Balker thrashed around for a moment then passed out. You dragged him first into one corner, then another. You didn't know what to do. He woke up and screamed, 'Pull it out!' You got a good grip of it in both hands and pulled. It seemed to come out easily, as if it was coming out of not muscle and bone but something soft and unstructured, but then stopped. There was no blood. You could see tight red runners, like wires, attached to it, radiating out into Balker's chest. It was made out of damp, slick fibres. You wouldn't say 'woven'. It looked fibrous but not woven: it was nothing so organised as that. You were afraid if you pulled any harder, they might rip something else out of him, something he couldn't do without.

'I'm sorry,' you said, 'It won't come any further.'

Balker shrieked. 'Why is this happening to me?' he called. Then he whispered:

'I went in there. They sent me in on foot.'

You let his head fall back. 'Oh god, you idiot, you idiot,' you said.

'They were losing all their good people,' Balker said. 'In the end they were sending anyone who'd taken the tests.'

'Balker —'

He looked confused, he wasn't sure what was happening to him. Neither were you. You noticed a kind of shadow around him, cobalt blue, blue almost to black. Out of that, small white feathers seemed to be spilling, as if someone had burst a pillowcase.

'Nothing's changed in there! Inside it's still perfect. It's only from our side of things that it's a war. The iGhetti don't see it like that. They just don't notice. Inside, it might be six o'clock on a Sunday morning in summer. I could hear the artillery and the bombers outside the zone, but nothing disturbs them in there. I never saw one. Only the 'blue effects' that told me one of them was near.' He groaned. 'I'm still there,' he said, clutching at you. 'In some way I'm still in there.' The air around him became syrupy and glutinous. That panicked you and you began to ask him questions, but it was too late. 'Everything's just such a nuisance,' he said conversationally. 'You know? When all you want to do is go to sleep?' By then he was sitting on the floor with his legs out straight and his hands between them; his voice seemed both thick and distant. 'I feel odd to be honest,' he said. My eyes feel odd. My face feels odd. I feel odd.' He thought for a moment. 'I feel tired.' After a pause he added: 'I'm sorry, Alan.' A minute or two later you saw he was dead.

'Jesus,' you said.

So that was it as far as Balker went, and now you sit over the one-bar electric fire in your rented room. Perhaps you think about him, perhaps you don't. As soon as you feel recovered from the commute you'll boil some potatoes on the gas ring, then, three minutes before they're done, drop an egg into the same water. You can hear the family downstairs laughing at something, some dressed-up cats or something, on the internet. It's minus ten outside tonight and you have no idea what's happening on the old housing estates by the river. 'Welcome to London,' someone in the office said today. That got a laugh. 'Welcome to the managerial classes.' All he really meant was that like everyone else he would do anything to look after himself, stay this side of the line and not have to make the kinds of choices Balker made.

The Theory Cadre

(1) THE THEORY CADRE IN SNOWDONIA

In its earliest years, the Ambiente Hotel's shadowy but powerful Theory Cadre committed itself to a regime of Crowleyism, mechanical engineering and systemic self-doubt. The accompanying docufictional image restages a crucial moment from the 1948 May Day Phenomenology Camp: an anonymous member of what was then little more than a clique retreats down the Watkins Path from 'a sudden organic lurching movement half-glimpsed along the lowering ridgeline'. 'Several hanging cubical structures,' AE Fenell was later to recall, 'were observed briefly during a lightning storm around the isolated peak of Yr Aran.' On the same day some younger members of the Camp, tragically decoding a shopping list as an instruction, became disoriented and committed political suicide by simultaneously immersing each other in one of the deeper pools of the Afon Cwm Llan. [Photograph and text courtesy Alice E Fennel, both from her forthcoming monograph 'Actioning the Optimal: The Theory Cadre in Wales'.]

(2) MORE ON THE THEORY CADRE

B writes, of my recent blogpost, 'The Theory Cadre in Snowdonia', 'Mike, although a 'docufictional image' is mentioned, there's no picture here.' Yes, B, there is a picture. But the Theory Cadre, unwilling to give away anything of itself even in such a deliberately revelatory document, has encoded it as text. Another way to look at this is that while the image exists, but is not present, 'AE Fenell' does not, and yet is. Pictured [left]: In 1979 someone calling herself 'Alicia Feignall' addressed the guests at the Ambiente Hotel from this location in the old kitchen garden.

(3) ROOM 121 AT THE AMBIENTE HOTEL

While endeavouring to stamp down the cracked and buckled lino in the first floor corridor I heard voices from Mrs Decateur's old room, number 121. When I put my ear to the door, they stopped. It was Tuesday, and the wind was rattling the balconies on that side of the building, bringing with it the sound of a siren, the faint yellow wail of a saxophone from one of the Parton Street bars. Flipping the cover off my uncle Mario's tarnished old silver hunter, I turned it so that its dial caught the 40 watt light: exactly 2:19. Ah, I thought, so the rumours are unfounded. The Theory Cadre was back. I made my way quietly down to the lobby and later sent Fleur, the girl who works in the back bar, up to 121 with a bottle of 60 year old British sherry and as many clean glasses as she could find. At midnight the lobby phone rang three times. I let a minute go by, then picked it up and said, 'Hello, Alice.'

(4) OCCUPANT OF ROOM 121

Few medical procedures are neccessary to maintain an occupancy once it is established. A bucket of disinfectant every two days, one or two injections of penicillin. The wiring, the other technical procedures, even the selection of the original subject all seem to have a preservative effect. What is meant by this? Well, not simply that the more durable guests are chosen. In fact, the reverse can be said: being chosen actually confers a quality of spiritual endurance the guest may not have possessed in ordinary life. Of course a certain physical toughness is also necessary, and guests can often surprise in that respect. Some won't survive the first two or three days; those I always recognise, and dispose of quickly. But others seem so frail and last so long.

(5) 'WINDOWS' IN THE 121/125 STUB CORRIDOR

Elements of the Theory Cadre believe that the structure of the hotel is rather older than appears. Speculation centres on the short corridor behind rooms 121 to 125, which is reached at one end from the rear stairwell and from the other by a flight of five descending stone steps, themselves perhaps the remains of a wider, older staircase. While this corridor is presently windowless, two or three tall, incomplete framelike structures can be detected beneath the plaster of the inner wall. 'Is it possible,' Alyssia Fignall asks, in the 42nd edition of *Wallpaper*, the Architectonics Committee Journal, 'that the 121/125 stub once gave on to a courtyard?' Unless this proves to be the case, she continues, the opposite conclusion – that an internal wall once looked outward – is 'as inescapable as it is impermissible.' Meanwhile, within the Architectonics Committee, a closed group consisting mainly of materials-technology students has already begun to discuss the possibility that an entirely different building occupied the ground as recently as twenty years ago.

(6) THE TRAFFIC OF THE SPECTACULAR

Narrative structure, AE Fennel has always believed, is the trunk route of the spectacle. Free flow of the spectacular is as necessary to a well-built secondary world as it is to the neoliberal state. Therefore, in every 'story' we tell, our ambition should be to achieve a calculated failure of service, a single perfect interruption of traffic. 'Failing that,' AE advises the Wednesday evening creative writing workshop in the refectory of the Ambiente Hotel's Cultural Wing & Conference Centre, 'do at least try to dig a hole in the road.'

(7) A KEY EVENT IN ROOM 121

Incidences of telekinesis disturb the hotel at night, rearranging small objects, papers, items of clothing. A pair of shoes moves an inch to the left. A cupboard door is rattled so quietly that no one wakes. Bunches of keys, placed on their hooks in Reception in the early evening, are discovered under a breakfast table at 8am. Some objects are moved once, others several times across two or three nights. 'An intellectual history founded on anthropocentrism,' writes Alicia Fennec in the Theory Cadre journal, 'encourages us to think of telekinesis as caused. In fact these events occur without agency, intent or telos. They are not communications. They do not support a narrative.' Tiny changes of air currents are recorded at the base of the kitchen range. A computer, switched off at eleven, is switched on again by seven. A brief flash of light is observed to have occurred in an empty fourth-floor bathroom. For several weeks, waves of improbability ripple nightly along the corridor outside Room 121 and, meeting the back bar staircase, which seems to act as a barrier, disperse.

(7) THE GUESTS AT THE AMBIENTE HOTEL

A reader from Leicestershire asks, Why are guests seen so rarely at the hotel? Reader, there are plenty of guests, but you only see them when you first arrive! The rest of the time they are stored in humane conditions. Deployed primarily in the dining room and the lobby, the guests in this picture are for the most part kept underground. Of the guest problematic, AE Funnel has written recently: 'Their hold on reality is tenuous. Although there is a sadness to their voracity and yearning, the behaviour of guests is determined by the same mathematics as that of any other school, swarm or murmuration. They pour constantly through a given room even though there is only one of them resident at a time. To the long term habitues of the hotel,' she concludes, 'they don't seem very robust.' For this reason, never address a guest seen in a corridor late at night.

(8) A HOTEL CHRISTMAS

The permanent residents at the Ambiente Hotel will be looking forward even more keenly than usual to both Christmas dinner in the Function Room and the traditional Boxing Day immanence vs transcendence debate (taking place this year in the downstairs back bar). Best of luck to everyone! Left: Alyssia Fignall is seen discussing the Christmas menu with an unnamed member of the Architectonics Committee. Below: A view of the Function Room windows, as viewed from the pavement in Codmorton Street.

(9) THE GUEST IN ROOM 444

K, who for some years has lived on the fourth floor rear corridor of the hotel's retirement wing, attributes an unremitting depressive disorder to (a) birth at the outset of the 'atomic age', (b) secondary school food in 1957, (c) the decaying John Calder publications which even now take up sixty percent of the bookshelves in Room 444. But the event that most shaped his view of the world was, indirectly, the death of Sacheverell Sitwell. Faced with the incompleteness of *Journey to the Ends of Time*, K's intellect – such as it was – became trapped forever in the first and only volume, a book he can't remember except by its dustjacket, which featured the layered colours of a dull yet ferocious sunset.

(10) PHOTOGRAPH DISCOVERED UNDER A HALL CARPET

This picture, apparently taken on a 1980s Polaroid format in Oaxaca in the late 2000s (microchemical analysis pending), shows (a) ornamental metal grille over a street door (b) adjacent exterior wall painted with the head of a laughing man in a hat, both viewed from the front seat of the modified WW2 Jeep which occupies the foreground of the image. A team led by Lisi Fearnall has established that the painted head, rendered in high contrast black and white, can still be found on the wall and displays 'gains and losses of clarity' on a twelve day cycle. ('Though it is always sharper and brighter,' Fearnall reported to a private session of the Steering Committee, 'whenever a vehicle is present.') Fearnall, emphasising the complexity of the physics, dismisses the view that the subject of the image is actually confined in the wall.

(11) THE LIBRARY AT THE AMBIENTE HOTEL

For some years a sub-basement beneath the hotel's parking facility was used to store texts generated by the guests. These, ranging from thin volumes of verse to literary horror novels the thousand pages of which might be read in any order, were discovered in predictable circumstances: an immaculately tidy room with 50 years of stored nail clippings and a mysteriously opened window; urgent written or recorded warnings against reading or even turning the pages of the manuscript; the death, wandering off or unexplained evaporation of the writer in circumstances which suggested they too had been an item in a text. During the pre-War period, the Theory Cadre threw open this library three times a year, but though its contents drew visitors from most major universities, no scholarship emerged and in May 1946 the sub-basement, along with the passage that leads to it, was sealed. Pictured below: Elements of the Closed Architectonics Committee of the Theory Cadre visit Le Tourniquet, circa 1930.

(11A): BROKEN SYMMETRIES

The historian K's function in the Cadre has been debated since the 1940s. Was he a member? Was he in fact, as RI Gaines suggests in issue 7 of *Wall Mart*, a founding member? The appearance in the Library of K's magnum opus after the sub-basement door was sealed (see left) suggests otherwise. But Alexia Ficknow puts it best when she writes: 'In those days a door might be sealed by the Architectonics Committee, but no door was ever sealed *to* the Architectonics Committee.' And we are left with the following tantalising passage from the manuscript itself: 'Project "Trap" was never completed. "Soul Gem" was a project to collect "evidence-free innuendo". Soul Gem was wound down in 1945 upon the death of the resource (see notes). Several similar projects wound down naturally with the resource itself. "Eat Cake", a hardened version of "Soul Gem 2": the Eat Cake abstract promised abjection, violence, denial. Eat Cake was unlisted. Various other projects: "Project Nineteen" (see appended material). "Mex Lite", "Max Eight" and "Lite Core" were clean product generated during varied initiatives and test runs. "Initiative B" ran successfully until 1978, when it was replaced under the *Dark Stork* programme. Project "Veil Grain" was an unsuccessful add-on to the *Main Stem* series. "Vague Heart": Project Vague Heart remains partially operational but is identified under recent initiatives as "2014". Resource appears to have retained motility & limited function. Project "121" is the shadow of something much larger.' [Italics & heavy underscore AF.]

Recovering the Rites

THE LAST TIME I went there it was a late Friday afternoon in October, coming on dark. The key took time going in the lock. As soon as I was up in the room I could see something had been there before me. As I entered, it was still disappearing, like an oily residue mixing in water. The air was almost as cold as the street outside.

I went to the window and pulled the blind. People were leaving work, walking quickly past with their heads down. Up and down the road the neon signs were going on one by one. October totters into November. London draws round itself for a second or two and seems comforting.

I looked along the street at the smear of light under the railway bridge. It was a place I would now do anything to avoid. It was a signal from the dead. It was all they had to say. They remembered being alive, they remembered a slick of light on old tiles on a wet day, the pavement becoming wetter and blacker as people tracked the rain into it. They remembered the cold draughts under the bridge there.

I rang the first number I could think of and said, 'We live in the thinnest of worlds, between the past and the future. They occupy more space than that. We never see the whole of them.'

The voice at the other end said, 'Jake, is it happening again?'

Everything becomes more itself, or what people have understood it to be. Under the bridge the dead are a cultural

135

force. 'Even when they're perfectly still,' I said, 'they seem to us to be moving. We only see them moving through.'

'Jake?'

Anti-Promethean

THAT WHOLE ENTERPRISE WAS a let-down. The star drive proved useful, but there was a war or two in consequence and when, after some centuries' travel, we reached the mysterious object at the edge of the universe, it turned out to be an advert for hair gel.

Animals

IN LATE JUNE, SUSAN rented a cottage for a fortnight. It was tucked away at the seaward end of a lane; beyond it there was only flat light on the sand dunes and open beach. The paperwork required her to collect the keys from a Mrs Lago, who lived at the other end of the lane where it joined the road. Mrs Lago turned out to be sixtyish, frail-looking but active, with watery blue eyes, bright red lipstick and a selection of cotton print dresses two generations too young for her. During the summer her grassy front garden, across which had been scattered some round white plastic tables, did duty as a café. She was in and out all day, carrying trays of cakes, fitting umbrellas into the sockets in the centre of the tables to keep the rain off. In the evening the onshore wind blew everything about, and it lay in the rain looking shabby.

Susan called as instructed and found the garden full of sparrows. They gathered round her while she waited for the keys, cocking their heads right and left. They ate cake crumbs, first from the ground, then the chairs, then the very edge of the table. Then they took off all at once and one of them flew through the open door into the house, where it fluttered inside the window just above the sill among the china ornaments and little vases. Its panic was terrible. Mrs Lago went inside and after some reckless stumbling about appeared with it in her hands at the door. It was squawking and cheeping miserably. As soon as she let it go it shot off across the garden.

'I thought it was going to break my lucky horseshoe,' she said, looking at Susan in a vague but excited way. 'It's been broken once before.'

'Has it?' Susan said.

You were always the junior partner in a conversation with Mrs Lago, your responses limited to, 'Yes. No. Isn't it?' and, 'I did!' Listening to yourself make them was a bit like listening to one end of a telephone conversation. She had a curious lurching or sloping walk. She owned two or three dogs that sometimes got out and ran up and down the lane, surprised by a freedom they couldn't seriously exploit.

Susan got up early and walked by the bay. She enjoyed the light on the waves. Every morning at six, rain showers rustled in off the sea, tapping on the windows like old women in a cheap seafront hotel. Susan, who ate her breakfast standing up in the kitchen where it was warm, stared out at the small ill-kept lawn. It filled her with nostalgia on behalf of the previous occupants of the cottage, whom she imagined as an active, kindly, but not very successful middle-aged couple a little surprised to find themselves still happy with their life after so many years.

'Do you remember,' she imagined them saying to one another, 'the year we planted the daffodils and nothing came up? What a laugh we had over that!'

In the same spirit she lived with their shopping lists, and the cardboard boxes full of Sunday newspapers stowed under the stairs. They had left behind a shelf or two of paperback books, dusty and stained with cigarette smoke – Virginia Woolf, Katherine Mansfield, Dorothy Richardson. Though she never managed to reconcile this library with the wallpaper in the kitchen, she felt as if she was looking after these things for them; as if, when she picked the cottage from the bewildering number offered by the internet, she had taken them on for a fortnight too.

After a few days Susan began to find the idea less friendly. The cottage could be quiet, especially in the early evening, when the lane, with its fringe of trees against the setting sun, filled up with shadows. She heard what she thought were movements, half drowned by the sound of the radio she kept in the kitchen, even in the day. 'It must be the central heating,' she thought, but soon it became clear that these sounds were actually voices. Whatever room Susan was in, she heard them somewhere else. They were the voices of a man and woman who, chafed by their circumstances, had became as fractious as children. At night in bed, for instance, discussing the house they would buy when the money came through, a really good lump sum rather than these stupid little dribs and drabs they kept getting, Alex would say:

'And no curtains in the study!' I want all the light I can get now, pouring in over the books.'

She would laugh offhandedly at this, and so would he. 'Anyway,' he'd say, 'curtains are vulgar. Or they were in Virginia's day – it's in her diary. Only the lower middle classes had to have curtains in every window.'

He always called Katherine Mansfield 'Katherine' and Virginia Woolf 'Virginia'. It often irritated her, but now she was amused.

'Alex, what snobs you three are!' she said.

'You will have some plants, though?' she asked anxiously after a moment. 'Just one or two of my best?'

'I don't want –'

'Oh, I won't fill up your precious window sills,' she said. She smiled. 'I won't need to, with the garden I'm going to have! Oh, it'll be fantastic just to have some room. Vegetables. A greenhouse. Everything!'

'A conservatory,' he said, 'with an old grey deal table to work on when it's too cold outside.' He was silent for a moment. 'A walled garden, where I can get away and sunbathe and not hear anything or think about anything. With the light pouring down like a post-Impressionist painting –'

'It will have to face south,' she said.

He writhed away from her suddenly and jumped out of bed.

'What's that?'

Susan jumped up too and went for a walk along the coastal path. She stood on one headland looking across at the next. They aren't the people I expected, she thought. Clouds blew in from the sea, and by ten o'clock the whole peninsula was locked in drizzle and mist.

On a wet day you could visit either the cathedral with its decaying and profitless stone stairs, or the aquarium. The aquarium was the more interesting of the two because at least its occupants were alive. In the main tanks, dogfish and small sharks circled endlessly in the hard light, which seemed, as much as water, to be their proper domain. Visitors shuffled round and round too, stopping to nose at a side tank, shoaling briefly around the interactive display. The children were excited, but their parents looked exhausted, and as if they weren't quite sure how they found themselves there.

Just before lunch, the rain stopped and everybody left. Susan walked up through a warren of steep streets until she came out on the hill above the town, where you could fly a kite from the bald patch of grass in front of the old chapel or sit on a bench with a view of the harbour composed along all the most formal curves: the sides of the stubby lighthouse on the granite mole; the bows of the fishing boats blue and white, red, green, yellow; an apostrophe of sand the exact colour of the coffee served in the Tudor Rooms. By then the tide was up: she could make out the surfers waiting in the calm water behind the long shallow silver waves. They stared out to sea with all the patience of primitive fishermen or pilgrims bathing, then in a brief, desperate flurry of activity tottered into the spume blown off the top of the first worthwhile wave and vanished. Further out in the bay two or three quite large ships, moored pointing west, seem to hover in the mist and blowing rain, not quite connected to sea or sky. Surfing here seemed as exotic and strange a gesture as the local TV ad for an Indian restaurant, of which Susan had caught only the words, 'the Ganges at Milford Haven', telling herself, Ah: so that's where it reaches the sea.

Walking back to the cottage after lunch, she considered the aquarium sharks again. They were less like the sisters of Jaws than of a whippet – small, quick, unassuagable. What distinguished them was a quality of patience, a Devonian strength of character no whippet – no mammal – could ever possess. When she got in she stood for a minute or two in the hallway, listening.

'It's a cranefly!' Alex said. 'Christ! How did that get in? I asked you to close the windows!'

It was clattering round the small untidy room dragging its legs and bumping against the wall. He missed it several times with a sheaf of rolled-up papers. It staggered into his books, fell, flew towards him suddenly so that he dodged back in spite of himself. 'Christ!' He hated them so much he could hardly get close enough to kill them. It had got down behind the desk among the box files and piles of old newspapers.

'It's dead now,' she said. She wanted to laugh.

She pulled the sheet over her mouth.

'I can still hear it buzzing,' he said. 'I shan't sleep if I know it's in here.'

He stood there in his pyjamas, breathing heavily, his eyes quite vacant. After a moment the poor cranefly lurched out into the air again and he hit it against the wall until it was a smear.

'You have to get their rhythm,' he said, throwing down the papers.

Now the wind turned southwesterly and blew onshore; several wet days followed in a row. Despite the weather, Susan felt like spending less time in the cottage. When the Oceanarium failed as an interest, she turned to the secondhand bookshops, in one of which she bought a volume entitled simply, 'Seashore'. This she took to the Tudor Rooms, an old fashioned place with faux leather banquettes, waitress service, and oak veneer to shoulder height. To feel comfortable in there, she felt, wasn't to live in the past, or, really, feel any kind of nostalgia; it was only that she understood its values better.

In an alcove at the back sat a couple in their fifties, who had with them their clinging, rather silent grandchild. The child moved its sickly eyes over the menu and couldn't make up its mind.

'He's panicking,' said the woman, 'because he thinks he won't be able to eat it all.' After that she began to talk about someone called Jonathan. 'There's something about Jonathan. For me he's like a sort of brother figure or something.'

Susan opened her new book.

'When waves break diagonal to a beach,' she read, 'material is pushed sideways by the swash before flowing down in the backwash, and is carried in this way along the beach, in a series of sawtooth movements called 'longshore drift'. The groyne — symbol of the Victorian middle-class bathing beach — traps and stabilises this sand. Left to itself it would only drift slowly along the line of least resistance and, at the dictates of the pleasure principle, form the strange thin hooks and curves which decorate the coastline lower down.'

Looking up from this paragraph, Susan heard the woman in the alcove prompt her husband: 'It would be so nice to see him again. Jonathan, I mean.'

'Which Jonathan?' the husband said.

It was his sole contribution, though at one point he ordered an ice-cream. When the waitress asked, 'What flavour would you like?' he seemed to answer, 'Vinegar,' but it must have been 'Vanilla'. The child stared at him as he ate it.

When they came to pay, his wife told the cashier: 'I've got him well trained in everything else but I never let him carry money.'

How awful for a man, Susan thought, to have to wear a vest under your shirt in humid summer weather and carry no money, and be discussed with a waitress while you are sitting there, and only grin vaguely. His eyebrows turned up at the ends like an eagle-owl's: it gave him a mildly ironic look, though on his part irony could only have been a gesture. Later, as she was letting herself into the cottage, she heard, very distinctly, the word, 'Don't.'

She heard the words, 'I'm warning you, Alex.'

She heard the words, spoken in a quiet almost conversational tone, 'I'll kill you if you do that.'

There was such depth of promise in those words, such a certainty of purpose. Susan tried to read a little more of her book. 'Mapped at yearly intervals, these delicate structures shift and change shape but do not die. If you were to animate their development, they would seem to eddy, like streams of smoke in broken air.' She slept badly.

A little before ten o'clock next morning, one of Mrs Lago's dogs broke into the cottage. It was a collie, quite well-behaved although a little overpowering, and it ate most of Susan's breakfast. When it saw itself in the mirror at the top of the stairs it wagged its tail furiously. It snuffled in the boxes of newspaper under the stairs, peed up the chairs and played with a mouldy tennis ball it teased out from under the cooker. Susan phoned Mrs Lago, who said, 'Oh dear, I didn't even know he was gone. He must have jumped out of the window,' and offered to come and fetch it. Susan, obscurely pleased by the whole incident, perhaps because it had been like having a real visitor, said she would return the dog herself.

'I'll put the kettle on,' Mrs Lago said.

The sea was out a long way; persistent, misty rain had been varnishing everything since before dawn. The dog ran about in the lane, lifting its leg amiably to the brambles. Almost anything made it happy. Later, Susan sat in Mrs Lago's small front room, looking round at the old china ornaments; the tacked-up postcards from customers gone home long ago; the rack of local history pamphlets devoted to mines and wrecks, their covers curled in the salt air.

'Are you lonely here?' she asked suddenly.

Mrs Lago laughed. 'Not since I got my Dell,' she said. 'I follow the horses.' The Dell enabled her to follow them realtime, all round the world. 'Be honest, look at this place, I'd never survive the winter without a couple of bets!' The collie whined suddenly and pushed its nose into her hand. She glanced down as if she was surprised to see it. Her skin seemed as delicate and cheap as the china. She tried to explain 'dutching' software to Susan.

'I'm always rather bad with numbers,' said Susan, who, in more ordinary circumstances, was not.

'It's changed the face of betting, the internet.'

'Has it?' Susan said.

She decided to have another cup of tea.

'While I'm here,' she said, 'what's the history of the cottage?'

'I don't think it's got one,' Mrs Lago told her. 'It's always been a holiday let.'

'Come back to bed. You look so funny when you get het up like that.'

'I'm having the bedroom empty,' Alex said, staring viciously at the desk and the files, the bookcases and dining chairs they had no room for downstairs. 'Completely bloody empty. I hope you've understood that. White walls and black woodwork, exactly as they'd have had it then. They knew how to get space round them. White walls and plain varnished floorboards. Maybe a chest of drawers. Christ!' He was shuddering. 'Christ!'

Sometimes it seemed to her, as they lay in bed like this, that they already lived in the new house. It would be, ideally, between the hills and the sea, somewhere in West Penwith for instance, so you could get the best of both worlds. They both loved the hills but neither of them wanted to give up the sea. They'd lived near the sea since they left college. He needed so much space. He could walk twenty miles a day when he needed to. He was actually physically better if he could do that. And he had to admit that she needed plants – really needed them – for the same reason. She needed something to grow.

'Of course, salt's not very good for most plants,' she said as he put the light out.

'That wasn't another of the bloody things was it?'

A few days after the dog came in, Susan returned from her morning walk to find the cottage door stuck shut. She pushed at it until she was out of breath. Looking through the window into the front room, she thought she saw a movement, a white face struggling with a strong emotion. 'Hello?' she called. Nothing. She stood there a long time. She couldn't see the face anymore. She wondered if she had ever seen it. When she went back to the door, it opened easily. As she stood in the hallway she heard a calm woman's voice say, 'Don't you dare come in here. I'll kill you if you come in here.'

She heard that voice say that three times, 'I'll kill you if you come in here.'

She went straight out again, down into the town, and walked about until she found herself in a little triangle of concrete at the corner of two lanes, chained off from the traffic and with a low parapet fronting on the sea. There were a couple of litter bins and some blue-painted benches. On the wall hung a red and white life belt with the letters PDC in black block capitals. Susan decided she would sit down there until she felt better. Across the bay the speedboats went in and out, boys standing rakishly in their bows. Closer, the Lamplighter Gallery, with its yellow shutters and careful resident landscape artist, advertised a clifftop outing, 'binoculars provided'. Susan coaxed a local cat on to her knee, where it sat amiably at first, thick-furred, tabby and self-involved.

'Well,' she thought, 'I am honoured.'

The Lamplighter closed for lunch and then opened again. The inshore lifeboat went quickly across the bay, returning about twenty minutes later. Tourists passed down the street behind her, saying, 'We'll have to see if there are enough towels,' and 'Here's a lady with a cat.' All of this was quite calming. She sat on with the cat. At first she had assumed it was a stray, independent in a town of discarded fish and chip wrappers but still on occasion lonely for human company. She felt pleased at how quickly they had taken to one another. But then an oldish man in a blue blazer came and told her its name. 'She's called Trixie,' he said. He smiled into the sun. 'And she likes corned beef.'

He was carrying a packet of frozen beefburgers in a thin plastic bag, the neck of which was twisted several times round his suntanned, square-tipped fingers. You could see, plainly, 'Birds Eye' through the plastic where it was stretched tight. After that everyone who came past, even some people who were only visitors like herself, seemed to know the cat. 'Soft thing!' they said, addressing it more than her. 'Anything for a warm lap, that one.'

'Go on home, Trixie!'

Somehow this made Susan feel cheated as well as left out. The cat not only had a home, it was part of a community from which she was excluded. She felt a fool. When the first drops of rain fell, and she wanted to shelter, the cat was reluctant to move off her lap. 'Off you go,' she said. She tried to pick it up and it bit her, as she had known it would. The rain drove her back to the aquarium, where the air was hot and curiously dry. The eyes of the sharks glittered suddenly in the clarified light. An octopus hung high up against the glass of its tank, stuck there motionless but pulsing gently, waiting, even more patient and alien than the sharks, for that change in the nature of things which would permit it to take up its rightful place.

'They've got fantastically developed vision,' said someone, 'apparently.' A pause. 'God knows what they use it for.'

Susan stared at the octopus and thought: I must go back. I must go back and pack my things. Outside it had stopped raining and the sun was out. As she stood in the doorway of the aquarium, blinking in the clean windy light, two women got out of a taxi in front of her. The older of them said in a voice rich with received pronunciation:

'One of us should look after the child.'

By then it was late afternoon, and raining again. The way the clouds toiled in over the sea, it could have been October. Susan packed her wheeled suitcase and tugged it along the lane to Mrs Lago's house. It bogged down in every puddle. She had called the local taxi on her mobile; the keys to the cottage, she kept in her hand all the way down the lane. 'I want to give you these,' she said, holding them out to Mrs Lago. 'I can't stay here another night.'

She would prefer to be back in London, she said.

'Something happened here,' she said.

Mrs Lago seemed slow to understand. She had been sitting in the gloom when Susan banged on the door, her face lit up in a faint but chaotic procession of colours by the screen of her cut-price laptop. There was a full ashtray near her hand; a cold cup of tea. She had folded an old tartan picnic blanket across her knees. The results of a bout of dutching at Far East courses had caused a bruised look to settle around her eyes. Her vagueness and lack of contact with the world only served to increase Susan's sense of urgency.

'Those two arrived here as nice a couple as you'd want to meet. But in the end –'

'Which couple?' Mrs Lago said.

'In the end,' Susan carried on, exasperated, 'they fought each other all over the place. She picked up the hammer and he picked up the axe. They fought each other all over the house, in the garden, and up and down the lane there. They stalked one another in the dark.'

She shivered.

'I saw them,' she said. 'Hit and chop, all afternoon and evening, waiting for each other, slipping behind the trees.'

The woman stared at Susan. She tapped the keys of the laptop, the screen of which darkened suddenly. It was clear she didn't know how to respond.

'Goodbye then,' said Susan.

She dragged her luggage to the end of the lane to wait for the taxi. She jumped at every sound. Every noise sounded like an axe or a hammer, and the sunset was like blood over the grey headland. *I don't know what I might see*, she kept saying to herself, *I don't know what I might see*. 'They were like animals,' she had said to the woman. 'Just like animals.' But she saw nothing and nothing happened to her, and soon enough she was on the train.

Back in London, she took to locking herself out of the house. She dreamed that her urine was corrosive, woke confused in her own bed. Her children were puzzled. It seemed to them that she had gone downhill quite suddenly; it was a pity, at that age, to be already forgetting your keys or phoning people late at night to talk. Things came to a head a month or two later, when a man in an unlabelled delivery van charged her five hundred and fifty pounds for bringing the roof of her bungalow up to European safety standards. It was evident he'd done nothing, but Susan allowed him to drive her down to the bank and wait outside to make sure he got his cash. She was upset when she thought about the incident later; but in a distant way, as if she was observing someone else's humiliation.

That night, unable to sleep, she went round and round the bungalow in the dark, touching a teacup here or a cushion there, boiling the kettle but letting it lay, listening to the distant thread of traffic on the M25, until she ended up at the sitting room window, staring into the dark.

Of course I knew really that I shouldn't pay him, she thought.

Dense shrubbery on either side gave the garden a sense of being larger than it was; its boundaries were postponed. Something moved out there briefly and she could smell the autumn leaves for the first time in years, a strange smell, acrid and exciting: the smell of change. *It's a smell,* she thought, *that you must never try to compare with anything else, or evoke by mentioning some other smell. It reminds you so forcibly of childhood, when every seasonal change had its excitements. Mist lying in under the north slopes of the low hills, making them dark and mysterious against the bright blue sky and dazzling winter sun. Chimney smoke from white cottages. Wisps and feathers of high icy cloud splitting the light like rainbows.*

Under the Ginger Moon

THE BIRD CALLS HERE get stranger and stranger. Sometimes we wonder if we're in Stoke-on-Trent at all. We sit counting our mosquito nets, while the 787 Dreamliners lug themselves into the air above us like suitcases full of cheap new clothes. Yesterday evening there was a wedding in the courtyard. The bride and groom processed slowly to their carved and decorated chairs, where they were soon surrounded by the traditional circle of softly-glowing camcorder screens.

In the Crime Quarter

HE WORKED OUT OF a small office the only feature of which was the clarity and interest of the screen saver images. They were beachscapes exotic and hard to place, with a sharp, travelogue quality. He had the screen positioned so it was impossible to ignore these glimpses as they dissolved into one another; while to the client he presented the city as a surf of buildings and people and consumer goods. The motives that powered it were tidal. Unpredictable winds played against masses of water, currents too complex to understand. Crimes were whipped off the crest of events like spray. 'A great wave,' he would explain, 'composed of the billion actions of the very citizens it curls so threateningly above!' It was the perfect experience of art, he said, in the perfect space – art as an aspect of architectonic and thence, with perfect logic, of lifestyle. His clientele were not so sure. These carefully groomed and dressed art tourists would look across the desk at him with a kind of puzzled distaste, wondering if they were in the process of making a mistake. They understood their own inauthenticity: they weren't, at the outset anyway, so certain about his. The women had come for the sensorium porn. The men, though they would pretend to enjoy 'seeing the world from a different point of view', were only interested in donkey crime.

The Good Detective

PRIMROSE HILL, THAT HOUR when things get hold of you, five o'clock on a dull Saturday afternoon. Single fathers are leading their little girls up and down the wet pathways and you can see the Regents Park birdhouse draped like fruit netting across the nearer trees. A systems manager walks away from his first wife. All she was doing was making a phonecall, answering a text. She looks up and he's gone. He's taken the children with him.

Where is she supposed to start looking for him? The world's full of harassed men his age, with two daughters and a suitcase. The trains and buses are full of them.

Eventually someone puts her on to me. She's upset. It's new to her, but frankly I'm used to it. People do this all the time. They're trying to get away from themselves. They're trying to reinvent, and why not? London's kind to the confident. Otherwise, what is there? Get on the tube in the morning and people stare straight into your face from less than one foot distance. That's no way to live. So they go missing, and I find them. I find kiddies and criminals, and people who would do crimes if they knew how. I find the people who paint themselves on to your walls, play their favourite music over and over again then leave you nothing but a picture in the night.

I never look for the ordinary ones. They're too easy to find. They've cashed in on the housing differential, abandoned Islington. They're off to the provinces: no mortgage, walk the children to school, grow your own vegetables. They've disqualified themselves.

Listen to this, though –

A man lives in Putney, Barnes, East Sheen, one of those places along the river. He's an actor, an investment banker, a publisher's editor – it doesn't matter. Or he sells something, say mobile phones. Say he sells mobile phones. One day he gets tired of that. He decides to write a travel book about the area he lives in. This area is two miles on a side, roughly square, no hard boundaries. That is, it's bounded on its north and west by the curve of the Thames: but he can cross that if he wants, and enjoy the other bank – willows, a couple of muddy playing fields and an old bandstand. A little road with allotments on one side which in the spring looks like a lane in the country. Over there it doesn't look like London at all.

This man buys several notebooks of the brand the famous Bruce Chatwin used to use for his writing. He buys some gel pens of different colours. He buys a Nikon 775 digital camera. Then he sets off into the streets which surround his house, intending to record everything he sees.

Winter. Late afternoon. Christmas is close. It's on his heels. The streets are dark and at the same time comfortable, narrowed by cars and a sense of warmth, a sense of drawing-together which seems to come from the houses on either side. The women have fetched their kids from playschool and finished parking their SUVs. In one street of little workingmen's cottages they close the curtains; in the next there are gleams of light from every window. Every street has its own culture. Here it's more BMWs than Audis; there, they'll keep a pedigree dog but a pedigree cat is extravagant. Wood floors, a child sitting on a sofa with its knees up, watching something you can't see. She stares out, startled by the flash of the Nikon. The traveller smiles, waves, moves on. Is that the river at the end of the street? Is that a Toyota? He's already lost.

To begin with, he brings all this back. From the Nikon

he downloads smoky still images of Barnes bridge, taken a few hundred yards downriver on an afternoon that makes it look like industrial archeology in Manchester or Bremen. His notes say: 'Every rivet stands out.'

When I claim some people are too easy to find, what do I mean?

Poll tax gave rise to a generation which lived in other people's houses. They formed strong personal ties yet remained evasive, incurious about one another. As a result, never fully sited, they suffered mild depressions and moved on. I'm not looking for them.

A train ride with someone you met yesterday. The smell of diesel fuel in carriage air. You look sideways at her face, you're not even sure you like her. The plain fact is she looks more grown up than you. Her house is cold and needs work. She has a kid. She says things like, 'I've always got by on my wits.' That's exciting but eventually you interpret it as a judgement. Later you see that's how she lives her life, as a judgement, as an ideological act. It's too forceful. It's too blunt. Worse, it doesn't work. She's just as compromised and vulnerable as you. Later still the pathos of that hits you, but by then she's long gone and you are too.

I'm not looking for her.

Afternoon, Old Compton Street. Rain makes it like an older version of itself. I'm doing the bars with a photograph. 'Can I just show you this? This is a sixteen year old boy who's gone missing. You haven't seen him round here have you? No? Can I just leave this with you?' Meanwhile in some other street – Ghost Town, Croydon, UK – the boy's parents have consulted a clairvoyant. She has a vision of him washed up in the waiting room at St Thomas' Hospital, Waterloo. Easy enough to check. I find he called there using a false name, but 'became frightened' and left without treatment. Treatment for what? They can't say. That's a bit more interesting to me, especially the clairvoyant, but it's still not quite what I mean.

Facts are the easiest things to come by. From age fourteen upwards, girls run away more often than boys. Yet twice as many adult men go missing as adult women. Men aged twenty four to thirty are likelier to disappear than any other group. More people go missing from the South East than any other region in the UK. What did they leave? Well, they left home. Why did they go? They can't tell you. People run away. They relocate, they go missing, as we've said. That's a geographical statement as much as a social one. It's what makes them easy to find.

The challenge is in the ones who go missing in their own lives. There's less to know about those people. They live inside us. They have very simple ideas. We rarely hear their voices before it's too late.

What does he want, this man from Barnes, whatever his name is? His intention is still unclear. Is he a traveller or only a tourist? Worse, is he a psychogeographer? To start with, he brings it all back. He comes home, seven every evening, just as if he's been to work. He's diligent. He keys his notes into the laptop; he downloads his pictures. It's an act of capture. For now, at least, his is the narrative of a man who begins to write a book about the immediate area he lives in – a radius of a few ordinary London streets – with every oriel window and garden ornament, every spalled brick wall, described as a feature. Then one day, from a narrow corner in 'Little Chelsea', East Sheen, he hears the following dialogue:

'Now she's begun to claim it's boring here.'

'Well of course, it is.'

He stands up close, but he can't see in. He imagines a room smelling of death, with two old people talking their dreary talk beneath the crosses, pietas, and old photographs on the walls.

'What's her name?'

'I only know her as Elaine.'

A long pause, and then:

'We wanted that war. All of us wanted that war. World War Three was the great imaginative act of its day.'

'Children are better in pairs.'

After that there's only a sound like someone doing the washing up. A cough. Later, at home, he realises he hasn't written any of it down. The next morning he takes the camera but forgets the notebook. Soon he's leaving them both behind. He feels relieved. A little guilty. He feels naked. Two years later his wife finds out he doesn't work in communications any more. That's when she calls me.

I listen to the family's ideas. It helps them. I appear receptive but that's a pretence. All I need is the facts. Who's missing. When it happened, or when the relatives first noticed it had happened. I don't want their theories. They come to my office and sit uncomfortably looking at the desk and the dusty filing cabinet, wishing they had gone somewhere else.

Whatever I say they always ask themselves:

'Why did he do this?'

I could tell them. From age forty he had the feeling of being spread very thin on the world, like a specialised coating. If people weren't careful with him, he felt, if he wasn't careful with himself, he'd crack or peel or flake away. Then one day he was trying to understand the instructions for some household appliance, and where it said, 'How to set up the timer,' he read instead: 'How to let things slip.' In the end, even the correct reading began to seem odd to him.

'Timer?' he thought.

That would have been the way it was.

For the sake of the family I ask all the usual questions. Did he seem to be getting thinner? Did he have – some evenings and in dim light – a kind of transparency, an abraded look which you could detect one minute but not the next?

161

For the sake of the family I look through the stuff he left behind: it's a collection of professional qualifications, Barbour jackets and Australian stable boots. It's a shelf of music CDs, English light classical, 80s pop. I find his laptop: it's a Sony. I find the travel notes and picture files, stored under Personal, passworded with the name of the family labrador, and it's all much as you'd expect — that naive, eviscerating attempt they always make to express their inner life as a record of the outer. I find the garage he sold the Audi to: it was a TT, very nice condition. I get positive responses at the White Hart, the Bull, and the Sun — he was seen in all three, last Boat Race day. But what did those locations mean to him?

Nothing, compared to the wall he puts his back against now, as, quaking with Thames fever, he rests after the long slog through the woods from the railway, past Marc Bolan's memorial and on to the Roehampton Gate. He's emaciated, stripped down. He's so far ahead of me! What began as observation became an adventure then a trajectory of relapse, a going-native. The long slow slide into the heartland of his imagination.

Eventually I'm on some windy hill, Richmond Park, early morning. I know he was here before me, quivering like an animal that's got the scent of distance in its nose, turning his head slowly so he can discover everything with those new eyes of his. But that was two years ago, and even if he was here yesterday I won't catch him. He's got his second or third wind by now. He's used to it. In his mind he's pushing an old bicycle loaded with his things, first towards Wimbledon then down the endless heartbreaking sweep of the A3 to the sea. It's his space now.

I call the wife.

I say, 'He's in your house but he's not there anymore.'

I say: 'You knew that already.'

I advise her: 'If you find the husk, leave it where it is. They're often in the garden somewhere; or the attic.'

Some of them you track down. Others you don't, and often that's the best thing. Because what are you going to do? Corner them in the loading bay behind a supermarket in Dalston? Chase them down a muddy path in Stoke Newington cemetery, calling out in a language they can't remember? Back them up against themselves until there's nowhere left to run and whatever dissatisfaction drove them inwards, whatever fire they're full of, bursts out of the neck and sleeves of their crap old raincoat and they go up in front of you like a bundle of dry sticks? I've seen that happen, believe me it's not worth it.

Another afternoon, another bar. I'm always on the lookout for the boy who called in at St Thomas' Hospital then, unable to control his anxieties, left before he could be treated.

'You can't keep them away,' the barman says. 'They're so bloody anxious to start their lives.' He treats the photo to his oblique, dismissing glance. 'They think of this as life,' it makes him say. He laughs. 'You should be here in the evenings.' Whatever he's seeing is so ordinary it's beyond his power to describe. 'Life!' he repeats.

'You run the place,' I remind him.

'Too true,' he admits, turning back to the spirit optic.

A missing person inside your own life. OK, I'm not sure what I mean by that. But the good detective shares some of those qualities of absence. Qualities of self-disenfranchisement, for instance. He's a torn place in the web which would otherwise detain him – home, family, profession, culture. I went missing from my own life years ago, but you don't need me to tell you that.

And what if, in the end, I'm wrong? What if Missing of Barnes only ran away, the way the majority of them do?

Well then I'll know.

One day I'll stand in an upper room in Harringay, looking out. The rain will be falling almost invisibly on the shiny black branches of the trees, dripping off again in big soft quick drops. At the bottom of the garden next door I'll see a man working in a shed. It'll be him.

I see him like this. He's wearing a blue plaid shirt and safety glasses. His dog sniffs round his feet. Every so often he stops what he's doing and comes to the door of the shed and looks out into his garden, or across it towards his house. The dog stands by his leg, its head just touching his knee. It's an old dog with a grey muzzle. After a moment they go back into the shed. He moves the wood from one place to another inside. He puts it up on the workbench. He takes it off again. Everything happens very quietly and comfortably under the yellow light above the bench, and the afternoon slowly gets dark around him. A growing pile of offcuts appears by the shed door and, absorbing the rain, turns from white to sandy brown.

Babies From Sand

(1) THE WATER HOUSE

A permanent exhibition of water paintings at the Holst House Gallery features *Crossing the River Styx* by Joachim Patinir, as well as some small canvases by John Atkinson Grimshaw, including *In Peril*, in the foreground of which several figures are seen running towards the sea at night across a vast, sloping, otherwise deserted quay. 'Though he is not known for his seascapes,' the catalogue remarks, 'when we re-examine Grimshaw, everything he painted seems to be located near water – wet estuarine streets in Leeds; Hampstead depicted on bluffs above a shallow sea at night.' Gericault's *The Raft of the Medusa* can be found in a side-room, along with a Philip James de Loutherbourg, *The Flood* – sometimes known as *The Deluge* – the composition of which eerily resembles that of *Sea Idyll* by Arnold Böcklin (1887). Loutherbourg died in Chiswick in 1812, having all his life 'pursued interests in alchemy, faith healing and the supernatural'. He was a follower of Cagliostro.

(2) THE DOGS OF ST MARGARETS

The twenty sixth of June: Cultural Day of Bad Luck all along the river as far as Windsor, but especially in the small enclave of St Margarets. A hot breeze moves the baskets of trailing flowers on the lamp posts. Faded looking men in red T shirts, a little bald, a little grey at the edges, gather outside Edward

Fail Solicitors, across the road from the bowel cancer charity. Later they will go down to the water, where every high tide briefly strands three lumps of wood known as 'the Three Marys'. These – large, black, asymmetrical, sodden as much with age as with water – are celebrated as the estuary's gift to the land, in a traditional call-and-response. (The dogs of the enclave howl: not just today, but on the anniversary of every one of the borough's many more private, more primitive tragedies. Each year when the light is right these animals remember events of five, ten, fifty years before. They remember not to the day but to the season. Things spread out. Whole months fill up with overlapping disasters.) Among the amusements on offer to visitors are: dream incubation, ritual bathing, and divination by the Lots of Mary.

(3) THE REVEREND HARRY PRICE

During the late 1990s, especially at high tide, the familiar figure of Harry Price could often be seen ascending the water stair at Hammersmith Bridge, dressed in dirty cotton chinos and an old-fashioned Belstaff waxed jacket, and carrying on a plastic strap round his neck the twenty year old Polaroid Sun 600 camera with which he recorded much of his data. Nightly excursions to the astral plane had emaciated the ageing psychogeographer, and his incomplete masterpiece *The Potassium Channel* – written in two hundred black Moleskine notebooks as he pursued, yard by yard, dérive by dérive, his minute investigations of the Brent River and its surrounds, from the boatyards at its confluence with the Thames, past Wharncliffe Viaduct and the zoo, towards the A40 at Greenford – lay abandoned. 'If the disaster can be said to be unevenly distributed,' he wrote to his wife, Fanny, by then a permanent resident in the old Barnes Fever Hospital, 'Brentford is one of the places it has been distributed to. Boatyards and their horrible refuse. High water one minute, the next only mud. Sudden drops bulwarked with rusty metal.'

(4) TRANSFORMATION REACH

'Oliver's Island', open six to seven most evenings, May to October: a small wood, frequented by foxes and wildfowl driven upriver by population pressures in the Barnes wetlands, has grown up on a late-Victorian dreadnought abandoned in midstream. Its iron plates have turned to stone. All down this stretch of the Thames, islands are becoming boats, boats are on their way to being islands. The boats fix themselves in the mud. They settle in the mud. Over the years they become mud. In the final stages of transformation, they support a thicket of buddleia often too dense to navigate. Between the bushes the old decks can sometimes be glimpsed, covered in rabbit-cropped turf and little winding trodden-down paths. Suddenly a passer-by makes out a new shape – planks! The curve of the bow!

(5) THE HUMAN FOOTPRINT

'Squalls of rain pursue each other southeast, the latest accompanied by a lurch of pressure and humidity that encourages waves of scent from the narcissi in the vase on my desk. Between squalls, light strikes half-opened petals, which, though individually white, wrap themselves round a smoky yellow tinge. It races in like the epileptic aura, at a surprising angle from the broken edge of the cloud cover, leaving the air quick and transparent against a dark sky. Ideally one should experience this kind of light on the riverbank near Putney, four o'clock in the afternoon; and perhaps remember later that the person who walked towards you was gone too quickly when you turned to get another look. Look for what rises to the surface in light like that! Not so much ghosts as visitors from the future, the past, or somewhere that is, simply, never quite there. People from under the water, who lose something of themselves on the shore. Babies from sand, at a loss beneath water. To us they seem robust, but their hold on reality is tenuous.' – from *The Seizure Journals of Fanny Price*.

(6) THE POTASSIUM CHANNEL

Notes for the incomplete final chapters of this work present as a sheaf of media reports and scientific abstracts. A seminar on ancient human migration (tracked via mitochondrial haplogroup); the Gnostic foundations of 20th Century Russian science; computer software designed to identify unknown locations by matching them with 'a library of sixty million landscape images': Harry Price's obsessions run together, hardening into unconformable layers of time and data. From a study of studies, robust evidence surfaces of a preCambrian micro continent along the Laccadive-Chagos Ridge; paragraphs from Wikipedia shed new light on metabolic byproducts found deep in the Juan de Fuca tectonic plate. Body parts wash up on a beach east of Southampton; while ('almost simultaneously' Price notes) in the Borough of Brent, a man of about forty, naked and with an inexplicable greenish tinge, is observed by passers-by to drag himself out of the Grand Union Canal near Gallows Bridge then run straight into heavy traffic on the nearby dual carriageway of the M4, where he is struck and killed by a black BMW Alpina with Swiss registration plates before being dragged for some distance underneath an unmarked Volvo FMX D13 truck painted Mediterranean blue.

(7) ARNOLD BÖCKLIN, 'SEA IDYLL'

Perhaps the best but least-known picture in the Holst House collection. The Swiss symbolist, known for his dream paintings of the English Cemetery in Florence, produced this item quite late in his career. In it, three figures – a woman and two children – are depicted sprawled on a lumpen, almost-submerged rock barely large enough to accomodate them; while a fourth – perhaps a man, perhaps some more powerfully ambivalent creature of myth – emerges waist-high from the water nearby. Their tenure on the rock seems anxious and marginal, their poses are awkward and strained. The woman, in yearning towards the man, is carelessly allowing her baby to fall into the sea; while the dwarfish older child, its enlarged buttocks stuck up into the air as a result of some deformity of the spine, appears to be trying to mount her from behind. The painting is too fraught to be any kind of idyll. A sense of confusion – of failed allegory – infuses the drab palette, the deformed anatomy.

(8) THE SEIZURE GENE

Somewhere along the Brent between the Thames confluence and the Fox Inn, for reasons unexamined or perhaps even unadmitted, the Prices became, in the days leading up to Fanny's illness, obsessed with the meaning of human gene Kv12.2. This gene originated 'more than 500 million years ago in the genomes of sea-dwelling species' and has a decisive role in spatial memory. A final note for *The Potassium Channel*, written some time in the early 2000s: 'Yesterday I watched a heron eating a live eel in bright sunshine on the South Pier mudbank. Today it was foggy: the mud was almost awash: the heron still waited there. I fear the hidden channels of the confluence and hate low tide as much as I hate the partly-foundered lighters.' And later: 'Kv12.2 is a very old gene. Even the fish have it.'

(9) EULOGY FOR THE AGEING HAUNTOLOGIST

Mystical sunsets behind the troubled roofs of East Sheen, the overgrown gravestones of Barnes Common, the grim Edwardian silhouette of the Elm Guest House. A smell drifts down the river which can't for a second be mistaken for that of the brewery. The tide is low, the water fast and turbulent between the piers of Barnes Bridge. Eddies thicken with the matted stuff left at high tide – bottle caps, tampon applicators, condoms in a matrix of sodden interwoven twigs rarely more than five or six inches long – it's a substance in itself. (The sexual health of a nation can always be judged by the state of its rivers.) Like the smear of light on the wet tiles under the bridge, it is a language, a signal from those who have gone before. It is what they have to say. They remember being alive, they remember a slick of light on old tiles on a wet day, the pavement becoming wetter and blacker as people track the rain into it and the human footprint blurs to black. They remember the cold draughts. Everything thus becomes more itself, or what people have understood it to be. The departed swirl forever under Barnes Bridge, a cultural attraction which draws visitors from all over the world. Come for the sunsets, we say in West London: stay for the funeral!

(10) THE LOTS OF MARY

Further along the tideway, the old Holst House fills up with depictions of people in the throes of some cultural stress difficult to understand. They recoil from one another and yet seem intertwined; they are bent back in the shapes of change, of seizure, of a body language of transformation which can have no meaning to the carefully groomed and dressed art tourists who pass in front of them. In his rooms directly above the Middle Gallery, Harry Price, puzzled by some implied but not quite demonstrable consonance between the celebrations of the St Margarets Day of the Dead and the central anxieties of Arnold Böcklin's masterpiece, which he feels as a powerful astral 'presence' in the hanging space below him, falls asleep thinking about the agitated gestures of the woman and her son, the smiling but curiously unreceptive expression of the older male. His dreams are filled with sounds both human and marine. At three in the morning the phone rings. A throat is cleared at the other end, but no one speaks and in the end it is Price who, looking down at his hands, feels he must whisper: 'I'm becoming something else.'

Name This City

A PRISON FOR THE heart. The heart's longings emerge squashed and distorted, in grimaces made inhuman by the sheer length of time they have been held in place: as if everyone you see there had spent their lives walking poorly-dressed into the wind and rain, which they have not. Hurt from the very beginning, the heart eats too many cakes. It deforms itself looking away from mirrors. It learns to ironise everything. At eighteen years old it has already collapsed like a senile face. You burst into tears on its behalf without knowing why. This city is no place for the heart, which therefore tries not to recognise itself in shop windows full of too-cheap clothes but keeps up a bright chat about its contact lenses, its colon and its high fibre diet. When the heart stares straight out at you here – as in children or lunatics – it's a frightening, exhilarating experience. A drawing of the town hall: the artist has subtly accentuated the portico, with its monolithic pillars and architrave, to make it seem menacing and gloomy. Old men sleep in the side doorways. There's a blanket, a pile of dirty coats. Further on, outside the mall, someone is hosing down the pavement.

Jack of Mercy's

HARDO CROME BEGAN HIS vast narrative poem, *Bream Into Man*, as soon as he arrived in the city. Most of the themes, obsessive images and techniques of the finished work – including its characteristic sabotage of narrative expectation – were already present in this most marginalised and often-misunderstood canto, 'The Gin Gun'. 'The Gin Gun', ostensibly a self-contained murder ballad, was published as a run of two hundred stapled pamphlets by Orcer Pust's Green Pony Epistemological Society Press (then situated in premises on the north bank of Allman's Reach) and not distributed widely. Reviews by Ray Inevort and Eric Desablier (Inevort famously called it 'a kind of metaphysical chancerism') served only to confuse its potential audience among the grisailles and midinettes of the Low City.

Over the next year, Crome moved restlessly across the old Cultural Industries Quarter. He became, briefly, a Starnist. He lived in no less than five different locations, including Monfourchet and along the Disclonal Avenue, until he settled on the edge of one of the city's more debatable spaces, in a fourth-floor room on the edges of Chenaniaguine where 21st Street meets Monsanto Avenue; and for the whole of a dry summer stared down nightly across New Rose Ground, to the dim lights of Atomic Avenue.

'Few here will admit to knowing the source of those lights,' he writes in his journal of the time. 'Those who do keep the knowledge from outsiders. Outsiders! As if any of us belong here. Leucaena Road is a parade of self-made dwarves down from Marg-Fawly, performers with quadriceps so developed that in the arena they are able to jump twenty feet into the air from a standing position. But they can barely walk and often their heads are tucked so deep into their displaced clavicles that they have to be led around by apprentices. Saturday morning, in the streets up behind the Zocala it's Particle Boys and Regulation Girls; whereas over here it's all 'poets', if that is what you want to call strummers like Ansel Verdigris and Echo Marsailles. An apparently endless column of artistic refugees, in retreat from the gentrification which began five years ago at the foot of the Gabelline Stair and now spreads into the Low City like mould on bread, we have been displaced. Paradoxically, there are no incomers here: we are all the most pathetic of insiders. We know nothing but we are *in the know*.'

After a month without entries, during which he seems to have pursued a less than satisfactory affair with Tamsene Field (later he will call her 'that decapitated princess', while in her history of the Starnist movement she refers to him only as 'a dissociated little man with red hair'), the journal adds, 'In the face of this, any adventure will do,' and Crome, abandoning Starnism, which he now described as 'rotten with self-reference, turn upon turn receding into meaninglessness', begins the series of unaccompanied forays into New Rose Ground which will lead to Cantos 2 through 7 of *Bream Into Man*.

'Letting myself in each night by the little iron gate on Mangot Street,' he tells us, 'I exchange entryism for the entrada.' In a sense, this is not hyperbole. Only someone desperate for subject matter would cast himself adrift in this way. Old Rose Ground — which, paradoxically, consists in a brand new park with a boating lake — used to be the city's graveyard. New Rose Ground (also known as Jack of Mercy's

Ground), differentiated by its position on the East or 'lower' side of the Royal Canal, has an air of industrial dereliction, as if the irregular hectare of overgrown water meadow it occupies was briefly the site of factories, quarries, rail yards, waste dumps and so on. Courses of brick rise above the couch grass and weeds. Litter is everywhere in the light scrub of hawthorn, gorse and elder. There are old bell pits and standing pools which drain or fill mysteriously; and a single shallow, circular lake filled with discarded machinery.

'Viewed at night,' Crome writes, 'it is a coming and going of denizens, animals, whole sudden holographic tableaux of inexplicable events. Corners of the space fold themselves up or unfold to reveal, briefly, a landscape difficult to interpret in terms of our world, along with glimpses of the mythical original inhabitants of the Quarter, who, in turn, displaced even earlier inhabitants.' These seem as elastic and self-modificatory as the space itself. An old couple and their dog, for instance, are said to be the last of an entire species of human beings called The Lords of Vule Portny, 'an individual of which was always comprised by this triad – although the third party doesn't always look like a dog.' It was an evolutionary choice long-abandoned, some way of being human pursued for a thousand years or so, 'as suddenly out of fashion as it was in.' Even in the day, the lighting seems odd. There are infinite opportunities for getting lost, and the ghosts of more tenuous human choices still haunt the open patches between elder groves. 'You go down by the river, on waste ground which still remembers itself as a water meadow. You see them there in front of you, flickering in and out of vision – it's only an effect of the long grass. Don't follow!' It's not clear who – or what – he means here; or why, after a year or eighteen months, he abandoned his exploration of the Ground. (His journals record only: 'Last time in, by the [illegible] Gate. All strata disturbed & buckled. Birdlike cry of the lar gibbons. Fresh shallow pits &

scrapes observed.' Then: 'To anyone who imagines entry to be possible through Omber Grove & the Electric Quarter, I say only: Look always to the right, never to the left!' And then, halfway down the page, heavily underscored: 'I swear that this is the last time.')

Towards the end of that period, he met the pianist Ingo Lympany. Of a planned collaboration between these two ex-Starnists, nothing remains. By then two further tranches of the poem had been published – 'On Greenmartin Swale' (*GPESB*, 1902), a memoir of Crome's childhood in the villages of the Hangline Estuary; and 'Tending rubbish fires' (*GPESB* 1903). These were received quietly, with Eric Desablier – by now editor of *New Rose Quarterly* – declaring, 'While he remains convincing as the conscience of Starnism, we sense in these stories a growing uneasiness with any kind of outer world.' Several works planned in this period have either vanished, or were never even begun and remained only in note form. Among the latter, 'The Mysterious Wife' stands out:

'A husband,' Crome wrote to Lympany, 'knows very little about his wife. Her arrival in the city is surrounded by mystery. Nothing she has told him about herself is true. She is both arriviste and adventuress; even her parents were counter-jumpers. One day she invites an old friend of hers to dinner. The husband asks this man what she was like as a child, and to protect her, the old friend begins to invent for a her a more convenient past. This myth is so beguiling that the two men soon begin to develop it, the husband subtly leading the reminiscences of the friend. Soon they are addicted, *to the exclusion of the wife*, who loses control of her own history to the extent that when, a year later, she announces that she will return to the provinces, they hardly notice. None of it is true! she shouts. They only blink and look away – that week they have begun embroidering a tale of her first communion. The husband will seem first a dupe.'

Crome began writing *Bream Into Man* again in the aftermath of the 'Force Publique' scandal in the early 1920s, with 'Prolepsis' and 'By Omber Grove'. The rest of the material was produced in a six-year stint beginning with the 20,000 lines of 'Bros Quai to Quai Mytho'. Throughout this period the sense of immanence which so saturates the early Cantos was being replaced by what the poet later named 'the unthought known'; and his sacralising of the mundane had given way to a kind of paranoia in which something literally unthinkable was seen to hide itself inside everyday events and, particularly, objects. 'The value of this unthinkable thing,' he wrote to Lympany, 'is in direct proportion to its horror.' (Lympany's side of this correspondence was destroyed by the great fire at Lowth in 1933; but Edio Bornfoth, who knew Lympany well, claims (*Indices* 47, 1950) that the pianist replied, 'Best not think about it then.') On the basis of this shift of emphasis, Crome decided to rewrite the Cantos to that date.

Some were revised out of existence – 'Organ 40' mutated into 'Christobel at the Atlantic Steps', for instance, retaining perhaps eight lines of the original text; while 'Events Recorded Last Wednesday in Iron Chine' was dropped entirely. Revision being as slow a process as primary composition, an interim volume was made available by Hart Volante, a short-lived enterprise of Paulinus Rack's, financed by proceeds of a ballet called 'The Little Hump-backed Horse'. Revisions up to about 1938 also made up the bulk of the Green Pony edition of 'Marks and Gravures'; further revision was carried out prior to the undistributed and now rare second edition in March 1939. The advertisments – for cold-cure and genever – bound into the Green Pony edition were described as 'part of the text', as was the dedication of the volume and a cover lino cut attributed to the expressionist portraitist L.A. Ashlyme; all of which was intended by the author to control and contextualise his overall system of allusion and imagery.

During this period his journals are full of the young woman who came in two or three days a week to look after him. A Lowth midinette who had arrived in the city less than a year before, she smelled, he records, 'of clean washing & geraniums'. In letters to Lympany and Rack, he calls her Genet or Ginny, although her real name seems to have been Marianne. Two or three pen sketches show her as having perhaps a less-formed character than the poet ascribes to her; nevertheless there is a sense of inevitability in the set of the head, the way the eyes meet the eye of the viewer. She loved dancing, music and the theatre. Their relationship was close. Crome sometimes referred to her as his niece; and once, in the hearing of Rack and Lympany, as 'my daughter': Lympany, perhaps remembering the story of the mysterious wife, seems to have remained unconvinced. Here, the journal is no help. A kind of shyness falls steadily across its pages for a year, a reserve which extends as far as the household accounts, from which even the midinette's salary disappears; although clearly it's her to whom Crome is referring when he records, 'G died last Wednesday at Lowth, of blood poisoning after a game of handsey-nailsey.'

Within a month of this laconic obituary he returned to his exploration of the shifting terrain of New Rose Ground. At first the journal gives up only brief, disconnected impressions – mainly of a failed attempt to enter from the south, between the vast deserted tenements of the Banlieue Lumianide, which led only to 'a deep sense of regret'; of 'a sticky darkness applied as if to the skin', a sensation of self-disgust from which it took weeks to rid himself. Then, after a return to his usual point of entry via the 'little iron gate on Mangot Street', we read this: 'Just after dawn, bright pale sunshine fell at an angle on to the bank of the Royal Canal. I was walking at the [illegible] pace. I observed two people and a dog perhaps a hundred yards ahead of me. They were doing something there, a little way back from the towpath in the green shade between scrub willow and elder.' He could see them coming and going between an abandoned lock and a little clearing. The project, whatever it was, seemed urgent, yet 'carried out in an atmosphere of calm'. He could hear two quiet voices; the dog panting and yelping and scraping. But by the time he arrived, they were gone, leaving only a long raw slot in the black, fibrous mud. 'Shallow at first, its lower edge packed and fluted by the dog's thick claws, this deepened and narrowed towards the back, where the tangled, freshly-broken roots of some plant protruded.'

He couldn't see much. His own shadow got in the way. He sifted some of the earth through his fingers. A rubbish tip from a hundred years ago: layers of beads and buttons interleaved with household waste rotted to soil; broken china and glass, no item more than a quarter-inch on a side. Bottle stoppers. Broken tools. 'It was the basic substrate of the city,' he records, 'packed yet somehow not dense. But then millions of tiny bits of rusty machinery!, compressed into a layer on their own, as if, a century or two ago, an extra layer of time had been laid down, here and perhaps all over the city. I rubbed my fingers together and watched the rust fall.'

Later he followed the dog's huge footprints east until they left the canal at a sudden angle and plunged into the interior of New Rose Ground, where it still seemed dark and he could hear not voices but musical instruments; or perhaps a factory. He didn't feel confident enough to follow. He had no sense of being observed in his turn, nevertheless he was careful how he made his way back to the Mangot Lane exit. Later the same day, exhausted by his attempts to sleep, he sat by his window and looked out over the waste, hoping to recognise something, or place himself on his night's travels. 'But as usual,' he noted in the journal, 'what can be seen from the window bears no resemblance to that which was endured on the ground.'

And then, inexplicably: 'Jack of Mercy's! I hate the thought of being buried alive.'

Late in 1939 he began to revise the middle sections of *Bream Into Man*, only to be defeated, as he wrote to Paulinus Rack in December, 'by earlier selves who won't let go'. Asked to nominate his favourite passages, he found they hadn't changed. '"Fire Parties" and "Antinomia",' he told Rack: 'Although I wish I'd called the latter something different, so as not to perpetuate the idea that these versions still orient themselves to the literary ideologies and aesthetics of Starnism and the Old Men.' The narrative had produced, he thought, 'a lively if terminal vegetation of secessionists, mummers, folklorists, paretic expressionists, Midland nature poets and consumptive Low City modernists, all mad with fear of the unthought known'. At the same time its infrastructure – as Shoshime Dollimore pointed out in a review of Cantos 34 through 51, published as 'The Fearful Hours of Night' – had become rotten with the very Starnism Crome had deplored when he abandoned it twenty years before. 'After a point,' Desablier says (locating it at about halfway through Canto Three of Chapter 46), 'nothing stays still long enough for you to trap it in the critical rhetoric'. Crome has found himself by locating with precision who he isn't.'

By then he was suffering from the paresis which would end his life. He had the slow form of the disease (called 'Discartia' or 'Mummy's Lobe' in the Low City where it had been endemic since the wars of the Analeptic Kings), with its distinct phases and curious effects on the spatial awareness of the sufferer, its accompanying parasitic infections and long incubation period. He seems to have welcomed the fevers and dysenteries, which he sometimes called 'my little holidays'. He was less sanguine about the pain in his lower limbs, which often crippled him for a week, and for which he required huge doses of morphia. In letters to Balfio Histamine he took to referring to the disease as 'her'. 'Mummy!' he says: 'my slow, careful lover.'

In the penultimate sequences of the poem, every vestige of Starnism has abandoned. From the broken-backed terza rima of 'Room 121' to the unpunctuated free verse of the 'Lullia', these Cantos resonate in the same way as the late paintings of Audsley King: for a time the world flares up like an autumn bonfire as the poet reverts to his earliest persona – 'Gifting,' as Desablier has it, 'himself to himself,' and becoming his own influence. He returns in his imagination to Greenmartin Swale, where 'unemployed boys build fires on waste ground, fight quietly under the bridges in the afternoon' and he remembers a geranium on the window sill of his mother's bedroom, 'its white petals more or less transparent as the clouds covered and uncovered the moon.' But for Crome this acknowledgement or recognition acts to flatten his perspective. From now on, lyricism will be strictly contained. The sublime will recede. The world will become for him, finally, the world. 'Neither blessed with immanence,' he wrote to Rack, who was by then himself ill, 'nor wrenched by the unthought known, the streets of the city are emptied and become streets; and there, unlike Audsley King, I am compelled to live.'

He was not to be 'compelled to live' there for long. By 1941, Maria Voolay had moved her elite cadres down from the North, and the city was under constant artillery bombardment from sites fifty miles off in Harpington and Beaumarchais. Many of the inhabitants of the Quarter removed themselves to Uwal Ease, the largest of the camps outside the walls. At first the journal seems optimistic, describing 'the amiable optimism of waking up in woods on a sunny morning. You hear birds. You hear other people beginning to stir. It's still cool but sunlight is falling through the branches and soon it will be warm. Insects loop past. You smell coffee. You're part but not part of everything that's going on – you're inside it somehow.' But he is soon enough complaining, 'On this long, muddy, partly-wooded slope beside the river we try and fail to introject the dreary vastness of the outside.' Running out of morphia, both his legs 'rich' with gangrene, he lay for three weeks on a low bed, distracted by airbursts and, closer-to, the cries of 'the chaotic middle classes, with their flapping tents and impractical demands, their attempt to face the inevitable by exporting the kitchens and dinner tables of Dynevor Road into a field in the middle of nowhere.' Every morning, he notes, the trodden earth is shimmed with water from the night's rain; the air fills with smoke and the 'brutal' cries of the children; while in verse after verse of the final cantos of *Bream Into Man* he depicts the city 'eating itself up in the distance like wood in a stove, like flames eating the work of the dead painter.'

At last, unsure whether he's awake or asleep, he begins to dream fantastically of the Vule Portny Lords, who, 'coming and going at unpredictable intervals on New Rose Ground, fuck half-clothed in the woods at night –

'Cold airs move around them. The dog sits looking away. It's brindled, with patches of bluish grey on a brown ground; as scabbed as they are. As thick-legged as a pony. Mist the colour of an exposed thigh – the colour of arsenic in milk – fills the wood for an hour to waist height, then pours suddenly away downhill. At dawn the sun falls on soft grey ashes tinged yellow or pink. The stones of the temporary hearth drips with solid candle grease. The Lords' curious old iron pots are caked with rust and ash; their barbeques, bricolaged into existence for a single night, are abandoned. Fragments of old furniture can be found scattered around a trampled glade, where they now begin to dig for a briony mandrake.' He writes with astonishment of the 'sheer effort of dragging this thing up out of the black and rusty strata – the crushed time in the earth – and then of hauling it away.' He writes with admiration of the courage of the dog: 'You can see that all its days this animal has drawn up bad luck. Yet it is still alive, and in its heavy poise and balance demonstrates the old couple's own qualities of persistence and endurance.

'On Greenmartin Swale,' he recalls suddenly, 'these roots were valued for their palliative effect. [Indistinct, but perhaps 'Poachers' or even 'Pochards'] would carve them into the shapes of babies, then sow the crudely-formed heads with rapeseed. The result was known as a 'genette' or 'jenny', and was sold to the newly bereaved across the months of May and June, sometimes into July.' He is not clear how the jenny worked, and asks himself: 'Was it herbalism or magic?' A jenny could weigh half a hundredweight and approach the dimensions of a seven year old child; later it might develop some rudimentary volition of its own. In the villages of the Hangline Estuary they never allowed a mature specimen to be brought within two hundred yards of a church, in case it gave up its true history and origins.

'The dog strains into its filthy old canvas harness. The old couple whisper and smile and click their tongues encouragingly. Where it falls on the aimless pathways between the bramble colonies and the thick stands of hawthorn, oak and sloe, the sun is warm; but the wood itself is always cool and damp. Branches with a laden curve, sagging close to the dark wet earth. Nettles lean out from the base of the dense growth. Small brown birds move in the undergrowth. They chip at the silence, hop into the sunlight. The Lords of Vule Portny wait until evening; then, themselves heavy and smelling of earth, join the dog in its harness and drag their treasure along the banks of the Royal Canal towards Omber Grove and into the city.' And then, inexplicably, 'I would have expected them to be dead by now, but they looked no different.'

Finally, sick of his own smell – 'which had stuck by then to every surface of the fabric' – and hardly able to move, Crome had himself carried out of the tent and into a nearby clearing, where he was left on his own. It was August the 8th, 1945. We can imagine the shouts of children in the twilight, the scents of bruised earth, rubbish and gangrene. Then, cutting across these sensations, the complex signature of the burning city: faint screams, the rumble of artillery, the red hot metal of sinking ships dowsed in the harbour. Night fell. After an hour or two without speaking, the poet became agitated. Indistinct sounds were heard. No one seems to have dared to go and see what was happening. Crome called out incoherently two or three times and was then silent. In the morning it became clear that he had left the camp for the wilderness outside. There was a shallow depression between the hawthorns, where in his pain he had tried to dig himself into the earth; a few scrapes and disturbances where he had dragged himself away. When Eric Desablier arrived at Uwal Ease three days later, Crome's tent was still intact. A woman from the camp had been paid to clean and tidy.

Crome left a box containing clothes, small ornaments and a framed pen drawing of a young woman in the style of Audsley King; while on a collapsible wooden table were arranged his favourite pen; his journal with its battered cover 'bound in wood & velvet'; and a full ream of paper, carefully squared-up, which proved to be the final raging cantos of *Bream Into Man*, with their liturgic and ultimately mysterious references to a 'King and Queen, installed, with garlands' and 'the dog that is not a dog'. On the bed lay a few stained but carefully folded bandages.

'It seems impossible to believe,' Desablier records, in his 'conditional biography', *A Poet of the Quarter* (New Light Press 1947), 'that this final act wasn't – like everything in the text itself – a considered and precise act of language. To Crome, village, city and wilderness were by then indistinguishable, his thoughts were indistinguishable from memories, and none of it was any longer distinguishable from the overgrown ruins of New Rose Ground.'

Last Transmission
From the Deep Halls

... SAYING, ONCE THOSE outsiders get in your tortured halls...
I'm saying we didn't have command of the vast fictions of the
day... The city wasn't, in the end, where those of us who lived
there thought it was. We had already lost it in all senses of that
word... All we knew of this place was the news... the halls are
aware that – in the end – they can never know what, exactly,
the plot was. It's only silence after that. Back at the beginning
there's the tapping sound, like metal on stone... then the call
signs, several of them, very amplified and confused... cries in
the halls... a cruel few words and then, 'We no longer know
which way to face.' The halls are still aware... What if the city
didn't 'fall'. What if nothing 'fell'? Nothing was lost but existed
just alongside everything else, fifty years later in the rubble by
a farm at the flat end of nowhere... who could write this...
everyone has a different story to sell... call signatures in rooks,
fresh plough, old silence: 'We don't know what to do.
Everything is the alongside of something else.'... Minor players
gesture helplessly... signals hard to make out in the chaos as the
big institutions go down... everyone desperate now.

Studio

MATTE WHITE WALLS. OVERALL hung on the back of the door. Black futon pushed against the wall. A Victorian hatbox, complete with travel stickers. A shelf of books high up along one wall, its line extended on the adjoining wall by four small square canvasses. A couple of larger, rectangular paintings on the walls and several small ones stored on a shelf in the chimney breast: the rest she keeps downstairs. 'Always sit,' she says, '*in* the room. Never along its edges.' She keeps turpentine in a Victorian inkwell, won't use white spirit because it's carcinogenic. 'Always have a lid on the bin for turpentine rags, especially in a small room, otherwise you have to live with the fumes.' Rectangular glass palette with a bevelled edge, resting on a pile of boxes, placed low to eliminate shine off the glass. A Stanley glass-cleaner to scrape the palette. Brushes – dull orange, blue and brown – laid out on the varnished floorboards, or next to the palette on ribbed or corrugated paper to stop them rolling about. A tub of acrylic gesso primer. A wire basket full of tubes of oils. Vandyke brown, Indian Red, crumpled tubes leaden in the dull light. Oxide of Chromium. Monestial Green. Rowney, Windsor and Newton. Speedball oils from America. Small sketches on French watercolour paper, wavering pencil lines and little dabs of paint, their edges torn neatly along a ruler. On the easel is an unfinished picture. A woman stares out at the viewer. Behind her, more men, women and children are caught.

The Old Fox

ALEXA WOULD LIE BACK with a glass of white wine and light the stub of a scented candle which she had cemented to the edge of the bath with its own juices. By its light you could see every bone in her body, brought up in relief like patterns in the sand. Even so, she regarded herself with bemusement: 'I've put on so much weight!' In a way this was true, though not to you or me with our skewed standards, the meaningless thins and fats of our social scale. I had seen the photographs of her. At five and half stone she looked saintly. She had the drawn yet peaceful face of a bog-burial, as if she had been killed but had got over it.

Alexa's father had doted on her until the age of twelve, while her mother looked on. Then he left them both, without saying why. It was a time of panic, first for him, then for Alexa's mother, then for Alexa. Panic conflated everything. One minute he was watching television, the next he had filed for divorce from Pasadena. 'He doesn't even know anyone in America,' Alexa's mother had said, looking down at the papers. The sense of him over there, working, living, opening and closing the door of some other house, getting by without her support while she sat at home in Holland Park, threw her into a worse panic than him leaving in the first place.

'Can he do that?' she asked Alexa.

Alexa shrugged. It was already clear he could. They sent letters care of his solicitor but never heard from him again.

'Why do you want to do this?' Alexa wrote. 'I don't feel you owe me an explanation. But if you could just help.'

A few months later, Alexa's mother went out into the garden one night because she thought she heard him coming back. After that she went out every night. Alexa couldn't disengage from either of them. She left home. She attended university. She put together some kind of life of her own. She was a successful theatre designer. Theatre suited her: she fell apart, she put herself back together, she fell apart again. It was a story of her own. She dreamed that if she stayed thin her father would return, in the guise of an animal. She was a survivor of all those late twentieth century wars. Family wars, self-image wars, wars of transformation and dysfunction: in those photos she had of herself at five and half stone, she was more soldier than victim.

I never knew what to make of her, or myself, or the relationship we had. I would manage to end it one way or another, meet someone else, involve myself elsewhere. Then I'd get a call. She would be coming in from Prague or New York, could I meet her at the airport? I would go there and find they had brought her off the plane in a wheelchair. I could see the relief on her face half way across the terminal.

'I'm *so* glad to see you!'

As soon as I heard that it would all start up again.

Her mother had been thin, too, Alexa said: but not really thin, 'just upset and not eating much.' Because this was back in the 70s, before the scales were loaded against thin people, before all the fuss. It was before the world over-reacted. 'My father always teased her about it,' Alexa told me. 'But she was never what I'd call thin.'

'Did you feel as if you were competing with her?' I said.

Alexa stared and didn't answer. A fleeting stubborness came into her face.

I never learned anything about the father. But from the things Alexa said I had a clear picture of her mother – a woman dark-haired and disorganised, nostalgic, a little deracinated, always missing something, even before he went away. After he'd gone, she spent her time in the garden. She halved the size of the big rectangular lawn, put in new paths and flowerbeds. She got rid of the vegetables. She grew roses. She was unlucky with one cat after another. 'Those cats!' Alexa remembered. 'Mum always had one rubbing round her legs, but they never lasted.' While her mother dug the garden, Alexa awaited her father's answer; which, of course, didn't come. By then she was seventeen and eating an eight ounce tin of green beans a day. 'Eight ounces. There was something so precise, so dependable about that!' Precision kept things at bay. But she worried how the strategy would evolve. 'I was going to want to eat less, I already knew that. Splitting a tin of beans wouldn't be so precise. I woke up one night in the dark in a panic. My father was in America, my mother was standing in the garden. How much of that weight was *water*? I had to get some scales, some *really dependable* scales, before I went to university.'

When Alexa talked like that she widened her eyes. Her voice took on tender, ironic values. In each wry shake of the head there was regret for a lost innocence, for the time before numbers began their flocking behaviour in her head – pounds, ounces, calories, ordering themselves by a few simple rules at the beginning, then paring down from there.

Sometimes she seemed to have an almost poetic insight into her own condition. Once she said: 'By the time I was thirteen all my fears had collapsed into one. That's the economics of it.' And then, after a pause: 'I need to grow up again. I need to grow up properly in some really safe place.' Later, I came across the same phrases in magazines and newspaper articles. In fact any rationale would do. 'Faced by the precariousness of tribal life,' she would misquote Italo Calvino, 'the shaman loses weight and flies to another world.'

I could usually take Alexa's mind off things.

'We all need to feel safe,' I told her. 'But what I want to know is this: what happened to those cats?'

She looked puzzled, even a little stubborn again.

'I don't see what you mean by that.'

'Those cats of your mother's.'

'Oh,' she said. 'Those.' She laughed. 'Run over mostly,' she said. 'All those pussies.'

Whenever I tried to make Alexa feel safe it ended in sex. 'Come and hug me before you go,' she would beg. 'Only a hug, I don't want anything else.' Hugging Alexa was like holding a child. She wriggled and fussed like a child settling itself, she smelt of soap and toothpaste. Then just as you thought she had fallen asleep she would murmur, 'Mm, that's nice, that's a nice thing you've got down there,' and that would be that. She was so obvious. I could hardly blame her for that because she was so completely cryptic too: she had her own motives for everything. It was some little internal ritual, you had to tuck her up in bed and give her a hug before she could do anything. She had to have a clean nightdress. And afterwards she would say something like, 'I always feel so safe with you!' as if she was at that moment discovering it. Other times she would just stop talking in the middle of a sentence and fall asleep. I would sit on the edge of the bed for another five minutes, then blow out the candles and leave. The nights were open and windy. I would walk down the empty street towards the tube station, thinking about Alexa asleep. She probably hadn't even heard the door closing. It gave me a feeling of satisfaction to think that.

Even when I ended it, Alexa continued to send me notes. They came as letters folded into airmail envelopes as flimsy as Alexa herself. Or home made cards with bits of sexy feathers or glitter stuck on. Or as mail from other people's computers in Hastings or the Hague. They ranged from the naive to the gnomic.

'I know you haven't got time for me at the moment,' she

would write, 'but I wondered if you wanted this.' Whatever it was, she had forgotten to enclose it.

At night her thoughts broke surface as mis-spellings, stories, puns accidental and deliberate; or at the other extreme, stripped themselves to a single bleak metaphor. 3am, and Alexa had woken up long enough to email me her dream: 'I was running back to you. You lived in an old hotel, in a small town where the last bus goes at eight. I didn't care if I missed the bus. I was suddenly filled with joy! It didn't matter how tired I was. I was going back to you! But when I arrived the hotel had been sold. There was nowhere for us to go.'

This was the kind of space Alexa's parents had bequeathed her. She tried to use it. She tried to rest there while everything else came and went. It was where she put up between episodes. It was where she tried to let go her baggage – which was always so heavy she couldn't bring it back from the airport on her own, yet without it to anchor her she'd float away.

Her house had a view over a park, with trees and shrubberies around some expanses of grass. After sex we would kneel on Alexa's bed together, slide the window up, and look out over the empty street into the trees. We were looking out one night when she saw a fox cross the street. It was April. The air was still warm, smelling faintly of the river, the day's traffic. Alexa clutched my arm urgently. 'Look!' The fox crossed the street with a quick, gliding gait. It was a sandy colour, greyed out by the streetlight. 'Look! Over there!'

I saw it too. I saw it quite plainly. But for some reason I said: 'Where? I don't see anything.'

'Crossing the road. Look, there!'

The fox paused on the opposite pavement, looked up at us for a second or two, then vanished into the park.

'Gone now,' Alexa said regretfully. She pulled the curtain across and got back under the covers. Her hands were hot. She smelled of cotton and soap. Her face took on that look of a bog-burial, serene, inturned, mummified by its own confusion. She was a survivor of human sacrifice. I sat on the edge of the bed.

'It was probably a cat,' I said. 'It was probably one of your mother's cats.'

Alexa laughed. 'No,' she said. 'It was definitely the old fox.'

I had a vision of her mother, tall and thin, out in the rainy garden every night after her husband left, burying yet another family pet while the traffic grumbled past two streets away on Holland Park Road. In her letters to America, it emerged later, she had accused the husband of not leaving at all. She had seen him, she claimed, or someone very like him, on the Central Line tube, every morning for weeks. 'You refused to speak to me, John, but I knew it was you.' Later still, she thought he had died and that she had experienced the moment of his death, suffering what she described as 'the most overwhelming feeling of grief' in Brompton Oratory on a wet morning in March. 'It took me so completely by surprise. I thought straight away, *Something must have happened to him.*' Alexa began to tell me the story, but I interrupted her. I had heard it before.

'You know I'm involved with someone else,' I said.

It would soon be too late to remind her of this. She wasn't concentrating well. She was back from Valencia or Venice or wherever, exhausted by the flight. Her luggage lay in the corner, still waiting to be unpacked. Soon we would no longer be sharing an indiscretion, we would be making a mistake. It would all have started up again.

'I know,' she said. 'Honestly, I do know.'

Next morning a helicopter took off from the park and hovered there indecisively in the strong sunshine. Alexa watched it with the matter-of-fact curiosity of a toddler. Later, in a café on Old Brompton Road, she touched my arm and said, 'When are you going away for Easter?' Meaning, 'When will I see you again?'

'I'm not sure,' I said.

'Sometimes I wish I could just curl up inside you and be safe.'

What I liked most about Alexa was her determination. Her work was killing her. She was never eating enough. She was always in crisis: the pure fiction of the last thirty years, authored by circumstance; by expectation and cumulative error; by herself. You can't not respond to determination like that, so I said:

'Sometimes I wish you could too.'

Awake Early

DAYBREAK AT THE SHIP hospital, dawn along the Dock of Dreams. May's my favourite month. It's a hairline fracture of the heart. It's a smear of flight across the back of an eye. I see your shadow on your wall, your small pile of objects. Those are my objects too. I'm alive to all of that. Meanwhile you whisper, 'I feel really different to myself this morning.' It's all right. You can get up now, they'll never hear us. There's a dry wind in the corners, smelling of salt and onions. But one day we'll feel warm again.

Explaining the
Undiscovered Continent

ALL THINGS METAL TAPPING together in the wind. Bleached
fishbones one thousand miles from the sea. Sheds where you
can get directions and diving apparatus. The inevitable
airstream trailer. The inevitable rusty boiler. The inevitable
graffito of a coelacanth. The highline of the last tide strewn
with yellowish swim bladders of unknown animals like
condoms inflated then varnished into fragility. Kilometer
upon kilometer of unravelled polypropylene rope. Tin signs.
Tied knots. A sense of petrol. Then the cliffs! with their
abandoned funicular slicing up through maroon sandstone 'to
the plateau above'. Windows of static ice cream parlours.
Buildings filled to the fourth storey with the grey flock from
old padded bags. 'This is where we'll dive.' As far as anyone can
tell, they lived in threes or fives, odd numbers anyway. Each
household kept a small allosaur on a bit of coloured string. We
have no idea who they were or when they were here or what
they wanted out of life. That's the attraction. (And afterwards
to sit in the boat, tired, happy, washing a small blue item in the
most gentle solvent: no one will ever know what it is.)

Self-Storage

I PUT MOST OF my things into storage when I returned to London. They've been there ever since, in a building at the end of a cul-de-sac somewhere in Hackney where, at that time, I had friends who could find the cheapest way of doing anything. I signed for one of the smaller units, and it's true that much of what went in there was junk. Kitchen equipment; some furniture, including the futon I had slept on for nine years, so impregnated with sweat it seemed much older; two ethnic rugs and a wicker table.

I could have left it all behind. I brought it home out of what I now understand to have been contradictory impulses. The smaller items were packed into cardboard boxes unwrapped and undusted, as if I didn't want to acknowledge them; as if their fragility might solve some problem for me. Personal electronics. Ornaments, including a china elephant. A thin gold wristwatch which had stopped working long before I set out in 1986. Why did I take it over there, let alone bring it back? There were a lot of books. There were a lot of cardboard files full of contracts, stuffed in among which I found three short, unpublished accounts of my stay.

Instead of boxing these, I kept them back to read on the flight home. Even now, after a decade back in London, they appear to me to have been written by someone else. They don't seem to belong to me, or to my present way of looking at things, or to any way of looking at things I might once have had. They contradict one another. All three have been generated on a typewriter rather than by computer. I don't recognise the typeface; and the pages, though roughly foolscap, are of uneven length, single-spaced, hastily written-over in red ink, cut up, pasted back together with a kind of patient hysteria.

'I lived the whole of that year,' the first begins, 'in a long house with a single corridor running past every room —'

While the corridor had no windows, the rooms looked out on to a harbour lively with heat and warships. Some rooms were dilapidated, with holes in the floors, collapsed ceilings, home to colonies of lizards and palm squirrels. Others were occupied by people like me who had never stayed in one place or situation long enough to learn to look after themselves. Yet others were really good rooms, cool, intact, full of contemporary sound equipment, interesting steamed plywood furniture and themes from Western lifestyle magazines. Tired of my original quarters, I was looking for somewhere quiet and without distractions. I had work that needed to be done: even more, perhaps, it needed to be organised.

It was impossible to calculate how many rooms there were in the long house. This information was known only to the figures of authority who often squatted in a line along one side of the corridor eating fish curry with rice. I soon found an unoccupied room, characterised by a large table full of neglected plants in pots and some veinous diagrams at different heights on the walls. Someone had built a shelter out of flattened cardboard boxes in one corner. The floor was littered with dirty flex, yellow cardboard boxes of nails, bags of chemicals that had burst in the heat, and the plastic toys you buy for hamsters. There was some sense that this was the detritus of not one but several previous attempts to inhabit the room.

I had to pick up that mess before I could start. But this is how puzzling the whole experience became: as I got rid of things, new things would appear. Someone's laundry, rammed into three or four binbags. Personal objects, such as: a broken Breitling chronometer, a framed photograph of the breakfast room at the Colonial Hotel. Confectionary. I would pack this stuff into other binbags and throw them into the corridor, then go back along the corridor for some things of my own. Each time I returned, there was more stuff. It was always different.

At lunchtime I hadn't done any work. I hadn't even taken my Mac out of its bag, that's how bad things were. I ate lunch with an old friend, who was anxious to be certain nothing of hers was among the belongings I had moved out of my original room. She was leaving later that day by air.

'These people,' she said, 'don't want help. They're cocking a snook at everything we think worthwhile.'

'"Cocking a snook",' I repeated. 'You don't often hear that.'

'It was what my father used to to say.'

We smiled at one another.

Then she took my wrist in one of her hands in a way she had and said, 'I want to be sure you'll be all right.'

I would be fine I said, I would be all right. But when I got back from lunch I surprised another man in the room. He was a local, younger than me, a bit scruffy, a bit ordinary. He wore cheap, ordinary clothes and even his stubble was worn-looking, as if he worked hard at some ordinary job. He had a radio playing the local music. He was stuffing my things into carrier bags and stacking them in the corridor. He thought the room was his.

'It has always been mine,' he said. 'It was always my room from when I came here.'

At first, I felt aggrieved. My work needed to be done. It needed, more than anything else, organising. Yet I was quickly convinced by the sincerity of this man's belief that it had been his room before I tried to occupy it. It had never been 'spare', or mine to organise. I went round picking up my remaining things, while he sat on the windowsill and watched me with a calm expression. Behind him the warships flickered in the heat haze in the harbour.

'If you had nowhere else to go,' he said, 'you could use this room. But you would have to share it with me.'

'No, no,' I said.

I was anxious to explain. I could easily go somewhere else, I was just looking for somewhere quiet to work. I was a writer. I was writing about the big changes that were going to happen here.

'They are bigger changes than you think,' he said.

I left him there, his head turned so that he could look out of the window while the radio filled the air with music, and went back down the long corridor, peeping into all the really good rooms, full of expensive old furniture or looking like the lobbies of comfortable hotels, thinking that I would never have a room like that, and rather dreading going back to the quarters I had come from, which would be unwelcoming, disordered, full of flies.

But when I got there I found that the figures of authority had inspected it while I was away. It was now the gateway to a rolling endless landscape of tall grass, under a lighting effect from the cover of a commercial fantasy novel. In the foreground, lying on the grass in front of a bench, was something which looked partly like a woman and partly like an oriental cat a kind of ivory white colour, which though it first seemed immobile, was slowly writhing and moving, struggling not to become one thing or the other but to remain both things at the same time. Something else was happening, too, maybe some people grouped in the foreground, I can't remember. I was struck by the potential of this landscape, rolling away under its alien light. I heard a voice say,

'You need never leave here.' A beautiful tranquility came over me, along with a sense of my own possibilities.

After a moment or two, the young man whose room I had tried to occupy came up behind me. He touched my shoulder.

'This room also belongs to me,' he said.

What surprises me most about this account is how much has been left out – the print media headlines, the troop movements, the international paralysis, the corporate betrayals. There is no question of me being as naive as I have presented myself here. Everything was a public psychodrama. Everyone knew full well they were behaving badly, whichever side they claimed to be on. There was nothing real left, nothing to be observed or reported-on except in terms of its reportedness. Any sense of what was actually happening had slipped away the previous winter; and the political windows were closing one by one, not just on the more exotic possibilities, but on any possibility at all.

Once I had decided to fly back to Europe, I knew I would have to see S again to say goodbye. We arranged to meet in the arts quarter, where the river swung inland and we could stroll between the playfully rusty sculptures, stainless-steel galleries and postmodern restaurants which had replaced the original shipyard furniture. It was a warm evening, with a slanting light the colour of egg yolk. The quays were crowded with people arguing pleasurably about where they would go to eat or have sex; I felt the same sense of pleasure at being with S.

'But this evening I hate you,' he said, when I told him.

'Why is that?'

'Because by being with you I lose the certainty of who I am; then, when you leave, I lose it further.'

Before S could explain what he meant, a young local man rushed past us and threw himself into the river, windmilling his arms and calling out something like, 'This is the way to do it!' The water cleared quickly where he had broken the surface, and he could be seen perhaps twenty feet below, not far out from the bank, trying to hold himself down in a foetal position, until several of his friends jumped in after him and pulled him out. They went away shouting and laughing, shaking themselves and wringing out their clothes.

'I think so many things about you,' S said.

Later I took him back to the long house, found my room, and encouraged him to have sex.

Afterwards I dreamed about the boy who had jumped into the water. In the dream I jumped in after him and found him floating upright just above the bottom, anchored in an envelope of air. He couldn't live and he couldn't die. I could hear him urging me to help, but when I tried to speak, a strong current pulled me away from the bank and the clear, shallow water, and into the cold, muddy, turbulent currents on the other side of the river. I soon realised that I was being carried away, among large boats and ships, towards something like a narrow, high-sided weir, on the other side of which, I knew, was a steep drop. In terror and confusion, I was swept away and died.

'You see!' I shouted at S, who was still on the bank. 'I went in there, and I'm dead! I'm dead!'

As I woke I was still dead but I was calming down.

In the morning I described the dream to S. 'What do you think about me now?' I asked him.

Instead of answering he said, 'Before you came here, I used to know exactly who I was. I used to be so certain who I was that I could reject anything – even something I liked and wanted – for the next thing that came along. There was a core of identity so hard it didn't need any form to make it visible and available to me. I knew who I was. I didn't care whether the stuff I owned – the things I did, the clothes I wore, the music I listened to, the people I knew – represented me or not.'

'I'm sick of being one of the things that doesn't have to represent you,' I said.

Years after the fact, with memory fading and in circumstances changed to the point of incongruity, I take out the second account of my time over there, leaf through its pages, and remember S's expression when I told him that.

'One evening a week,' the account begins, 'I have supper in their garden with my friend Bernard and his family, who live on the hill above the port –'

The history of that quarter is of a fall from grace. It begins with some medieval prince covering the hill with flowers and ends with a fashionable suburb where the prices now reach European levels. Everyone who's anyone lives there, diplomat or businessman, or in the case of Bernard, 'cultural ambassador'. The flowers have long gone. The cheaper streets at the base of the hill, drenched in a rich sunset light, are lined with wrecked cars.

'Not that we mind,' Bernard's wife told me, with not a hint of irony, the first time I arrived for supper, 'because they're really rather lively and attractive, almost art. All the different colours! And people use them as storage, their houses are so small.'

The end wall of Bernard's garden is rough-plastered a shade of terra cotta. On to the plaster a previous owner has painted a *trompe l'oeil* gateway a little less than life size, opening on to a trodden-earth path through a wooded landscape. The path leads away in its flat sine curve into distant hills planted with olives. Secondary growth is applied as a mist of green, while the trunks of a hundred trees, very slim and straight, stand away from the path like spectators.

On that side of things, it's morning perhaps. At this distance it's really quite hard to tell. You're too aware of the brushstrokes, the stipple. The effect is best gained not from the garden itself but from Bernard's kitchen, sixty feet away. From there the faded quality of the paint blurs everything together, turning the garden into an extension of that mysteriously inviting path, a merging effect heightened by the ivies which spill thick and glossy over the wicker fences on either side. Plantings of arum lily, fuchsia and false orange lead your eye to the small acacia tree artfully overhanging the gate itself.

For a moment, especially in twilight, it can have a brief magic.

This evening, as we sit out in the garden waiting for his other guests, I tell Bernard:

'The door in the wall was an icon beloved by late Victorian and Edwardian alike. The symbol of lost opportunity, or of opportunities not fully taken. If you pass through the door, the story goes, you cannot be anything less than changed. If you don't pass through it, you still cannot be anything less than changed.

'Choice, here, offers a fifth major compass point, an unnamed direction or plane. It's the plane of nostalgia, and of nostalgia's inverse, a kind of weightless but abiding regret.'

'Bloody hell,' Bernard says. 'I bet you can't repeat that.'

'Don't tease each other you two,' his wife tells us. 'The children are bad enough.'

Her three older girls are in bed, but she is having a problem with the youngest. 'Ella, if you can stop crying now,' she says patiently, 'Ella, if you can really get control and stop crying, I'll give you a big bottle of milk. But if you don't I'll only give you half a bottle. All right, Ella?'

'If I was Ella,' Bernard whispers, 'I'd be pretending to get control now and take revenge later.'

'Bide her time then get revenge on all adults,' I agree.

'Don't be so bloody horrible,' warns Ella's mother.

All afternoon the children have worked hard to personalise the gate, surrounding it with art of their own, bold, determined representations of people and stars in unmodified poster reds and yellows, done directly on to opened-out cardboard boxes left over from their recent move from Europe. They have propped their pictures up around the door in the wall like mirror portals, entrances to quite different kinds of imaginary worlds – lively, jarring and expressionistic. Ella's efforts are particularly determined. Later I will write, 'These worlds of hers are not alternatives to anything. Instead they are real, explosive acts of creation.'

The air is warm and soft. The other guests arrive. We talk, we laugh. We eat beautifully cooked garlic fish.

Trompe l'oeil is a con, and not much of one really. Everyone who sits in Bernard's garden that evening is grown up enough to relish this. They would never call the view the other side of the door a 'world' or insist that, to function as art or even as a mild joke, it must successfully suspend their disbelief. After the youngest child has gone at last to bed, the adults smile and stretch and help clear away the supper things. They go to the end of the garden and gently collect up the children's art to protect it from the dew. 'Aren't these wonderful? Aren't they so energetic?'

Then they yawn and smile, and say goodnight to one another, and one by one pass through the gate, under the unpainted transom with its moulded flowers.

For a moment I watch them run away into the trees, calling and laughing softly. I leave them to it. In the harbour the tide is down, there's dark algae on the surface of the mud. A swan sleeps amid the yellowing fibreglass litter between the moored boats. I look back at the hill and, parked round its base, all the wrecked cars. Before each one ends its working life, it has already become so patched and repaired that every panel is a different colour. Pea green. Talbot blue. Maroon. Rich yellow of city sunlight. Their wheels are gone. Their seats are long gone. They are held together with bits of string or leather belts, and full of obsolete TVs, hat boxes, bales of clothes, paper sacks of cement!

I don't know anyone called Bernard. I never did. I have friends who live in the 'alphabet ladder' off Fulham Palace Road. They own a little garden that ends in a trompe l'oeil gateway. But their lives are not like this.

On the morning of my last day over there I packed the three manuscripts in a carry-on bag, crossed the river by the new metal footbridge and walked to the airport. The river was muddy and agitated. I saw an old fashioned boat, painted white. I saw fruit bats hanging in a tree like oily leather bags. I looked into the sunlight where it dissolved the sidestreets and made the world seem both ended and endless. There were fretted shadows and dry brown palm fronds everywhere underfoot. I felt free. I felt ready to write whatever I saw. I saw the red and yellow tuk tuks, the children walking to school along the railway tracks, the soldiers with their assault rifles hanging from a webbing loop. In the suburbs the sun was all over the humid morning air; but in the town the streets were still dark and chilly. A whole quarter smelled of petrol, and every street I looked down seemed more interesting than the one I was on. I stood for a moment or two in a cul-de-sac with fallen-down walls. A cat came out on to the rubble-strewn cobbles in the sun to say hello.

My return flight on the 787 'Dreamliner' was via Paris. I remember the slow, measured descent into Charles de Gaulle; brown fields, long shadows, low sun on autumn trees; a graveyard experienced as a pocket of greater density in the city viewed from above – smaller objects of the same type, crushed into a smaller space. We hurried through the airport, only to find we had missed our connection. I hate to travel in groups. Other people are less a comfort than you expect. You catch their anxieties. They edge their way into your head.

There are two classes of memories: the ones you keep and the ones you don't. Which of them constructs you best? The second account I brought back with me ended, 'I've lived with a lot less intensity since I arrived here. You might say that was age, but I would have to call it self-preservation. If I felt things as much as I used to – if I allowed things to take their proper space inside me – I'd be in trouble.' The third account, which I read on the short flight between De Gaulle and Heathrow, seemed to take up from this proposition –

I didn't have much, for most of that year in the city, but I liked what I had. I could look up from my worktable and see a wooden chair, a small chest of drawers painted green, some paper flowers full of dust. Each of these objects became valuable because it crystalised a feeling, an event, a memory of my time there; I allowed them space into which they could comfortably leak their meanings.

But towards the end of my assignment I became involved with another expatriot who immediately began filling my rooms with things of her own. She dragged bits of furniture across the city – tables, sidetables, occasional tables, folding tables. Cardboard boxes of old clothes, old records, old books. Childhood books, and books from other people's childhoods. I put them behind a folding screen. Piles of newspapers and magazines gathered on the tables, then underneath them. Sometimes she would place five or six newspapers in a plastic bag, twist the ends of the bag together in a loose knot, and put that in a corner. She brought me these things but she wouldn't stay with me. Sometimes I didn't see her for days. Instead she sent an email.

'According to this map I found,' she wrote, 'we're in The World. Did we plan on that?'

She gave me a chess set. She gave me an old shirt of her father's; it came down to my knees but the collar wouldn't fasten. I couldn't help trying to interpret these gifts. When I asked, 'Why have you brought me this?' or, 'What part of your life do these things come from?', she would look confused for a moment then carry on doing whatever she was doing. She wanted to answer but here was a check between what she knew about herself and what she wanted me to know.

Once or twice a week I was compelled to take a tuk tuk across town to the harbour where she lived. When I got out to pay the driver, I found only the usual tangled mess of receipts, keys, change and low-denomination notes in the narrow upper pockets of my jacket. Half-sunken warships lay rusting in the hot evening light. The harbour streets, wide and empty yet at the same time maze-like, stretched into the dusty hinterland in a confused dream of sagging telephone wires and heatstruck dogs. That was where I visited her, in a long house in the local style, with a single corridor running past every room. The corridor had no windows; the rooms overlooked the harbour. Some were dilapidated, with holes in the floors, collapsed ceilings and an air of abandonment. Others were traditionally occupied by western journalists. She had lived there three years, she said, but it was always like the first day of college or university. 'I can never find my room.' We walked up and down the corridor for fifteen minutes, trying door after door. We stepped over the caretakers who sprawled unconcernedly on the floor, drinking arak, involved in their own conversation.

When we found it her room was almost empty of furniture. It was empty of almost everything except a pile of newspapers, a mattress, a Turkish cat asleep on the computer keyboard. 'We should have some tea,' she said. We drank it from faded old china cups with a silver rim and a rose motif so worn away you seemed to be seeing it through a mist, while she read to me from the advertisements in the newspapers. 'The sky is the limit for Rhino Roofing!' 'Elephant House Ice Cream.' 'Try something from our sandwich menu, fast and quick.' Immediately outside her window lay a slough of black mud-thickened water, the remains of a system of sluices and culverts which had once conducted the river to the harbour. It looked rusty and poisonous. When I tried to embrace her she pointed out of the window and said –

'We can go swimming if I get the caretakers to open the sluice!'

'I'm not swimming in that,' I said.

The caretakers opened the sluice. She jumped in vertically, her arms stiff by her sides, and went straight under. When she bobbed up again the water looked clearer and shallower and fresher, with sunshine falling on to it; but it remained cold, and I was still reluctant. My friend seemed to have forgotten me. She was off! She was sliding down a sort of steep shallow pebbly stream like a waterslide, towards the main body of water. The harbour, such a feature of the view, had receded to the horizon, where I caught glimpses of its massive stone moles and cranes like a tiny heat mirage. My friend was already in the distance, shouting and laughing.

'Come on,' she called. 'Come on!'

Sometimes we had sex on the mattress, but not today. I picked up the cat and put it down. When I looked out of the window again, she was already out of sight. I didn't know what would happen next, so I left. The following day I received an email which read: 'This city is pure freedom in the neoliberal sense. It's all freedom to exploit and no freedom from being exploited. All you can be here is a tourist or a businessman. Better still, something that combines both.'

'If you don't want to live with me,' I emailed in return, 'why are you bringing me all your furniture? I feel you are weighing me down with things.' I looked round my room and added: 'I'm leaving soon, anyway.'

She knocked on my door late that night. 'We often swim in there,' she said. 'I don't know why you're making such a fuss.'

For months after my return I still felt exhausted. I felt as if I was still over there. I stored my belongings in Hackney; then, as if I couldn't wait to get away from them, moved almost immediately to a rented four-storey house in West London. There, I tried to put my memories in order. That failing, I ignored them. After perhaps a year I had the following dream:

I was back over there, unpacking my things in a room on the top floor of the two-hundred-dollar-a-night Colonial Hotel. I had arrived after a ten-hour flight, about an hour before dawn. I was looking forward to an hour or two's sleep before my first meeting. I could hear the surf on the hotel beach; the crows waking up in the palm trees. On the warm air was that smell you never get used to, dried fish, faeces, rotten papaya, exhaust fumes. It fills the world, I thought, while you smell it – dry, dusty, organic, aggressive. It won't let you think of anything else. It might be the smell of vomit. If you *did* vomit, it would be the smell of that forever after, the smell associated with a stroke or a brain disease, the smell of an irreversible transformation. While I was thinking this, and wondering if I had brought enough shirts, I noticed some activity in the street below.

The reflections of flashing blue lights flickered across the walls of my room. Three or four of the old and mismatched appliances you see in every fire station over there had pulled up in front of the hotel, and a wooden ladder was already leaning against the window ledge. I thought: 'I didn't know the place was on fire.' Then a fireman who was literally a child, very chubby and a bit like a spoiled boy actor in a Bollywood film, appeared at the window. By now I could see that the back wall of my room was glowing red and sagging, though I felt very little heat or sense of urgency. We chatted about this and that. I wondered how he was going to rescue me, being so small. But I still wasn't worried. After a moment he asked me for a cup of tea.

While he was drinking it he admitted that he didn't know how he would rescue me, either: 'You're a bit big to carry.'

I couldn't imagine myself on his little shoulder as he

swayed and tottered back down the ladder. But I still felt a perfectly steady sense of optimism and good will. I said, 'Oh, never mind mate, I've got my climbing rope here. I'll just tie it off and abseil out.' Then I remembered there was no rope anywhere in my luggage.

I woke up from this dream with a tremendous sense of happiness and energy which lasted for two or three hours.

The things I brought back remain in storage. The fee goes out by standing order every month. Every two or three years an adjustment has to be made, to the fee or the contractual terms. I sign something. At the time I stored it, that stuff had value for me, even if I wasn't sure why. Now I never think about it and I'm not sure I could find my way back there without the paperwork and an A-to-Z. Perhaps, before I'm tempted to try, I'll store the paperwork, too, at the bottom of a box of unrelated papers, in the cheapest self storage I can find in West London.

A Web

DEEP COLD AIR. TRIANGULAR spiderweb, curved like a sail, attached at two points to the house and at the third to an old dry poppy-head in a pot on the balcony. Most of it invisible, but the edges and all the rigging picked out with frost. One patch of frost, about three inches in from the leading edge, minutely cross-hatched in the shape of a section through an ammonite; I can't see if the spider's part of that little structure. The effect is of a journey in a regime different to ours. Whatever medium is inflating the sail – whatever medium, conversely, is rushing past it – is not a property of our universe and cannot be defined by our way of relating to things. That's why we have a duty of care to the spider. She's sailing into an idea of winter we can't have. Her perceptions, acted out as this structure of hers, are a valuable resource. I've watched her mother and her grandmother make webs here, and their mothers and grandmothers, right back to the historical times. They all built ships but none of them built quite like this.

Back to the Island

LAST NIGHT I WAS in Autotelia again, in the town I have decided to call 'the provincial capital'. In the garden, I found the elephant still chained to the tree where I had left it, its small eye full of knowledge. All the animals seemed amused by their own humiliation. Despite a good night's sleep – despite two or three good nights' sleep – on our side of things, I was tired by eight in the evening. Whatever was happening to me had taken another turn for the worse. But I felt happy, not anxious or afraid or ill. Only warm and tired and, now I had got back there, full of the deep Eros of the island. Fireflies began to gather in the corner of the summer house from which, later, the voice I had grown to love would comment on the intimate events of my life in a matter-of-fact whisper.

Cave & Julia

WHEN CAVE MET JULIA Vicente, she was living quietly in one of the four storey houses on the hill which overlooks the harbour.

People still gave her space. They knew her founding narrative — the loss of her brother and the subsequent prosecution for manslaughter. They knew more about those two events than the life that had followed — the long struggle to adjust to self-imposed exile on our side of things, the bouts of post traumatic stress which made her work difficult, the disastrous marriages to bankers and minor celebrities, the failed film career, the eventual return to Autotelia to live quietly in a postindustrial port which, though it reminded her daily of her tragedy, seemed at a safe remove from some other concept that frightened her more. She was a gaunt woman by then, tallish, full of an energy that rarely showed. A heavy smoker. She liked to walk in the gentrified dockyards, where art galleries were replacing ships, and restaurants the old dock furniture. She had a daughter, three or four years old, from her third marriage.

Cave, a cultural journalist with a broad remit, took her to restaurants she claimed she was no longer able to afford. In return she showed him the town's prized possessions: a collection of early Doul Kiminic watercolours of eviscerated horses and grieving women; and the municipal crematorium, the curious truncated cylinder of which was decorated on the outside with a wrap-around mural like a 1920s woodcut, showing the dead silhouetted by the invisible sun of the afterlife.

'This is awful,' Cave said.

'Isn't it?'

They got on well together. Then one morning she telephoned him and said: 'You don't ask me about my life.'

She was known to be difficult, and Cave had come to Autotelia to write a piece about someone else. He didn't want complications; he wanted his relationship with Julia to remain personal. More importantly, perhaps, he felt emotionally disqualified by the central event of her history. He felt he had nothing to offer. All of this made him wary, so he replied:

'No one likes to pry.'

'Are you dishonest, or only naive?' she asked, and hung up.

Perhaps an hour later he called her back. 'I'm sorry,' he said. He thought she would put the phone down again but instead she said:

'I don't see my brother any more.'

'That's a curious way to put it.'

'I mean literally. For years afterwards I saw him almost every day. He wasn't here, obviously: he was dead. But I saw him.' She still dreamed of the event itself – if, she said, that word could be used to describe what she remembered. 'But I don't see him any more. He's invisible now. I don't even miss him. He's just one of the fictions that lives here.'

She was silent for a moment. Then she said:

'I'm sorry, my daughter has woken up. Will you wait a moment while I see to her? Do you mind?'

Cave said he didn't mind, and for some time all he heard was the child's voice, thin and distant at the other end of the connection. He began to think Julia Vicente had forgotten him. 'Hello?' he said. If the child had turned out to be ill, he should ring off and try later. Instead he hung on, listening to that long, unassuagable, archaic complaint. 'She's always disoriented when she wakes up,' Julia said when she returned to the phone. 'Always at a loss.' For a moment she seemed both impatient and puzzled. Then she laughed. 'I'm her mother,' she said, as if this wasn't just a new discovery but a new kind of fact.

When Autotelians say 'those who came before us', it's clear they aren't talking about genetic precursors. There is archeological evidence all over the continent, but the Autotelians resist connection to it.

Age fourteen, Julia Vicente had taken her brother up to one of the mysterious sites on the karst plateau above the town and there, she claimed, 'lost him'. Since this was clearly unlikely, it was assumed by the court that they had approached one of the flimsily fenced sink-holes which penetrate the limestone foundations of the site, and that he had fallen in. Subsequently the girl had wandered distractedly about in the ruins, being found asleep near a dry fountain after a week-long search by police and local quarry workers. Some months later, on her fifteenth birthday, she was still unable to provide a coherent account of what had happened. No one, the court concluded, could mistake such a tragic incident for 'manslaughter'; the child – eight years old and dark-eyed, skinny, lively, beloved by everyone – had been as difficult to control as his sister. But by then, as far as Julia Vicente was concerned, the damage was done.

The Autotelian karst drains itself, through a complex of vast underground caverns – many of which have never been entered – directly into the sea. That whole year, and to a lesser extent the year after, bodies were washed up all along that part of the coast, some whole, some in pieces. A proportion were claimed; many – like the mysterious 'Mr English', delivered by a high tide one summer afternoon on what the European news services referred to as 'Autotelia's Riviera' – were not.

The sexes tended to be evenly represented. The oldest item was the lower left leg of a woman of at least sixty years; the youngest a complete male toddler wearing a wristband with the name Ellis, never identified. There were pairs of hands in an expensive suitcase, and heads wrapped carefully in clingfilm or hastily tied up, bunny-ears, in plastic bags. In the south of Autotelia, especially, it was a bad year for bodies; but the body of the vanished brother didn't show up among them. Passive and silent, full of some incommunicable anger, the sister attempted suicide, spent time in institutions; then, her work suddenly becoming popular, left the country for a new life on our side of things.

All of this, Julia rehearsed for Cave over supper in the maze of old docks not far from his hotel, adding nothing to the popular account.

They had spent the afternoon in the port's only cinema, lit by a dull greenish light from above while the sound system produced faint tango music and they waited for a film that never played. Cave had been as delighted by the cinema – the mossy folds of the curtain, the faintly glowing exit sign, the rows of grubby empty seats – as by the incompetence of the projectionist. Now the lamp swung above their table, moving the shadows of the wineglasses regularly but uncomfortably across the tablecloth, like the umbrae and penumbrae of planets. They were the only customers there. The cook came out of his kitchen to look at them. The woman talked, the man bent towards her. Their voices were quiet. The shadows of their hands touched, flickered, then lay flat. The cook watched them with a kind of suppressed amusement.

'So now you know,' Julia Vicente said.

'I'm not sure I know any more than I did.'

She shrugged. 'We'll go there then,' she said, 'and I'll show you things I told no-one at the time.'

The restaurant's pink napery and white wrought-iron partitions reminded Cave of a hairdresser's in 1968. Unsure of what he was being offered, but certain that this bald proposition could only move things in a direction he didn't trust, he explained that his visa only had two days left to run. 'There wouldn't be time.' She pretended not to understand this. 'You should come,' she said. 'If you had any courage you'd come.' It was one thirty in the morning: a waiter dragged a chair around. By then only the casino across the square remained open, drawing people in, fixing them like insects under a jam jar, where they buzzed about energetically without much sign of getting anywhere. A wind came up off the sea, blew sand across the neat cobbles, died away.

'All right,' Cave said.

He waited for her early next morning at the tourist beach, a deserted, artificial curve of white sand. The day was already sullen and humid, with hidden light penetrating the cloud and heat resonating from the limestone buttresses above the town. Faint residual smells clung in the corners of the sea wall: the previous day's fish, salt, perfume, fried food. For a moment it seemed to Cave like a language, but when he listened it had nothing to say. While he was considering this, Julia came down between the houses towards him, wearing a white sleeveless frock with a picture hat and gloves, waving happily like a much younger woman. 'Isn't this awful?' she called. 'I bet you hate it!' And when she got close enough to stir the sand with her toe: 'Every grain imported from the other side of the country.'

Round the point at the south end, she showed him, lay a different kind of beach: brisk inshore winds drove the sea up over the jumbled rocks, the water was a detergent of grey and green, and huge banks of black weed had formed on the tideline. A few yards inland, a path wound its way into the hinterland between undercut slabs of shale. Julia set off along this so quickly Cave was hard put to keep up. His mouth soon became dry, the glare made his eyes sore. The path climbed and climbed. Away from the sea, the air smelled of leafless, thorny vegetation, and behind that its own dry heat. Thirsty and irritable, dazzled by Julia Vicente's bone white frock, he called: 'How much further?' She didn't answer. Perhaps she hadn't heard him. A hot breeze rose among the vegetation; her hand went up in a graceful gesture to secure her picture hat. When, a moment later, she stopped and said, 'There,' in a curiously flat voice, Cave saw the plateau stepping away from him in every direction, a series of shallow, imbricated terraces linked by the remains of broad white avenues. Each terrace supported a clutter of patterned mounds, platforms and ramps – some more sophisticated than others – beneath which, he knew, an elaborate system of tunnels opened into the karst below.

'My god,' he said.

'But hardly a new story.'

'I don't know what you mean when you say that.'

Cave had got to Autotelia by credit card and asking, 'Do you speak English?' The day he arrived he had emailed a friend: 'Travel is no longer measured by change, only by the time it takes to go the distance. It's tedious, but it's not a journey.' Now he wasn't so sure.

In recent centuries, some attempt had been made to reoccupy the ruins. It was hard to see why. There was no water above ground. Shade trees were few and far between. Successive waves of colonialists had fought each other over water rights, relics and ideological interpretation of the remains, and were as long gone now, you felt, as their enigmatic predecessors. Their buildings, assembled from the rubble and set down at the junctions of avenues where they could command the longest view, resembled fortified abbeys or monasteries, the cloisters of which often guarded the only well for miles around. It was to the courtyard of one of these structures that Julia Vicente now led him, via dark shiny passageways, the old laundry, the household gardens choked with a plant that reminded Cave of amarynth, its seedheads like accretions of oily dust at a city corner.

'This is much later than the rest.'

Pale rhiolite columns. The sense of an unending afternoon. Light slanted in from the right. Each side of the cloister was six arches long. The courtyard was cobbled with smooth oval stones tipped up on their thin edges. In its centre an octagonal pavement at four corners of which were placed two fluted pillars. From each point of the pavement radiated star-shapes in cobbles of a darker colour, between which a short, parched vegetation grew – not grass but some herb. In the centre stood the fountain, a shallow basin supported by a plinth of caryatids. There was a thin, intermittent central jet of water. A veil of droplets hung down from the edges of the basin.

'Isn't it wonderful?'

'It's very striking,' Cave said.

'Why don't you have a closer look?' she invited him.

After three or four paces into the sunlight, Cave was disoriented. He could see the fountain in front of him, but it appeared to be further away than when he had started. From above, the structure was four-lobed, like a clover. The sun baked down on it but it was as if all the heat were generated there between the eight pillars and the pistil of the fountain, then projected upward and outward. Heat ripple affected Cave's vision in some way he didn't understand: everything remained sharp, but he was experiencing a mild vertigo, a stretching-out of things. His lips felt numb and he could no longer feel the cobbles under his feet. 'This was a culture of engines,' Julia Vicente said. 'Some architectural, some sacrificial, some both.' Her voice seemed close and intimate. The woman herself leaned out of the cloister, shading her eyes as if Cave had become difficult to see. 'What fourteen year old could understand that?'

'I don't care why it was constructed,' Cave said, retreating hastily to the cloister. 'I don't want to know.'

She laughed at him from the shadows.

'If you had any courage you would go all the way,' she said.

Cave, who still couldn't see well, took a moment to locate her. She had turned away and was trying to light a cigarette like someone in a strong wind. He made her look at him. '*This* is where the boy disappeared,' he said. 'This is where you lost him.' She shrugged. 'Jesus,' he said. 'When they found you, you'd been here all along.' He stared at her for a moment, then pushed her against the back wall of the cloister.

'You weren't lost. You were never lost.'

She pulled away from him, took his hand and led him out of the cloister as if he were blind. 'Listen,' she said, and after a moment or two he thought he heard water rushing through the limestone somewhere deep beneath his feet. By the time they got down from the plateau, it was afternoon and rain was falling on the sea.

'Do you want to swim?'

'In this?'

They sat in the empty cinema again. Cave found he couldn't stop talking. She in turn seemed preoccupied. Eventually she said:

'There are sites like that one all over Autotelia. It's a heritage, but not our own. We've failed to colonise or commodify it. The local town is always named after a flower. The women make fabrics. The men drive around in pick-up trucks trying to sell one another liquid propane. After two or three days it's the most boring place you've ever been. Those old priests convinced each other that the world wouldn't work without intervention. But they're long dead. The gods don't come forth and the approaching thundercloud stays on top of the hill. After a few grand but silent flashes of light, nothing happens. And do you know what?' she said. 'That's a good thing, because they were all quite clearly mad anyway.'

'Astonishing,' Cave said, but only because he felt he had to say something.

His dreams that night were full of mirages.

The next morning he had to leave. He had closed out his other project a little early, but in the end he thought he'd probably done enough. He left his hotel and went down to the tourist beach, where he found the sea calm. Two men were running about on the tideline, throwing something between them. It didn't look like a ball. Heat already blurred the air, resonated from the steep cliffs of the plateau. Cave sat on the sand, and around him everything was suspended in light; everything like a film, wrapped in cameraman sublime, documentary sublime. Light, silhouettes, warmth like a perfect saturated colour, all at once. Distant objects seemed too large. In the end, he told himself for the hundredth time in his life, you are the only description of what there is. All that counts is to be there. A little later, wandering up into the town through the maze of net shops and fish stalls, he read the words 'locally sourced' as 'locally soured'. He knocked on Julia Vicente's door, and she let him in.

'I feel scared this morning,' she said: 'I don't know what you feel.'

'Neither do I,' Cave said.

He sat reluctantly watching her prepare the little girl's breakfast, perhaps deliberately allowing a silence to grow.

'Don't you see,' she said suddenly, 'I can't talk now?'

She studied the base of an enamel milk pan. 'The life I'm living,' she said, 'the life I've been living – I wasn't like this but now I am.' And then, suddenly: 'I wasn't like this but now I am. Can you see that?' Cave, though he couldn't, said he could. 'My brother, all those years ago!' He had no idea what she was trying to say. She put the pan down, then picked it up again. 'If nothing happened in the cloister I can't explain the life I've had.' She stared at him. 'Everything that happened in the cloister was already there. It was already present in some way,' she said. 'My brother knew that. At the end it tired him out.'

'At the end?'

She shrugged but didn't reply.

'I think you've been defending for a long time now,' Cave offered.

Julia Vicente considered this. 'I have,' she said. 'I've been defending *so heavily*, but I don't know why. It was all those years ago.' She sniffed back a tear. Her daughter looked up instantly from the floor.

Later, unable to make himself leave, Cave tried to work. The sun shone across his eyes. It was impossible to concentrate. Julia had finished the ironing. She was upstairs dressing. She was putting on her make up. Her little girl followed her from room to room, talking softly in the local language and making kissing noises; later, came downstairs and rode a scooter shyly round the tiled floor of the lounge, stopping every so often to make sure Cave was paying attention. The phone rang; rang again. The shutters banged in the wind under an eggshell sky. Eventually he got up and took a taxi to the airport.

If it's difficult to understand Autotelia as a place which is both here and not here, a place congruent with what we used to know as the North Sea, the idea that it was once inhabited by something neither human nor pre-human is almost impossible to grasp. In other circumstances, Cave would have described the site on the plateau as a kind of cultural chewing gum, something irritating stuck to the sole of everyone's shoe. He would have dismissed its history, and described his morning among the ruins by describing the landscape – the footprint planed off the top of the hill thousands of years ago for reasons he could never hope to understand; the white cloud bouffant above the mountains to the south; the black smoke on an adjacent hilltop. A single shade tree in the high, dry heat.

Two months later he was back. He wasn't sure why. He pushed a note under the door of her empty house, discovered the next morning that she was halfway through a tour of provincial theatres and scheduled to return the exact day he left. He spent his mornings visiting by bus the official archeological sites on the plateau, and in the evenings recovered his expenses by writing lacklustre reviews of the beach cafés. He photographed the crematorium murals. He bought a small, not-very-well-known Doul Kiminic – *The Ruined Harvest*, oil on canvas with some water damage in one corner – intending to have it reframed and shipped back to our side of things where he could profit from its mildew tones and desperate body language. He drank. 'When the menu offers "tiny fishes",' he warned his readers, 'be cautious. For me, whitebait are tiny fishes. These fishes are three inches long. On the whole, they eat like whitebait; but tiny is a misnomer. 'Quite small' would be better.'

Back in London he barely thought of her, yet soon found himself outbound again on a 787 Dreamliner from Heathrow. 'Before you ask,' he told her when she found him on her doorstep five hours later, 'I have no memory of buying the ticket, let alone making the decision.' He'd brought the clothes he stood up in, he said; a credit card and his passport.

She laughed.

'I've got someone here,' she said. 'But I can get rid of him tomorrow.'

'I don't mind,' Cave said.

She shut the door. 'Yes you do,' she called from inside.

After that, he made the crossing two or three times a year; visits between which the rest of his life suspended itself like a bridge. He drifted across London from employer to employer, assignment to assignment. His career, never spectacular, scaled down to a sort of lucrative pastime. He travelled the Americas, photographing the monastic architecture of the Spanish and Portugese colonial eras; he bought a garden flat in Barnsbury, Islington. Moving into his forties and perhaps a little fearful, he drank determinedly; as a consequence broke his hip cycling along the bank of the Regents Canal to an interview with two narcissistic conceptual artists in Hackney. Otherwise things remained quiet. He felt his age. He felt his surfaces change and soften, but detected beneath them a concreted layer of debris, an identity he could date very accurately to his struggle across the cloister, a condition of anxiety which founded not just his memories of Autotelia but of himself.

'The fact is,' he emailed Julia Vicente, 'I can recover so little of that time. The shoreline cliffs crumble into side-streets of tall pastel-coloured apartments. The old dockyard, with its rusty machinery revisioned as art, is an endlessly fragmenting dream, endlessly reconstructing itself. As for you and me, we seem like characters in a film. You never stopped smoking cigarettes; I bought a yellow notebook which I never wrote in. For years I've kept these fragments floating around one another – it's such an effort – attracted into patterns less by the order in which they occurred or by any 'story' I can make about them than by gravity or animal magnetism. But I have no memory at all of the experience as it fell out. Perhaps if I could see you more often, I'd remember more.'

It was hard to know what she made of that.

'I've grown used to you being here just the once or twice a year,' she replied. 'Don't come again too soon, I wouldn't know what to think.' In an effort to lessen the impact of this, he saw, she had struck through the word 'think' and replaced it with 'cook'.

He was grateful for the joke. But that night he dreamed he was back in the cloister. This dream was to recur for the rest of his life, presenting as many outcomes as iterations; from it, he would always wake to an emotion he couldn't account for: not quite anxiety, not quite despair. He dreamed the white blur of Julia Vicente's face watching from the shadows, immobile and fascinated until the procession of search-and-rescue teams found her and bore her triumphantly home on a stretcher in the bald light and shimmering air of the plateau. The fountain seemed to roar silently. The cloister cobbles softened and parted in the heat, encouraging Cave to slip easily between them into the vast system of varnished-looking natural tubes and slots which, he now saw, underlay everything. It was cold down there; damp, but not fully dark. He could not describe himself as lost, because he had never known where he was. He heard water gushing over faults and lips in tunnels a hundred miles away. Full of terror, he began counting his arms and legs; before he could finish, woke alone. A feeling of bleakness and approaching disaster came out of the dream with him. His room was full of cold grey light. 5am, and *traffic* was already grinding along Caledonian Road into Kings Cross. He made some coffee, took it back to bed, opened his laptop. Although he knew it would mean nothing, he emailed her:

'What can any of us do but move on? How?' And then: 'Did I ever have the slightest idea of your motives?', to which she could only reply puzzledly:

'Of course you did. Of course you did.'

Work remained central in Julia's life. She continued to write and publish, though none of her books had the same impact on our side of things as her first. Still pursued, though now by cultural historians rather than cultural journalists, she made hasty public statements about herself which she came to regret. She and Cave exchanged emails, argued, fell out, made friends again. In her fifties she entered a fourth marriage, which lasted as long as any of the others. (At around that time, Cave wrote in his journal, 'She arrives at the airport either an hour early or an hour late but in any case attractively deranged. She has no money and her car won't start. She greets you by saying in a loud voice, 'Oh god, things have been horrible,' and doesn't stop talking for some hours. She will insist on driving you somewhere and then forget how to get there and phone husband #4 – who is at that time in another town – for directions.') She dyed the grey out of her hair but rejected all forms of cosmetic surgery; experienced some symptoms of mild arthritis in the fingers of her right hand.

'It's sad to think,' she wrote, 'that people long ago stopped making full use of you as a human being. You feel as if you have let them down by somehow not being persuasive enough.'

The daughter, meanwhile, grew up, evolving from a curious olive-skinned scrap with very black hair into a tall, graceful adolescent obsessed with dogs. This surprised Julia as much as it did Cave. 'One moment she was five, the next she was fifteen. I was a little upset at first, but now I'm delighted. Luckily she's very self-absorbed.' And then, out of nowhere, a year or two later: 'She wants to be an archeologist. I think I might come to London now. There's nothing to keep me here.' Cave looked forward to a new beginning, but it was more as if something had ended. The closer they came geographically, the further they drew apart. Sometimes it was as if they had simply changed places: Cave buried himself in his Autotelian journals and memories, revisiting a relationship that had changed so much it was to all intents and purposes over; while Julia Vicente, camped less than two miles away from him in a rather nice house on the banks of the Regents Canal, waited impatiently for his return.

They were drinking red wine in Islington one afternoon when part of the sky went dark. Eddies of wind bullied the street trees around. A single feather floated into view, made its way across Cave's lawn and out over the garden wall, its weird calm transit defining a layer of privileged air at about twice the height of a person. 'People don't give in to age now the way they used to,' said Julia. The windows behind her blurred with rain, rattled a little in their frames. A summer squall always made her excited. 'Age has to find its expression in new ways.' It was her topic of the moment. 'I don't know anyone, for instance – not anyone who really accepts and understands what age means to them – who hasn't experienced the urge to act out the coming journey.'

'Which journey is that?' he teased her.

'You know exactly what I mean!' And then: 'Some kind of walkabout: as soon as you get the idea, you feel relief. Here's a way of recognising and accepting that urge to leave everything behind. A way of being thrown by it.' Cave considered these rationalisations with as much dignity as he could, then poured her another half glass of red and wondered out loud what would happen to the feather. The rain stopped. 'Seriously,' she said: 'What kind of a map would you use for a journey like that? A final journey?'

Then she laughed and added: 'You don't have to answer.'

When he first met her, Cave had sometimes glimpsed for an instant the older, tireder woman she would become; now that she was tired all the time, there were brief instants in which the younger woman showed through. Seeing what he thought might be his last chance, he offered:

'I'll answer if you answer.'

She stared at him intently. 'Answer what?' she said.

'Tell me what you expected to happen in the cloister.'

She seemed to relax, as if she had been afraid he might ask something else. 'To you? The same as him, perhaps. To me?' She shrugged. 'Who knows. Something new.'

A child, playing in a garden several houses away, began shouting, 'I said I can't do it! I said I can't do it! I said I *can't do it*!' over and over again. At first it was part of a game with friends or siblings, with a pause for laughter between each iteration. Then the other children dropped out and the chant took on values and momentum of its own, on and on, real meaning, real confusion, real rage. After two or three minutes Cave realised it wasn't even the child's own rage, any more than the sentence itself was the child's sentence. It was the rage of some significant adult, overheard in god knew what circumstances.

Alternate World

LONG HORIZONS, RISING DOWNS. West Sussex pub, full of the ghouls of money. 1947 Concours d'Elegance Bentley in the car park. Light aircraft float to and fro across the ghouls' own sky won in single combat from the Nazis all those years ago. The weather is fine, blowy mid–May, but when we say we'll sit outside, the barman responds with a kind of knowing servility, 'You're going to brave it, then?' Yes, we're going to brave it. We're going to meet today's minor but satisfying challenge, we're going to brave the May weather and have our lunch outside, the way the ghouls braved the Nazis in the blue enduring sky to protect their power and money all those years ago. You can't be the rulers if you have no country to rule.

A Bad Dream

I WOKE UP FROM a dream about losing my identity and not being able to find anything that would confirm it. It wasn't a dream about the problem of losing your identity; neither was it a dream about, say, the horror of not having a financial identity. In the dream, loss of identity was not a condition that required explanation or a way of escape in either of those senses or in any other sense: it was just a condition. I was in the town of my birth. I hadn't been there for decades. I was at the station, at a sort of advice counter. The man behind the counter was amused. It was as if he didn't understand the extent of the problem. It was as if he couldn't believe anyone could lose their identity. I was trying to appear cheerful about the situation. I had a tarpaulin travel bag containing a few clothes and other personal items. It was also full of bits of waste paper and receipts. Each time I went through this litter in the hope that a credit card or phone or other identifier would turn up, it seemed to be more useless. Who would help me? Though I couldn't remember any addresses I knew I could physically make my way to one person's house. But I had long ago fallen out with them.

Getting Out of There

HAMPSON CAME BACK AFTER some years, to the seaside in the rain, to this town built around a small estuary where a river broke through the chalk downs. Everything – everything people knew about, anyway – came in through that gap, by road or rail; and that's the way Hampson came too, down from London, midweek, in a rental van, unsure of what he would find for himself after so long. He had options, but since he wasn't sure about them either, he rented a single room on one of the quiet wide roads that run down from the old town.

The day he moved in, he realised that not all the things he had brought back with him – bits of furniture, endless half-filled cardboard boxes sealed with gaffa tape – would fit in there, so he drove the van to a self-storage under some railway arches where the London Road left the centre of town. It was a bit back from the seafront, the usual kind of place, not very modern, with untreated breeze-block cubicles of different sizes, behind doors that were little more than plywood. He spent a morning carrying things around in there, then looked into the office on his way out. Behind the desk he found a woman he recognised.

'My god,' she said.

At the same time Hampson said: 'I knew you when we were kids!'

'You wouldn't leave me alone,' she said.

'I was quite stricken.'

'I know you were,' the woman said.

Hampson paid the bill. 'I was seven years old,' he said, 'and you were, what? Thirteen?'

She laughed. 'I bet you can't remember my name either.'

Hampson had a couple of tries but she was right. As he was leaving, she called after him, 'It's Beatrice.' And then: 'Are you going to be stricken again?'

Hampson said he didn't know how to answer that one.

'*You* haven't changed,' she said, as if he'd already done something which demonstrated it.

The house – it was called 'Pendene', everything had to be called 'dene' round there – was large, square, detached, surrounded on three sides with empty parking space and, at the back, a long, overgrown garden. It wasn't much. Hampson's room wasn't much either. It lay at the end of a long, badly-lit second-floor landing, which still smelt of food cooked there in the 1960s: a section of a room – perhaps twelve feet by ten, painted white, accessed from a fire-door with the remains of broken bolts laced down the inside – so literalistically partitioned out of the original Victorian space that the light filtered in from about two-thirds of a bay window. The day he moved in, before he went down to the storage with his things and met Beatrice again, he had looked out of the window and watched a woman, thirtyish, long hair and nice legs in skinny jeans, walking diagonally across the road towards him from a house twenty yards down.

The garden wall, so overgrown with ivy it was bowing into the street, cut off his view of her. Shortly afterwards she was followed by a man in a pale blue shirt, who vanished in the same way. The next time Hampson looked up she was walking towards him again. The wall obscured her. The man followed about a minute later, and the wall obscured him. This happened three times, in bright sunshine. Hampson never saw either of them walk back towards their house. They didn't speak to one another. Up the street – towards the square where the buildings began to look a little less bleak, more as if they housed families of human beings – the gardens were full of camelias and early-flowering clematis.

For the first three or four days he didn't do much. He had a job to go to, pushing software in a local design firm, but it wouldn't start for a week. He pottered around, refamiliarising himself, feeling his way across the joins between the old town – with its herringbone brick and lapboard architecture, its carefully cultivated links to notable soldiers and writers of the Edwardian afternoon, and its quiet graveyard backwatered behind yews – and the new, which wasn't much more than a housing estate, some car parks, and a loop or two of bleak, dusty pubs and charity shops tucked between the chalk cliffs and brutalist sea defences known for lost geographical reasons as Shining Dene. There wasn't a lot to it, but Hampson already knew that. The promenade. The beach with its reclaimed Victorian railway track. A couple of Regency crescents on a hill which attracted a dry cold wind.

If you were bored – and Hampson soon was – you could go up on to West Hill and stare out towards France. One lunchtime he went into the English Channel, a pub about a hundred yards back from the clifftop, and Beatrice was sitting there at the back. He got a drink and went over to her. He asked if she minded him joining her, she asked him why she should mind. Unable to disentangle anything from that, he said:

'This is a weird place.'

'It's a town of the dead,' she said.

'I meant the pub,' Hampson said.

At the back it was hollow with plastic beams and tobacco-stained artex; a whitish sea-light crept in among the tables nearest the window, overexposing the floorboards, the sleeping dogs, the customers' feet. Every support pillar was papered with posters – 'Club Chat Noir', 'Maximum Rock &

Roll' – and a sign behind the bar advised, 'No bloody swearing.' For a moment Hampson and Beatrice stared companionably around, then she said:

'So. London.'

'London,' he agreed.

'I'd kill to be in London,' she said. 'Why'd you leave?'

He couldn't answer that. He hadn't answered it for himself.

'I suppose you get sick of it,' he said. 'You get sick of pretending it's not crap.' But it had been less about London and more about not fitting into your own life, not being described by the place you live in. Not being seen into life, by others or yourself. He had been lonely there even though he knew people: but Hampson told her a different story. 'Vomit's the London keynote,' he said. 'If you like to stand in a puddle of someone else's in a tube train on a Friday night, London's the place to be.'

'But why come here?' she said. 'Nothing happens here.'

'Nothing happens there, either.'

She laughed at that. 'Except the vomit,' she said.

'The vomit's world class. Good solid stuff. We can be proud of that.'

She made a face.

'I don't think I'll have another drink.'

'Of course you will,' Hampson said.

After that, he often popped into the storage at lunchtime. He took a couple of things out then put them back. She teased him about that. Hampson was a small man, perhaps five foot six. He couldn't see anything wrong with that. In her high heeled shoes Beatrice sometimes had an inch or two on him. He was excited by her and didn't see why he shouldn't show it. They chatted. They shared this funny small-town teenage history. It was all very pleasant and explicable but it wasn't going any further. Then, after a fortnight or so, Hampson was dawdling through the centre of town on his way to the cinema to see a film called *Shame*. It was a warm evening, just after dark, with a light rain and static patches of mist out to sea. As he crossed one of the High Street junctions Beatrice walked straight out of a house about a hundred yards in front of him. In the moment the door slammed, she was just a figure to him, in a pencil skirt and some sort of jacket with a pinched-in waist; then he recognised her from her walk, short tapping steps echoing back to him. He followed her without a thought. They were soon out of the centre, heading up the Bourne past the Ship Museum into the Old Town, where she knocked on a door; waited for a moment or two; called, 'Emily? Can I leave them with you tomorrow? Emily?' and receiving no answer went up a steep, narrow little passage and out into one of the Regency enclaves that faced the sea. It wasn't an area Hampson remembered. She was too far ahead to call her name; anyway shyness kept him from calling out to anyone in public. He thought he would make himself known when he caught up with her, but he never did. Instead he hung back, listening to the sound of her heels on the pavement. He never saw where she went. The cloud broke: moonlight gave the deserted streets a flattened perspective, as if the two of them were in a picture: suddenly Hampson became anxious and turned off.

Next day he went to the storage at lunchtime and asked her out.

'You took your time,' she said. 'What about Sunday afternoon?'

They rode the West Hill funicular railway to the park at the top of the cliffs. She stretched her arms and looked out to sea. 'It's great,' she said, 'that you can get so high above it all.' A moment later she was gone. Hampson sat on a bench looking out to sea, waiting for her to come back. There was a strong smell of cut grass, then fried food from the café at the top of the funicular. If he looked off to his left he could see her sitting on a bench about a hundred yards away. Behind her the town fell away towards the sea. Was she looking back towards him? He couldn't be sure. Suddenly a great flock of gulls poured down the Bourne and circled over the shops and houses, screaming and calling; then spread out along the esplanade and diffused like fog.

'I just went off for a bit of a wander,' she said when she came back.

'No problem,' Hampson said.

'It's a bit neat, this park. Don't you think?'

'I quite like it.'

'I was just sitting on a bench down the path,' she said.

Two or three boys were kicking a ball about on the grass behind them, and in front the sea was dissolving into the sky behind the tall black net shops and the art gallery. 'That yellow lichen on the roofs down there,' Hampson said, 'I wonder what it is?'

She laughed.

'I thought you were a local?' she said.

From there they went up on to the golf course, where groups of children hunted around all weekend for lost golf balls, paying particular attention to the base of the old black smock mill. There was a constant wind which seemed, Beatrice said, to come all the way from France. 'Look!' she said. From up there you could see clearly how the houses flowed between the downs, filling up the valley with humanity or something like it. Hawthorn and sloe grew on the edge, low, lichenous, wind-sculpted, dense. Lower down a fox sat calmly in a small sloping field between woods and allotments, watching some people tend horses. There were little valleys, warm, still and full of life, a few hundred yards from the sea. 'Anything can happen here,' she said, 'safe and out of the wind.' They ended up at the Open Art café, which offered an all-day breakfast sandwich, fragile-looking wildflowers in old glass bottles and the Sunday afternoon gathering of the Philosophical Society.

'What's the topic for this afternoon?' someone asked Hampson, as if he and Beatrice were members too. For him, Hampson said, to some laughter, it would have to be the existential quality of the art on the walls: several versions, in different sizes, of a sunbather sitting naked on the shingle, seen from behind, hugging her knees, framed in such a way as to render the whole experience anxious and claustrophobic – the sunshine, the beach, the wideness of the air, all denied. They were all called 'Woman from the Sea', with a hashmark and a number.

'Well I enjoyed that,' Beatrice said when they were back in town.

'Come out one evening,' Hampson suggested.

'I can't,' she said.

She stood awkwardly on the pavement outside a pub called the Plough, waiting for him to kiss her cheek; then laughed and walked off up the hill. 'But we could do this again,' she called back. Then she stopped and turned round and added: 'I've got kiddies. Two.'

He couldn't imagine that. He sat in his room later that night, watching the TV with the sound turned down, and tried to remember what she had looked like when they were younger. He couldn't remember much of anything. A smile, a pleated uniform skirt. Wet light shining off the seafront benches, streets steepening away north and east into middleclass cul-de-sacs. A gang of Year Ten girls laughing about something they had seen, or perhaps done, in the Shining Dene public toilets where moths with fawn pillowy heads and eyes like cheap red jewels lay stunned and immobile on the windowsills of the lavatory stalls. If he tried, he could remember how he felt – it was a crush – and someone giving him a sweet; but he was afraid that if he tried too hard he would begin inventing things, so he put it out of his mind and went to bed.

A couple of evenings later he waited beneath the old railway arches until he saw her come out of the storage place, then allowed her 40 yards' start and followed her home. There was a qualitative difference between this time and the last: he understood what he was doing. Also what he was feeling. Curiosity. Excitement. On top of that, a kind of peculiar self-satisfaction, as if following her made him superior.

It was cold and lively up there. The shabby white stucco facades, the columned doorways peeling and cracked in daylight, had under the moon a pure, abstract look. By day you could tell from their mismatched curtains and rows of doorbells that they had been divided as thoughtlessly into flats as 'Pendene'; at night they curved away like fresh illustrations of themselves in watercolour and architectural ink. Beatrice approached a house. He watched her put key to lock, listened for her footfall in the hall, waited until a ground floor window lit up; then turned up his coat collar and went back down into the town.

After that he followed her most evenings. Sometimes he was tempted to make his way straight to the house and wait for her to arrive; but something kept him honest. He wanted the sound of her heels, the lucky emptiness of the streets, the sense of the two of them being figures caught moving on an almost abstract ground. Her life seemed simple. Hampson couldn't see much of it. The children ran about playing some game upstairs. They had a television up there. Beatrice called out to them from the bathroom or the kitchen. They seemed happy. Later, she might sit for an hour on her own in the yellow-lit front room, staring ahead of herself. Crouched painfully in a soft patch of the bit of garden at the back of the house, he found himself shaking with attention. His hearing sharpened until he thought he could hear her breathe. When she leaned forward to pick up a magazine he could feel his heartbeat rocking his upper body. Walking home afterwards, he felt dizzy – as if he had been released from some vast effort

– and at the same time quite unreal. It would have been easy to believe that, at night, the town had no existence except as a picture – or not one but several of them, stacked planes, layered and imbricated in the rising salt air and faint sound of waves, implying three dimensions yet completely two-dimensional.

One evening as he hid in the garden, he realised someone else was in the room with her. She was listening to someone he couldn't see; someone, perhaps, who had been there all along; a male voice, first questioning then reassuring. From then on, Hampson wondered if he too had company. Though he never saw anyone, might other men be crouched in the garden near him at night, their attention as excited and obsessive as his own?

All the time he was following her at night, they had an easy familiarity by day. They sat in the English Channel at lunchtime, eating a pint of prawns each. When she could organise childcare they visited the art cinema and had arguments about Michael Haneke. It was a normal relationship, although Hampson often felt she was trying to tell him something without actually saying it. She took him to a famous house a few miles inland. This confection of butter-and-honey stone, built by an Edwardian author to enclose the memory of his dead son, had first passed into the hands of the Bloomsbury group – who, in their anxiety to control the cultural conversation and contribute to English post-Impressionism, had painted watery greyish designs on the wallpaper and doors – and now belonged to the Nation. Standing in extensive gardens, behind warm brick walls and tall yew hedges, it boasted an oast house, a box maze and a fully operational watermill from which the public were encouraged to buy flour. Beatrice and Hampson took the Saturday tour, after which she led him through a little wooden gate into one of the more intimate gardens, which featured a rectangular pool and some statuary among exuberant cottage garden plantings. There, she sat him down on a bench.

'Look!' she said. 'I love this!'

Hampson wasn't so impressed. The rim of the pool had been tiled by amateurs – an effect less of Tuscany than of the mouldy bathroom in a Spanish holiday villa – and all you could make out in the clouded water was a kind of feathery weed moving to and fro. It might have been growing on something, Hampson thought, some shape he couldn't quite bring to mind. Overseeing the pool from a short plinth of home-made concrete was a ten-inch figure without head or legs but with detailed, slightly disproportionate male genitals. There were similarly broken or partial bodies all over the garden – both sexes reduced to loins and buttocks half hidden by foliage.

'Isn't it calm?' she said.

'Very calm,' Hampson agreed. But he hated the place and couldn't wait to get away: within a week he was having a dream in which it seemed less like a garden than the site of a crime. Limbs had been torn off for reasons unfathomable; the aesthetic of careful disarrangement – of humorous disarray – tried but failed to dissimulate the rage that lay behind it all. Hampson knew he wasn't looking at a celebration of Mediterranean influences and classical forms, or even the operations of a disturbed mind. One night he woke up understanding the difference between the garden and his dream of it: in the dream all those dismembered trunks and torsos were real. The knowledge exhausted him. He groaned and turned over. He fell asleep again. He had begun the night throwing body parts into the pool: he spent the rest of it trying to force an object the colour of a plastic lobster into an open pipe.

When he woke again it was six the next morning and the sun was out. He walked down the hill to Shining Dene, where he found two old women already swimming from the shingle. They ran laughing into the sea, carrying between them a child's bright blue-and-yellow plastic inflatable upon which was printed the words HIGH VELOCITY SPORT, which they lost for a moment in the surf; then, still laughing, ran out again. They shouted and waved to someone on the cliff above, stumbled about in the shallows chasing one another. Hampson, puzzled by their energy, sat under the sea-defences, pulling up clumps of chamomile and yellow horned poppy. Down among the roots he found beads of a material resembling cloudy plastic, washed in by the tide. It was difficult to tell what they had been; on the shingle, the difference between organic and inorganic was constantly eroded by water, weather, sun. This idea made him think about the object in his dream. It had looked crustacean but felt fleshy and limp. It had been about the size of a seven year old boy. The old women finished swimming, dried themselves and pulled on their vast shorts. Soon after that, he began avoiding Beatrice during the day and stopped following her at night.

He couldn't have said why. He was angry. He didn't like the pool, he blamed her for the dream; he was angry that he had to follow her. He didn't phone and he didn't answer when she phoned. He took the train up to London once or twice a week. It was the same as ever: he would spend the evening in Soho getting pissed, wind up outside the Bar Italia with all the other digital creatives, clutch a beaker of hot chocolate too glutinous to drink. He would grin vaguely into the warm drizzle and wonder what to do next. He missed her. He missed their walks together. In a week or two, he felt, he would be all right again: meanwhile this was the best his personality would let him do. Eventually she came to find him.

Thursday, after midnight. The corridors and studios of 'Pendene' exuded a false warmth; the smell of old cooking oil hung in the corners. The residents were locked-down in silence for the night, while, outside, strong winds came blustering down the Channel from the Hook of Holland. Hampson sat in his room playing *Death Camp 3* for the X-Box through an old Sony TV set, out of which issued faint hissing noises he couldn't fix. When Beatrice knocked on his door he opened it but sat down again immediately. She was wearing black jeggings and a short white lozenge-quilted parka with fake fur round the hood. The cold came in with her. 'I don't know how you got in,' was all Hampson could think of to say. He kept his eyes on the screen, after a minute adding: 'They're supposed to keep the outside door locked at night.'

'You're going too far with this,' Beatrice said, looking around as if the room were part of it.

'How far is that?' Hampson said.

'Don't be puerile.'

She lifted the lids of the as-yet-unpacked boxes of books, poked the bin bags into which Hampson had compacted his clothes when he left London. 'It's like the back room of a charity shop in here,' she concluded. 'You should be ashamed of yourself.' She switched the electric kettle on and the TV off, then knelt down in front of him so that he had to look at her. Her hands were cold. He wondered briefly if she had come to have sex with him. Instead she smiled with a kind of painful intensity and urged him: 'Listen to me.'

'How are the kiddies?' Hampson said.

'Listen,' she said, 'no one can show you anything if you won't involve yourself.'

'I don't know what you mean by that.'

She shrugged and let go of him.

'Come and find me when you do,' she said.

A few nights later he turned on the TV and a woman was striding around in a derelict house shouting, 'We could put a pa sha in here! Plenty of space for a pa sha!' For a moment Hampson had absolutely no idea what she could be talking about. Then he saw that it was the bathroom she was in.

He turned the TV off again and went out to look for Beatrice, and soon he was following her once more, every night, up the quiet steep streets on the landward side of the town, or along the deserted sweep of the seafront. They were a hundred, two hundred yards apart, the two of them, in the night wind and strange light. Everything was very silent. There never seemed to be an ordinary passer-by. Hampson felt rapturous, even though, after a while, he saw that after all they weren't alone. Other men were following her too, two or three at a time; some women, too. Though Hampson saw them, they didn't seem to see him. They had the look of the figures in Stanley Spencer's 'Beatitudes of Love' paintings, shabby, collapsed and watery, rather grotesque. He wondered if he looked like that to other people.

To a degree, he felt relieved by this turn of events. He felt as if some weight had been lifted; a weight and perhaps a barrier. But his dreams didn't improve. He dreamed of Beatrice's children, who he'd never seen: they were a boy and a girl, toddlers in matching woollen coats, their little gloves dangling on elastic from the ends of their sleeves. He dreamed of the beach at Shining Dene. He dreamed of a hollow below the Downs, where the sun fell through dense, wind-sculpted hawthorn on to ashes, on to candle grease dripped over the stones of a temporary hearth. An event enacted itself in front of him, some episode which transfigured everything, in which a madwoman strode across the golf course to the smock mill, carrying her coat across her arms like a child. Soon there were lots of women, all carrying their coats that way, like sleepy children across their arms; but now they were throwing them off a pier into the sea. Lines of people followed a leader down to the sea, where they first sang an old Morrissey number, 'Every Day Is Like Sunday' and then something, coat or child, was let fall into the water. All this dream-content seemed so distant! At first it was musing, lyrical but simple and matter-of-fact. It seemed strange but kind: the arms of the coats fluttered and gestured as they fell: they were like the expressive arms of performers in a charming traditional drama. But then someone was being killed and dismembered at a distance, in a rusty enamel bath or perhaps an empty brick sump. Hampson was helping with it. Great chunks of translucent, whitish flesh were falling heavily apart along clean cutlines. They were weighty and substantial, but there was no blood. It was more like fat. On waking he thought, I can't do this any more. He didn't really know what that meant: it was just the kind of thing you thought. But he knew he had to get things out into the open.

'You know full well what's going on,' he said, when they were alone in the storage place next day. 'You always knew.'

She smiled. She looked at him sidelong.

'I don't get it,' Hampson said.

'Why should you,' she said. 'Why should you get it, after all?'

'You've made me into a voyeur,' Hampson said. 'That's not what I am.'

'I know. You're a man escaping the London vomit. Ask yourself if that's all you are.' She came out from behind the counter and offered him her hand. When he took it, she led him through the office and into the storage itself. Rows of shoddy cubicles stretched away in all directions, their plyboard doors fastened with little cheap padlocks. 'People leave stuff here for a decade or more,' she said. 'When they come for it again, their lives have changed. They might as well be going through someone else's things. A lot of it they don't recognise. They don't know why they didn't just throw the rest away and save themselves the trouble.'

'Other people are following you too,' Hampson said.

That made her compress her lips and turn away abruptly. 'I don't want to know,' she said. 'I don't want to know what you see.'

'What have you got that they want?'
No answer.

That night he followed her down towards the sea. She knew he was there, and he knew she knew: there was a satisfaction to that. He knew she was smiling, though she never looked back. He was one among many, but Hampson didn't mind: he had seen them all before, trailing after her up and down the windy streets; they were easily recognisable. He could also identify other groups of followers, following other individuals. Some were women, some were men; some were members of the Philosophical Society. It resembled a midnight *passeo*, in which everyone in the town went down on to the vast, brutalist sweep of the sea-defences and filed along them in the transparent, motionless dark. After crossing Marine Drive to the seaward stub of the High Street, they all paused for a moment on the apron between the car park and the Brazilian JuJitsu Academy, halted, apparently, by the smell of the salt. For a moment they had an air of being discarded, agitated by a breeze too faint to feel in their world. And the thoughts you had when you watched them were the same, like the continual blowing or silting-down of the chalk detritus from the cliffs. Groins of piled rock, with acres of flint shingle strung between them so that from above they looked like webbed fingers, reached out from the land; the sea, though calm as a pool, gave the impression of hidden disorder. Beatrice walked down between her followers to where the shingle steepened. Everyone was smiling. They were all watching her. They all shared the secret now, even Hampson. He watched Beatrice walk slowly into the water until it closed over her head. Her hair was left floating for a fraction of a second, then it vanished too. But he knew not to follow her, or call out to anyone, or otherwise raise the alarm.

When he turned away at last, he was alone on the sea-defenses and it was morning. The blunt chalk headlands, already busy with commuter traffic, stretched away east, decreasing mistily into the distances of Peacehaven and Hastings. He looked at his watch. Beatrice was waiting for him in the shadow of the sea wall. She had the two kids with her, peaky-looking little things about two years apart, one girl, one boy, who stared up at him as if they were thinking something that couldn't be put into speech.

She said, 'I thought I might find you here.'

'Are you following me?' Hampson said.

Beatrice laughed. The kids laughed. Hampson tousled their heads. They went all four of them and got some breakfast.

He had never thought life was infinite. He had always understood that focus was the key, although he was prepared to admit he had often focussed on the wrong things. Earlier in life he had felt too much anxiety over that. From now on he wouldn't feel enough, even though he knew his focus was slipping off the right things. Like everyone else he would begin to look forward to the evening, two or three glasses of wine. He would eat too much.

I've Left You my Kettle
and Some Money

TEN YEARS AGO I looked up and saw in my garden a layer of fluid ice, the exact blue of the chemicals in a cold pack, trapped between two layers of air. It was still there an hour later. It was still there the next day, like a temperature inversion hanging above the lawn. I took a chair out and climbed up on it and put my hand in. There was no resistance. Nothing leaked out. I could see my hand in there. Once I got inside I could breathe, though there was some discomfort to begin with. I've been hauling my stuff up there ever since, stashing it item by item until I was ready to leave. I'll have to crawl, because I'm not sure what I'd find if my head broke out of the top. I know I can keep warm. I've got enough food for a month. After that I plan to live on my wits, always moving east, pushing the furniture in front of me. None of the others know. Don't tell them until you're sure I've gone.

Special Thanks

Thanks for every kind of help, encouragement and support to: Nina Allan, Barbara Campbell, Jon Catty, Deb Chadbourn, Mic Cheetham, The Collective, Sarah Cunningham, Lindsay Duguid, Will Eaves, Tim Etchells and everyone at Forced Ent, Fiona Hugget-Ling, Simon Ings, Justine Jordan, Zali Krishna, Dave McKean, Farah Mendelsohn, China Miéville, John O'Connell, Ra Page, Ian Patterson, Lara Pawson, Christopher Priest, Julian Richards, Andrew Rosenheim, William Schafer, Penny Schenk, Simon Spanton – and especially Cath Phillips, without whom.

About the Author

M. John Harrison is the author of eleven novels (including *In Viriconium*, *The Course of the Heart* and *Light*), as well as four previous short story collections, two graphic novels, and collaborations with Jane Johnson, writing as Gabriel King. He won the Boardman Tasker Award for *Climbers* (1989), the James Tiptree Jr. Award for *Light* (2002) and the Arthur C. Clarke Award for *Nova Swing* (2007). He reviews fiction for the *Guardian* and the *Times Literary Supplement*, and lives in Shropshire.